'Mama! Mama!

Max stopped and looked back to see a small golden-haired boy standing halfway down the stairs. Ellen gave a little cry and rushed to catch the child in her arms. The child laid his head on her shoulder but for a moment looked directly at Max—a long, unblinking stare before his eyelids drooped. He was already asleep as Ellen handed him to the nursemaid.

'Take him back to bed, Hannah. And this time please make sure the door is properly closed.'

Max's brain was working frantically. When he had first seen the boy on the stairs he had been forcibly reminded of the portrait hanging in the drawing room at Rossenhall—the one of Hugo and himself as children. When he had been barely four years old. Then he had seen the child's eyes, green as emeralds, and suspicion had hardened into certainty. He stared at Ellen as she turned and made her way back down the stairs towards him and his simmering anger turned again to ice-cold fury.

He forced out his next words through gritted teeth.

'This, madam, changes everything.'

Author Note

When I finished writing The Infamous Arrandales there was one character who just wouldn't go away. Little Ellen Tatham, the spirited young heiress who appeared in the books, was quite adamant that she wanted her own story.

So that is how *The Duke's Secret Heir* came about. We have moved on several years, and Ellen is now in her mid-twenties. She is enjoying life as a rich and independent young woman when she meets Major Max Colnebrooke. The setting, on the banks of the Nile, is perfect for romance, so is it any wonder that Ellen falls head over heels in love with the dashing Major?

Unfortunately the course of true love does not run smoothly for our lovers, but Ellen is not one to sit and pine, and she makes a new life for herself in the north of England—quite a contrast with the Egyptian desert—content to be the diamond of Harrogate society. Until one day she comes face to face with Max again. Only now he is the Duke of Rossenhall.

After four years, can our lovers put the pain and misunderstandings of the past behind them and find true happiness?

I do hope you enjoy Ellen and Max's journey, and if you would like to share your thoughts on the story with me then do feel free to contact me on my website, www.sarahmallory.com, or on Twitter @SarahMRomance.

THE DUKE'S
SECRET HEIR

Sarah Mallory

MILLS &
BOON

Published in Great Britain 2017
by Mills & Boon, an imprint of HarperCollins*Publishers*
1 London Bridge Street, London, SE1 9GF

© 2017 Sarah Mallory

ISBN: 978-0-263-92558-6

Sarah Mallory was born in the West Country and now lives on the beautiful Yorkshire moors. She has been writing for more than three decades—mainly historical romances set in the Georgian and Regency period. She has won several awards for her writing, including the Romantic Novelists' Association RoNA Rose Award for *The Dangerous Lord Darrington* and for *Beneath the Major's Scars*.

Books by Sarah Mallory

Mills & Boon Historical Romance and Mills & Boon Historical *Undone!* eBook

The Infamous Arrandales

The Chaperon's Seduction
Temptation of a Governess
Return of the Runaway
The Outcast's Redemption

Brides of Waterloo

A Lady for Lord Randall

The Notorious Coale Brothers

Beneath the Major's Scars
Behind the Rake's Wicked Wager
The Tantalising Miss Coale (Undone!)

Stand-Alone Novels

The Dangerous Lord Darrington
Bought for Revenge
The Scarlet Gown
Never Trust a Rebel
The Duke's Secret Heir

Visit the Author Profile page
at millsandboon.co.uk for more titles.

For lovers everywhere

Chapter One

High Harrogate was in a state of excitement. A most illustrious visitor was expected to grace the ball at the Granby that evening. True, the rumours had not been confirmed, but the visitor was an old friend of a regular patron, so everyone was in high hopes. To add to the excitement, it was known that the golden widow had returned from London. Some might wonder why such a rich and attractive young widow as Mrs Ellen Furnell did not choose to make her home in the capital, where she would doubtless be one of the top society hostesses, but admirers such as old General Dingwall were only too happy that she did not and declared gallantly that London's loss was High Harrogate's gain.

The lady in question was currently at her desk in her house on Paradise Row, looking through the correspondence that had accumulated during her absence. Ellen had only yesterday returned from her annual stay in London. To be accurate, she had hired a house just outside the capital, in Kensington, where she resided very quietly, no invitations, no callers. However, from there she might walk into town if she wished, or go to the theatre or museums. And it was convenient for visiting the fashionable *modistes* and warehouses she patronised to replenish her wardrobe.

The bills and notes from tradesmen she put aside for another day and after a brief hesitation she added to that pile the letter from Lady Phyllida Arrandale. Ellen was sincerely attached to her step-mama, but her letters always exuded an air of calm domestic felicity, and this morning Ellen did not wish to read about such things for it would exacerbate the vague feelings of dissatisfaction that had been growing over the past few months. Ellen pushed aside such thoughts, refusing to indulge in self-pity. She had chosen her life and she did not regret anything she had done since she had stepped off the boat at Portsmouth four years ago. She was very happy living in High Harrogate. She *was*.

Ellen began to sort through the remaining papers and cards in front of her. There was an invitation to join a house party in Leicestershire for the summer, a politely worded note from the

Reverend Robert Mitton soliciting her attendance at a forthcoming recital—which would naturally involve making a generous donation towards the repair of the chapel roof—and numerous invitations for tea-drinking, breakfasts, balls and evening parties. Ellen decided against the house party in Leicestershire, but the rest she would most likely attend, including tonight's ball at the Granby Hotel. After all, that was what she did in Harrogate: attend lectures and debates, support charitable causes and go to parties. As a wealthy woman of independent means she must always be welcome and her many admirers declared she was a jewel, the brightest ornament of Harrogate society. Ellen might laugh when they paid her fulsome compliments, admired her ready wit or went into raptures over her golden-haired loveliness and sparkling blue eyes, but it would have been false modesty for Ellen to deny her beauty, when her looking glass confirmed it.

'And you should be thankful for it,' she muttered, scooping the invitations into a tidy pile. 'Your pretty face has always made life much easier for you.'

Except once.

She was aware of a sudden contraction of the heart and an unexpected lump in her throat, and she found herself blinking back tears. Perhaps she should stay at home, claim she was fatigued from her journey.

'But who would believe it?' she argued with herself. Since her arrival in Harrogate four years ago she had worked hard at her image, becoming an important part of every social event whilst maintaining a spotless reputation. 'So now everyone knows Mrs Ellen Furnell is indefatigable.'

Because you are afraid to stop and remember.

Ellen rose and made her way upstairs to the nursery. This was where her heart lay now. Not in some distant memory. She reached the top floor and went quietly into the nursery, where a grey-haired woman was sitting on the floor helping a very young boy to build a castle with wooden blocks. The blocks went flying as the child jumped up and ran towards Ellen as fast as his little legs would allow.

'Mama!'

'Jamie!' Ellen dropped down and opened her arms.

With a shriek of delight, the little boy ran into her embrace. The maid climbed slowly to her feet, tutting.

'You shouldn't encourage him, ma'am. He's wild enough as it is.'

Ellen scooped up the boy and carried him

across the room. 'Nonsense, Matty, he is only three, still a babe, aren't you, my pet?'

'Aye, and in my day he would not yet be breeched.'

'And you would probably have left his hair to grow,' laughed Ellen, ruffling the short curls that were even fairer than her own. 'Now what are we doing here, are we building a house, Jamie? Perhaps you will let Mama help you.'

Playing with her son did much to restore Ellen's spirits and she remained in the nursery until it was time to change into her ball gown. She had no qualms about leaving Jamie: Matlock had been Ellen's own nursemaid and later, her dresser. Matty loved the little boy as much as she did.

After a solitary dinner Ellen went back up to the nursery. Little James was tucked up in his bed by then and fast asleep, so she dropped a gentle kiss on his golden head.

'He looks like an angel,' she murmured, gazing lovingly at her son. 'I could stay here looking at him for ever.'

'And what good would that do either of you, ma'am?' asked Matlock, bustling around the room. 'You go off and enjoy yourself. Master James will be perfectly safe with Hannah and me.'

Ellen sighed. 'Ah, Matty, do you really think I enjoy these parties?'

'Well, you says not, ma'am, but there's no doubting you need to mix with people and to have some sensible conversation, which you won't get with a three-year-old, and that's a fact.'

Ellen laughed. 'Sensible conversation! There is little enough of that to be had in society, Matty, I assure you. But you are right, it will serve no one if I become a recluse.'

With a smile and a wave of her hand she went downstairs and out to the waiting carriage.

'Your Grace? Duke?'

Max started and turned to his hostess, quickly begging her pardon. He had been Duke of Rossenhall for over a year, but he had still not grown accustomed to the title. His hostess brushed aside his apology, not at all offended by his inattention. It was as if polite manners were unnecessary for a duke.

'I was merely saying that it is time we were leaving for the Granby, Your Grace.'

'Must we, Georgiana?' Max grimaced, but followed it quickly with a smile, to show he meant no offence. 'I would as lief enjoy a quiet evening here with you and Fred.'

'Well, that ain't possible,' Frederick Arncliffe

told him bluntly. 'Georgie promised that she'd bring you to the ball tonight.'

Max threw him a look of pained reproach. 'And I thought you were my friends. I am beginning to regret my decision to visit you.'

'You know Georgie and I would do anything for you, old boy, but your presence here ain't a secret. Dash it all, Max, you are even *staying* at the Granby!'

'I had little choice, at such short notice,' Max retorted. 'If my business in York had not been concluded so swiftly I should not have come at all.' Which they all knew was not the truth. Georgiana had written to him, explaining that Fred's health was deteriorating rapidly, and Max had always intended to cut short his visit to York and call on his friend. Not that he would ever admit as much to Fred, of course, so now he scowled and added, 'I should not have come near Harrogate if I had known you would want to show me off in this absurd fashion.'

Fred grinned. 'What is the point of being acquainted with a duke if we can't make use of him?'

'And everyone knows you are here to visit Frederick, so they would naturally expect you to attend the ball with us,' added Georgie. 'Think what an honour you will be conferring on the hotel.'

'I am thinking of it,' said Max bitterly.

Frederick laughed. 'I know you are not one for dancing and gaiety, my friend, but it will look very odd if you shut yourself in your rooms while Georgie and I are in the building.' He sobered a little when he saw the look on Max's face. 'Do you think that because I am dying I should spend my remaining months hidden away?'

'No, of course I don't think that,' said Max at once. 'I beg your pardon, Fred. I am being odiously selfish, but having read Georgie's letter I expected to find you at death's door.'

'And so I am,' said his friend with brutal frankness. 'I can no longer exert myself on the dance floor, but I love to sit and watch, and to see Georgie enjoying herself.'

Max regarded him in silence. Frederick Arncliffe was a former shadow of the strong soldier Max had known, but although the doctors had only given him months to live his zest for life was undimmed, and Max knew that any attempt at sympathy would offend him, so he offered none.

'So I am to be paraded through the rooms,' he said as they made their way out to the carriage. 'Like some strange creature in a menagerie!'

'That's right.' Fred chuckled, taking his arm. 'You'll be courted and toadied as if you were Prinny himself.'

Max shot him a look. 'I am growing accustomed to that.'

Was he really? As a younger son he had never expected to succeed to the title. His father had bought him a commission in the army and convinced Max that his presence at Rossenhall was unnecessary. Even when the old Duke died Max was informed by his brother that he was not needed at home. That had caught Max on the raw, but Hugo had only recently taken a bride and Max understood that they would want time alone together. Everyone had expected an heir to follow the marriage, it was just a matter of time. Five years later there were still no children and Hugo's untimely death just over a year ago had been a shock. For six months Max had refused to accept that he was now Duke of Rossenhall and continued with his military duties, convinced that the estates could go on very well without him. In his decision he was supported by Atherwell, his chief steward, and he had left the administration of his affairs to him and the Duchess, his widowed sister-in-law. The new Duke of Rossenhall was content to let the world pass him by.

Unfortunately for Max, the world had other ideas. He had thought remaining in the army would protect him from scheming parents with daughters to marry off, but he soon realised his mistake. Everywhere he was courted, fêted and pursued as England's most eligible bachelor and he hated it. Even his best friend was not above matchmaking. Fred had written to Max, hinting that his little sister would make a fine duchess. Since Clare Arncliffe was barely sixteen, more than ten years Max's junior, he had ignored the suggestion, but the subsequent letters suggested that Fred had taken his silence for acquiescence.

Max had always planned to tell Fred at some point that such a match was out of the question, but had never got around to it, deciding it was something that should be done face to face. Now Georgie's most recent letter, informing him that the doctors had given Fred only months to live, had put paid to that. He had come to High Harrogate, determined to spend what little time was left with his friend, and if that involved accompanying him to the odd ball, then so be it.

Having resigned himself to the inevitable, Max climbed into the carriage with his friends for the short journey from their rented house in Low Harrogate up the hill to the Granby. The approach to the hotel was already choked with carriages when they arrived and Fred muttered darkly, 'Confound it, Georgie, you must have told the world and his wife His Grace the Duke of Rossenhall would be present tonight.'

'Nonsense,' she replied comfortably. 'I told only Lady Bilbrough.'

'Which means it was all over Harrogate within the hour,' retorted her fond spouse. 'Oh, well, I suppose we had best go in. Never mind, Max, you can tell them you do not dance tonight and sit at the side with me.'

'Oh, no, he cannot,' said Georgie as she prepared to alight. 'Max is the best dancer I know and I intend to have him as my partner at least for the first dance!'

The Granby Hotel might be more than two hundred miles from London, but the ball was no different from all the others Max had attended. Too many people squeezed into a warm room and all talking far too loudly for comfort. It was not in his nature to be rude or impolite, so he smiled as he was introduced to an endless line of guests, exchanged civilities with gushing matrons, avoided toadying sycophants and, after leading Georgie out for the first two dances, obligingly stood up with any number of blushing debutantes. He had done it all before, so many times, and when there was a break in the dancing he went in search of Georgie and Fred, wondering how soon they could leave without causing offence.

It was then he heard it, from across the room. A laugh, merry and joyful, clear as a peal of bells. The familiar sound that stopped him in his tracks and sliced into his heart like a sword.

When Ellen arrived at the Granby she was surprised to see how many carriages were still waiting on the drive and still more surprised at the crush of guests thronging the ballroom. As her name was announced at the door, Lady Bilbrough came hurrying over to greet her.

'My dear Mrs Furnell, I am so *pleased* you could come tonight. And a new gown, too! Let me look at you… I adore that red silk net with the underdress of white satin just peeping through. Quite beautiful, and it suits you perfectly. One of your new creations from London, if I am not mistaken. How did you go on there, I hope you enjoyed yourself?'

'Town was very hot, ma'am, and I am very glad to be back,' replied Ellen, moving away from the door as another crowd of guests arrived. She glanced around the room. 'Harrogate has turned out in force this evening.'

'It has indeed,' agreed my lady, but all the time her eyes were darting around, as if looking for someone. 'I vow the landlords of the Crown and the Dragon will be kicking themselves that their balls have not been so honoured!'

'Honoured, ma'am?' Ellen gave a puzzled laugh. Surely the lady could not be talking of her own return from London.

Lady Bilbrough reached out and touched her arm, saying in a voice trembling with excitement, 'Oh, Mrs Furnell, only *wait* until you have heard the news!'

But before she could continue General Dingwall came bustling up.

'My dear Mrs Furnell, delighted to have you back with us. I have been looking out for you, for you promised me the first dance when we met again and they are striking up already, ma'am, so let us make haste. You know I am loath to stand up with anyone else, my dear lady, for I swear no one else is so light on their feet.'

Ellen had no time for more than an apologetic smile for Lady Bilbrough before her elderly gallant carried her away. It was always the same; at any ball she attended there was never any shortage of dance partners and in tonight's crush there were more than ever. No sooner had a dance ended than she was snapped up for the next. It was gratifying, but she was glad when the music stopped for a while and she was able to catch her breath and talk to her friends. She was drawn into a laughing, chattering group at the side of the room and was giving them a lively account of her time in the capital when she realised her companions were not attending. The men were standing to attention and straightening their neckcloths, while without exception the ladies were simpering and blushing as they looked at someone behind her.

Ellen turned and found herself face to face with the man she had tried so hard to forget.

The room began to spin. At a great distance she could hear Lady Bilbrough performing the introductions. So he was now the Duke of Rossenhall. He had not lied to her about everything, then. Only about the marriage. Only about loving her. But why had he come to find her? She realised she was being presented to him as if they were complete strangers. Which of course, her struggling brain fought to tell her, everyone thought they were.

As Ellen sank down into the required obeisance she wondered if she would be able to rise again, for her knees felt too weak to support her.

'Your Grace.'

By a supreme effort of will she kept her voice

steady and rose gracefully from her curtsy. When she forced herself to look at the Duke she was momentarily dazzled, for the candles glinted off his fair hair and it gleamed like molten gold. A halo, although she knew to her cost he was no saint. She schooled her face into a smile. His eyes, green as a cat's but cold as ice, pierced her to the soul. The handsome face was achingly familiar, yet now it was stony and uncaring, so different from the way she remembered him. He looked as if this encounter was as unwelcome to him as it was to her and she knew in that moment he had not planned it; he had not sought her out. Ellen's hands were tightly wrapped about her fan and she felt one of the sticks break beneath her grip.

'Mrs Furnell.' No one else noticed the steely menace behind the softly spoken words. But then, thought Ellen, no one else here was so well acquainted with the Duke. 'If you are not engaged, madam, perhaps you would do me the honour of standing up with me for the next dance?'

No. That would break her. She said, with spurious regret, 'Alas, Your Grace, I have promised the next to Mr Leeming.'

Ellen turned to smile at that gentleman, but he immediately coughed and bowed and assured His Grace that he was happy to forgo the pleasure of dancing with Mrs Furnell. He then lost himself in a tangle of words as he tried to assure Ellen that he meant no disrespect to her. His sacrifice earned him a bow from the Duke.

'Normally I would not dream of taking another man's partner,' said His Grace, with smiling civility, 'but in this instance, I confess the temptation is too great to be resisted. Mr Leeming, is it not? I am indebted to you, sir.' As if on cue, the orchestra struck up the first notes of the next country dance and the Duke offered his arm. 'Madam?'

Time stopped. Ellen felt as if she had grown roots and could not move. She was aware of the interested stares of everyone around her, the smiling face of Lady Bilbrough, who was nodding encouragement, but most of all she was aware of the man standing before her, fair, tall and broad-shouldered, his back ramrod straight. Solid as a rock and dangerous as sin.

Ellen's eyes dropped to the dark sleeve. She would as lief put her hand in the jaws of a crocodile, but she was trapped. To turn away would cause talk and speculation. Ruin. Slowly and with infinite care she placed her fingers on his arm. Beneath the fine material he was tense, hard as iron, and as he led her to the dance floor she could feel the anger emanating from him.

It was like a physical wave, trying to wash her off balance. She put up her chin. Why should he feel aggrieved, when she was the one who had been betrayed? They took their places in the set, facing one another more like opponents than partners.

'It has been a long time,' he said. 'Four years.'

She smiled politely. During those years she had practised hiding her true feelings and now that training came to her aid.

'Is it really so long? I had forgotten.'

A lie. She had counted every one of the days since they had parted, but she did not cry over the past. At least, only in her sleep, and no one could help their dreams. They moved forward and back. They circled, changed partners and back again. His next words, little more than a fierce whisper as they passed, caused her to miss her step.

'I thought you were in France.'

She corrected quickly and hissed at him as they circled, 'That was the intention.'

'But you came here.'

'I had to live somewhere.'

'But not with me.'

She kept smiling, but inside a sharp blade sliced deep into her heart. 'No, never with you.'

They separated. Only her familiarity with

the dance kept Ellen moving. Only pride and strength of will kept her smiling, while her mind wandered back to those heady days in the Egyptian desert. The stuffy warmth of the ballroom disappeared, replaced by a dry heat and the scouring sand carried by the Simoon, the wind that could blow up ferociously and without warning. The chatter of guests became the shouts and menacing cries of the Mamelukes as they thundered up on their horses and surrounded the camel train, bristling with weapons and clearly hostile.

Ellen heard again Mrs Ackroyd's impatient tut. The little Englishwoman had been Ellen's schoolteacher and was now her friend and mentor, and her indomitable spirit was in no way cowed by a threatening tribe of desert horsemen. Or perhaps it was being perched high on a camel that enhanced her sense of superiority.

'For heaven's sake,' she admonished their trembling guide, 'tell them I am a personal friend of Bernardino Drovetti, the French Consul General. Tell them he has arranged safe passage for us with the Governor of Egypt.' She drew out a paper and waved it at the nearest rider. 'Look, we have permission to visit the antiquities at Giza and our permit is signed by Muhammed Ali himself!'

At the name of Egypt's current ruler, the horsemen muttered and growled and looked even more threatening. One rider, taller and broader than the rest, pushed his way through the throng and approached them. He was dressed as the others in loose white trousers, a blue waistcoat over the billowing white shirt and a turban with a scrap of cloth over his face to protect him from the windborne sand, but Ellen noticed that his skin was paler than his companions, and there was a glint in his emerald-green eyes that was strangely compelling.

'Perhaps I can help?' His voice was deep and well-modulated. She remembered feeling no surprise to hear the aristocratic English accent in this foreign land. 'No doubt you paid good money for that pass, but I'm afraid your dependence upon the Pasha's protection is misplaced. Outside the walls of Cairo his power is limited.' The green eyes narrowed and gleamed, as if he was laughing at them. 'Let me see what I can do.'

The memory of that mocking glance had haunted Ellen's dreams for four years. Now, as the dance brought them back together, she could perceive no laughter in his eyes, just an ice-cold fury that chilled her blood. If only she had known he would be here, if only she had enquired who was in town before venturing out this evening, but she had thought herself safe enough in Harrogate. The Duke had no properties and no family this far north. Her mind, normally so sharp and clear, refused to work. She could not think what she should do, save continue to dance and smile.

When the music ended she ignored the Duke's hand as they walked off the floor.

She said coldly, 'Pray do not feel obliged to accompany me, Your Grace. If you think I am honoured by your attentions, you are mistaken.'

'I want to talk to you.'

'We have nothing to say to one another.'

He put his hand on her arm, obliging her to stop and face him. There was barely contained anger in every line of him, but before he could speak they were interrupted by General Dingwall.

'Well, now, Your Grace, you have had your dance and it is time to give up your fair partner!' The old soldier gave a fat chuckle. 'Oh, yes, you may look daggers at me, young man, but when you get to my age you will find that a title is not nearly so intimidating. Besides, I know you for a military man, sir. A major, so I outrank you!'

For a moment Ellen feared the Duke would ignore General Dingwall and actually drag her away with him, but at last he released his iron grip. He held her eyes, his own full of chilling ferocity, but his voice when he spoke was politeness itself.

'Your superior strategy carries the day, General,' he said. 'I relinquish my prize. For the present.'

He bowed, but the look he gave Ellen as he walked away told her it was only a temporary reprieve.

Ellen's elderly admirer led her back to the dance floor for a lively gavotte and when it ended she was approached by several other gentlemen, all hopeful of a dance, but she announced her intention of sitting out for the rest of the evening. She could not see Max, but she knew he was somewhere in the crowded room, watching her. She could feel his presence, menacing and dangerous. She considered leaving early, but was afraid he might follow her home and that was the last thing she wanted.

When supper was announced Ellen decided there was safety in numbers and headed for the large table that ran down the centre of the room. With relief she saw an empty chair beside Georgie Arncliffe and she hurried towards it.

The Arncliffes had come to Harrogate two years ago, when Frederick's doctors had advised him to try the spa waters, and Ellen and Georgie had immediately struck up an acquaintance. The fact that they both had young children had drawn them together, but their lively minds were very much in harmony and the acquaintance soon blossomed into a firm friendship. Now, Georgie's smile of welcome was balm to Ellen's battered emotions.

'I did not know you had returned, Ellen. Welcome back, my dear.'

'Thank you.' Ellen took the outstretched hand and squeezed it gratefully as she sank down on to the chair. 'I am so pleased to see you and Frederick tonight.'

'As if you did not know almost everyone here.' Georgie laughed. 'And I had been hoping to impress you by introducing Frederick's good friend, but alas Lady Bilbrough has stolen my thunder.'

Georgie turned to smile across the table and Ellen's heart sank when she saw the Duke of Rossenhall lowering himself into the vacant seat opposite. He gave her a look that was nothing short of predatory.

'So,' he said. 'We meet again, *Mrs Furnell*.'

Frederick Arncliffe looked up. 'You two are acquainted?'

Ellen kept her eyes on Max, wondering if he would tell them the truth; that they had met in

Egypt four years ago, when he and his men, a mixture of English deserters and Mameluke warriors, had come upon two Englishwomen with their woefully few guards and had offered them protection. But it was Georgie who laughingly replied.

'Why, yes, they are, my love,' she said. 'His Grace requested an introduction from Lady Bilbrough.'

'What man would not?' Max murmured with a smile that did not reach his eyes.

'Indeed, Mrs Furnell is one of the diamonds of our society,' put in Mr Rudby, sitting close by.

'So I am informed,' replied Max. 'The golden widow.'

Ellen's cheeks flamed. He made it sound like an insult, although no one else appeared to notice. True, Georgie gave a little tut of disapproval, but Frederick merely laughed and shook his head at her.

'Pho, my dear, Mrs Furnell is not offended. She knows it is a compliment to her radiant beauty.'

'Yes,' the Duke agreed quietly. 'I have been unable to think of anyone else all evening.'

'Indeed?' Ellen's brows rose. She turned to Fred and said coolly, 'I fear your friend is a breaker of hearts, Mr Arncliffe.'

Sitting a few seats along from the Duke, General Dingwall gave a bark of laughter. 'How could he not be? Handsome young dog, with a title *and* a fortune, 'tis no wonder that all the ladies are hot for him.'

'But I was not always titled, or rich. A few years ago I was merely Major Colnebrooke of a Regiment of Foot.' He leaned back, his long, lean fingers, playing with the stem of his wineglass. '*Then* ladies were more inclined to run away.'

There was uproar at this, hoots of laughter from the gentlemen while from the ladies came disclaimers that their sex would be so fickle. Only the Duke and Ellen appeared unmoved. She felt his eyes upon her as she concentrated on her supper, cutting the meat into precise little portions. Each mouthful tasted of ashes, but pride forced her to continue. How dared he chastise her? What had he expected her to do, once his deceit was discovered?

And your own deception?

She would not think of that. She had done what was necessary to survive.

The scrape of fiddles heralded the start of another dance and the supper party began to disperse. The Duke pushed back his chair.

'May I escort you back to the ballroom, Mrs Furnell?'

'Thank you, Your Grace, but that will not be necessary.'

'What, madam, are you afraid of me?'

Slowly she came to her feet, saying with a laugh, 'Of course not, Your Grace.'

But the look in his eyes told her she should be. Very afraid.

Chapter Two

Ellen stood, waiting, while the Duke made his way around the table to join her. His step was firm, assured, and he had the lithe grace of a big cat. When they had first met she had likened him to a lion, with his shaggy mane of thick, wavy fair hair. It was shorter now, and darker than she remembered, but four years ago his locks had been bleached by the Egyptian sun. Now it had golden highlights that glinted in the candlelight.

All that glitters...

Mrs Ackroyd had called them a golden couple, but Ellen had quickly discovered that Max was not gold but dross. Foolishly she had allowed herself to be taken in by his charm, so blinded by love that she had ignored her friend's advice to wait, and had entered into a hasty marriage, only to discover within weeks that it was all a pretence.

Now the man who had broken her heart and ruined her life was towering over her.

'Well, madam, shall we go?'

With a smile she took his arm. She had vowed that no one would ever know how foolish she had been, how much she had suffered. Least of all Max Colnebrooke.

Max kept his pace slow, measured, as he escorted Ellen back to the ballroom. The shock of seeing her again after all these years had abated. Upon his return to England, four years ago, he had searched for her, hoping against all the evidence that she had come back to him and not forsaken him for the French Consul, but it had been in vain. She had left Egypt under her new lover's protection, leaving him no word of explanation. Not even goodbye. His temper was under control now and it must stay that way. His anger against the woman beside him had cooled long ago, he would not give her the satisfaction of knowing that her betrayal had almost destroyed him. But there were questions he wanted to ask, things he needed to know.

'We must talk,' he said.

'No, we must dance.' She was smiling, but not at him. She lifted her hand to acknowledge those already on the dance floor who were inviting them to join in.

He could refuse, he could drag her away to some secluded spot, but how would that look? Everyone would say he was besotted with the golden widow and he had no intention of adding to her consequence in that way. Max took his place in the line. It was a country dance and would go on for some time, perhaps as much as an hour. He almost ground his teeth in frustration, but there was nothing he could do now. Talking would have to wait.

The fellow standing beside him, a Mr Rudby, Max recalled, looked at Ellen in surprise.

'Dash it, I thought you was not going to dance again tonight, ma'am.' He laughed and threw a sly glance at Max. 'I am glad you persuaded her, Your Grace, for now I can reserve the next for myself. And I'll take no denials, madam, it would be dashed uncivil of you to refuse!'

Max saw the look of distaste in Ellen's eyes at this forthright speech. She could not reject Rudby without giving serious offence and Max knew *he* could not stand up with her again. He silently cursed these rigid ballroom conventions; he would be obliged to invite other ladies to join him on the dance floor if he wanted to avoid speculation, even though there was only one woman he wanted to dance with.

There had only ever been one woman and that annoyed him more than all the rest.

Unbidden, the picture of Ellen in the desert came into his mind. She had been untrammelled by convention then. When he had first seen her she was dressed like a man in a fine silk shirt, scarlet waistcoat and long, loose trousers tucked into her riding boots. Very practical attire for riding a camel, he had thought, and with the scarlet *khafiya* covering her luxuriant golden hair she might have passed as a boy, although Max had never had any doubts about her sex, even though at first all he could see of her were those laughing eyes, blue as sapphire.

She had wanted to visit Giza and he had escorted her there, despite the risks of being discovered so close to Cairo by soldiers loyal to Muhammed Ali. It was night by the time they reached the pyramids, but the full moon provided light enough, although the shadows were black and sharp. The night air was balmy, the warm breeze a refreshing change from the oven-like heat of the day. Ellen had laughed and exclaimed at how ragged the pyramids appeared when one was close, and Max had challenged her to climb with him. She had not hesitated. He remembered how nimbly she had scrambled over the large stone blocks, how they had rested together in companionable silence on their high perch. How he had stolen a kiss.

Ellen smiled and skipped her way through the dance and when the music stopped she accepted Mr Rudby's hand to join the next set. She had never felt less like dancing, but it was almost obligatory and besides, the alternative was a tête-à-tête with Max, which she wanted to avoid at all costs. With mixed feelings she watched the Duke lead out Mr Rudby's previous partner. She would much rather he had taken himself off, but she could not help feeling a little grateful that he had taken pity on poor Miss Glossop. His attentions would go a long way to make up for the offence Mr Rudby had offered the poor girl in discarding her so quickly for the golden widow.

Ellen was exhausted. Her face ached with the effort of smiling and she felt sure her dance shoes were worn through. She had danced continuously since supper, putting off the evil moment when she would have to face Max alone. It would come, she knew it, and it must be this evening. There was no help for it. Even as she skipped and laughed and twirled she was planning how quickly she could remove her household from Harrogate.

When the last dance ended Ellen looked about for the Duke, steeling herself for a confrontation. She was a little surprised that she could not see him, because she had expected him to be standing at the side of the room, ready to pounce. She was even more surprised when Lady Bilbrough told her that the Duke had already left.

'Although he has the advantage of us,' said the lady, with a regal smile. 'He is staying here at the Granby, so he does not have to wait for his carriage.'

Ellen was relieved, but that relief was tinged with anger. He had ruined her evening and now she had lost the chance to give him the verbal flaying he deserved. However, her natural common sense reasserted itself as she went off to collect her cloak and change her shoes. If he had grown tired of taunting her so much the better. She really did not want to relive all those painful memories.

But it was already too late. As she sat down to replace her worn slippers with more serviceable footwear, recollections of their last night together were already crowding in. She was once again in the luxurious and gaily painted cabin of the *dahabiya*, rocking gently at anchor on the

Nile. She could feel the soft cotton bed quilt on her naked skin as she lay in Max's arms, sleepy and replete from their lovemaking.

'There is trouble coming, my love,' he told her between kisses. 'I cannot tell you more, but believe me when I say it would be dangerous for you to remain in Egypt. You must leave the country with all speed. I would escort you to Alexandria myself, if I could, but that is not possible, so tomorrow I will arrange an escort to take you there. Seek out the British Resident, Major Missett. He will arrange a passage for you back to England. Go to Portsmouth and wait for me there.' She felt again the soft touch of his lips on her neck, heard his smooth voice in her ear. 'Forgive me, love, but it will be safer if you travel as Miss Tatham. If the enemy learns you are my wife, it would put you in much greater danger.'

A tear dropped on to her shoe and Ellen quickly blinked the rest of them away. Honeyed words. Honeyed lies, all of it. Yet she had thought it perfectly sensible at the time, and then he had made love to her again and she had ceased to think anything at all.

What a besotted fool she had been! Angrily Ellen threw her cloak about her shoulders and went downstairs. In the entrance hall she met the Arncliffes and as they said their goodbyes she noticed the dark shadows beneath Frederick's eyes.

'You must be fatigued, Mr Arncliffe,' she said quickly, her own concerns forgotten for the moment. 'Look, my carriage is at the door, I could take you up, if you wish...'

He acknowledged and declined her offer in one wave of his hand.

'That's kind of you, m'dear, but the Duke has put his own chaise at our disposal. We are waiting upon it now. It will not be long behind yours, I am sure.'

He ended with a wheezing cough and Ellen noted how anxiously Georgie urged him to sit down. When he demurred Ellen took his arm and gently pushed him down on to the bench.

'Yes, sir, rest yourself,' she said. 'Do not think I shall be offended. Quite the reverse; we are such old friends I shall be hurt if you do not sit down. It has been a long evening for you.'

'Nonsense, I would not have missed it for the world. It does my heart good to see everyone enjoying themselves. And to see *you* dancing with my old friend Rossenhall was a high treat, I assure you, ma'am. And very good you looked together, too, although I warn you not to lose your heart to His Grace, for he is as good as promised to m'sister. Ain't that so, Georgie?'

Ellen's hand crept to her throat. Promised? Could Max be in love with another woman?

'*You* would like it to be so, at all events, my love.' Georgiana laughed, rolling her eyes.

Ellen tried to smile, wondering how much more her beleaguered spirit could take. She allowed Georgie to enfold her in a warm, scented embrace, promised to visit her very soon and at last she could leave. Torches flared on each side of the doorway, lighting up the hotel entrance and her footman, who scrambled down from the chaise to open the door for her. She climbed in and as the carriage jolted into motion she sank back with a sigh against the thickly padded squabs.

'We are alone at last. *Mrs Furnell.*'

Ellen sat up with a gasp and peered into the velvety blackness of the far corner. There was no mistaking that deep voice and as her eyes grew more accustomed to the dark, she could make out his cloaked figure, although it was little more than a deeper black shadow against the gloom.

'How did you get in here?' she demanded angrily.

'Once I had ascertained which was your coach, it was easy to slip inside.'

Max sat up, pushing away the black cloak. He

wondered if its owner was even now berating some hapless footman over its loss. Little matter. He would hand it back to the hotel manager tomorrow and he could return it.

'Do you expect me to fall into your arms?' Ellen's voice was scathing. 'I am surprised you dare to approach me.'

'Oh, I dare, madam.'

'Then you are shameless.'

'Hah, that's rich indeed, coming from you. You were the one who put yourself under the protection of the French Consul. I suppose he was more to your taste than a poor major.'

'How dare you? Monsieur Drovetti arranged safe passage for us out of Egypt—that is all.'

'And why should he do that if you were not lovers?'

'I told you at the time that he and Mrs Ackroyd had been in correspondence long before our visit to Egypt. They share an interest in antiquities.'

His lip curled. 'Do you really expect me to believe that?' Max scowled. 'When I reached Alexandria I learned Drovetti had sent you off on a ship to France. I have always been intrigued to know why you did not go back to him, when everything settled down. Or did you play him false, too?'

She flushed, but ignored this taunt.

'We never went to France. It was just…easier to let the world think it. I wanted to make a new life for myself.' Her hands fluttered in her lap. 'In the confusion of the British invading Alexandria it was not difficult. Monsieur Drovetti arranged passage for us on a French ship and from there we were smuggled back to England.'

'Where you hid yourself away. I suppose you thought I would come after you.'

'Why should you?' she said bitterly. 'You had had your pleasure.'

'Had my *pleasure*? Confound it, woman, I married you!'

'That was nothing but a trick. You had one of your friends impersonate a chaplain and I am ashamed I fell for it.'

'Impersonate! Why the deuce should I do that?'

'To trick me into your bed.'

He bared his teeth. 'Unnecessary. You would have come there very willingly without marrying me. Admit it.'

Ellen would never admit such a thing, although she knew it to be the truth. She had been so in love she would have died for him. But not now. The carriage slowed and she looked out of the window. She said coldly, 'I am home. My coachman will take you back to the Granby.'

'Oh, no,' he said, following her out of the carriage. 'We have not yet finished our business.'

She gasped in outrage as he dismissed her coachman.

'How dare you! I do not want you in my house.'

'I think you will find, madam, that it is *my* house. As my wife, any property you own is mine.'

'We were never married.'

'Oh, yes, we were,' he said grimly. 'And I have the papers to prove it.' He caught Ellen's arm, marching her up the steps and past the astonished butler who was holding open the door. 'Which way?' he growled. 'Or do you want to discuss this in the hall?'

For a long moment Ellen glared at him in silence before leading the way into the drawing room. Only two candles were burning and the butler followed them into the room to light the others. Ellen walked over to the mirror that was fixed above the mantelshelf. She pretended to give her attention to tucking a stray curl back into place, but all the time she noted what was going on behind her. While Snow made his stately progress around the room lighting the candles, Max took off his cloak and tossed it on to a chair before inspecting the decanters arranged on a side table. She pressed her lips together. If he thought she would be offering him refreshment, he was very much mistaken!

'Will that be all, madam?' The butler's tone was perfectly polite, but she knew he was reluctant to leave her alone. Her servants were all very loyal and protective, but even if she asked them, they could hardly manhandle a duke from the house. She turned, hiding her anxiety behind a cool smile.

'Yes, thank you, Snow. You may go. I shall ring when I need you.' As soon as the butler had withdrawn she said coldly, 'I will spare you five minutes, no more. It is late and I am very tired.'

'You surprise me. I was informed the golden widow could dance until dawn.'

'We are not dancing.'

'Very true. Shall we sit down? But first, brandy, I think.' She curbed her indignation as he turned away from her and pulled the stopper from one of the decanters. 'Will you take a glass with me, or there is Madeira. I remember you saying you liked it, although we never drank it during our time together. The best I could offer you then was strong coffee and rose syrup. Or mint tea. I remember you liked that.'

Ellen sank on to a chair, trying not to shiver. She did not wish to remember those heady days, nor the nights they had spent together.

'I want nothing,' she told him. 'Only for you to leave.'

'I am sure you do,' he said, taking a chair opposite her. He crossed one long leg over the other, very much at his ease, which irritated her immensely.

She stared at the fireplace, determined not to begin any conversation.

'I was surprised when you did not write to me upon my brother's death,' he said at last. 'I thought if anything might bring you back to me, it would be the knowledge that you were a duchess.'

'I—' She stopped and after a heartbeat's pause she said icily, 'You forget, I know we are not married.'

Max sipped his brandy, pretending to savour it although in truth he was too intent on controlling his anger to taste anything. Seeing Ellen again had shaken him to the core. He had thought he was over her, but to hear her laugh, as if she had not a care in the world, when for the past four years he had known nothing but grief and guilt and emptiness, had brought back all the bitterness of her betrayal. It took all his iron will to remain outwardly calm.

'It certainly did not take you long to forget me,' he remarked, swirling the brandy around in the glass. 'By the by, what happened to your new husband? If he had been alive I should have had to tell him you had committed bigamy.'

She gave a bitter laugh. 'You need not pretend any more that we were ever married. Do you think I did not make enquiries as soon as I returned to England? I had my lawyers inspect the regimental registers and they confirmed what Missett had told me, that there were no British soldiers south of Cairo at that time. Unless they were deserters.'

'I explained it to you, my unit was on special duties that even the Consul knew nothing about.'

'But why could I find no evidence? The men you were with, the chaplain—'

'Dr Angus went to South America after we left Egypt. The others—' pain twisted like a knife in his gut '—they are all dead. Killed in action either in Egypt or the Peninsula.'

All except me.

Max felt the bitter taste of his guilt welling up in his throat again. He had cared so little for life after Ellen had left him, yet he was the one who had been spared, time and again, however fearful the odds. He had seen his men, his friends and colleagues slaughtered in the field of battle, yet he had survived.

'Why should I believe you?' Ellen threw at

him now. 'When Major Missett told me only deserters could be south of Cairo I assumed you had taken a false name, too. Now it is clear that your desertion was concealed. After all, your family would not want their good name disgraced, would they? Any more than they would want you to marry a tradesman's chit.' There was something in her tone, something more than bitterness and it made him frown at her, but she waved one hand dismissively and continued. 'But whatever your own situation, the marriage was a fraud. Dr Angus, the chaplain you say married us, was in Sicily at that time. Missett was quite clear about that.'

'Confound the man!'

'Do not try to blame the Consul, you tricked me!'

'No, you *wanted* to believe that, because you had found yourself another lover.'

She flew out of her chair. 'That is a lie.'

'Is it, madam? Why not admit that you decided to throw your lot in with the French? After all, they had the upper hand in Egypt at that time, I had told you as much. I was trying to negotiate alliances with the Mamelukes, but they were fighting so much amongst themselves that it was impossible to form a cohesive resistance to the Pasha. And despite losing the Battle of the Nile,

Bonaparte looked set to conquer the world, so who could blame you for switching your allegiance?'

'I did nothing of the kind. I merely deemed it safer to leave Egypt under the French Consul's protection.'

'And leave me to learn of it from Missett. Fine behaviour from my wife, madam!'

'I am *not* your wife!' She flung out her hand to silence him. 'I was taken in once by your lies, it will not happen again.'

'You need not take my word for it,' he retorted. 'If you check now you will find the records have been amended.'

'I do not believe you. I made thorough enquiries when I returned to England. I even had my lawyers go through the Chaplains' Returns. There is no record of our marriage.'

'All the papers have now been returned to England. Send your lawyers to look again, if you do not trust my word.' He saw the first flicker of doubt in her eyes and his lip curled. 'You are my wife, madam, like it or not.'

Ellen felt as if she was standing on the edge of a precipice. She could still recall the hurt and disillusionment she had felt when she and Mrs Ackroyd had arrived in Alexandria and the English

Consul had told them categorically that there were no British soldiers south of Cairo. He had waved a sheaf of papers at them, detailed information on ship and troop movements.

'Believe me, ladies, if there were any British units in the area I would know of it. I am afraid you have been duped by deserters who have thrown in their lot with the Mamelukes.'

'And the chaplain?' Mrs Ackroyd had asked him the question, since Ellen had been too distraught to speak.

'I am personally acquainted with Dr Angus and if he were in Egypt he would have come to see me. The last letter I had from him was from Sicily and he was even then talking of a posting to South America. You have been grossly deceived, ladies, the soldiers you met could only have been deserters.'

Ellen remembered his words all too clearly, felt again her shock. Shock and mortification so great that it had sent her into a dead faint. She had been foolish beyond reason to accept Max with no proof at all of his identity. She had fallen head over heels in love and within two weeks of their meeting she had married him. She had never before let down her guard and trusted any man, which was why his deception had broken her completely. When she had learned of it, all she had wanted was to leave the country as quickly as possible. Mrs Ackroyd had pointed out that the French Consul's sphere of influence was far greater than that of the Allies and he could get them quickly and safely out of the country. Ellen had known how that would look to Max, if he found out, but she had not cared for that. In fact, she had been glad. It would be some small revenge for what he had done to her.

But now, as he sat in her house, coolly refuting her arguments, the doubts crept in. Why would he suggest her lawyers should investigate unless he was sure of his facts? What if she had misjudged him all these years? She looked up to find he was watching her and his cold, assured smile chilled her to the bone.

'Yes, madam, you are my wife, but not for long.'

Ellen felt the blood draining from her face and put her hands to her cheeks. Max gave a scornful laugh and pushed himself out of his chair. As if in a dream she watched him place his empty glass carefully on the side table before turning back to her.

'You should not have been so hasty in casting me off, Ellen. But four years ago neither of us dreamed I would ever become Duke. That makes you a duchess, but you may be sure I mean to obtain a divorce as soon as possible. I do not think it will be difficult, do you?' he drawled. 'A wife who abandons her husband for another man and a French official at that. And there is the bigamy charge, too. Divorce will be expensive, difficult and we will be a laughing stock, but I will endure it all to be free of you.'

She barely heard him, too horrified by her own thoughts to understand his words. She had been so devastated by what she thought was his betrayal that on her return to England she had taken a false name and hidden herself away. She had given him no chance to explain himself. But if she had indeed been mistaken, this anger, this hatred he was displaying was perfectly understandable. She bit her lip and looked at him.

'Oh, Max,' she whispered. 'I am more sorry than I can say...'

His lip curled. 'I am sure you are, but you should have thought of that before you deserted me.' He picked up his hat and gloves. 'I shall write to my lawyers tomorrow to free us both from this damnable mess.'

Ellen looked into that cold, implacable face and her spirit crumbled. She felt physically sick at the thought that she had been wrong and she could not blame him for hating her. Leaving Alexandria under the protection of the French Consul was an insult Max would never forgive, but she had believed then that she was the injured party. Her head was reeling. If the marriage was indeed legal, then she needed to consider her situation, but that was impossible in his presence.

She drew a breath and steadied her nerves. 'Very well. I will show you out.'

She waited until he had picked up his cloak, then preceded him to the empty hall, anxious to get him out of the house as quickly as possible. They had just stepped into the hall when a little voice called from the top of the stairs.

'Mama! Mama!'

Max stopped and looked back to see a small, golden-haired boy standing halfway down the stairs. Ellen gave a little cry and rushed up to catch the child in her arms just as a flustered housemaid appeared on the landing.

'Ooh, madam, I am sorry, I must have left the door ajar. I thought Master James was asleep and I'd only turned my back for a minute!'

Ellen gathered the little boy up, hugging him close. The child laid his head on her shoulder, but for a moment he looked directly at Max, a long, unblinking stare, before his eyelids drooped. He was already asleep as Ellen handed him back to the nursemaid.

'Take him back to bed, Hannah. And this time please make sure the door is properly closed.'

She turned back, ready to usher him out, but Max did not move.

He said, through gritted teeth, 'This, madam, changes everything.'

Chapter Three

'Well, were you going to tell me I had a son?'

He bit out the words, his mind working frantically. When he had first seen the boy on the stairs he had been forcibly reminded of the portrait hanging in the drawing room at Rossenhall, the one of Hugo and himself as children. When he had been barely four years old. Then he had seen the child's eyes, green as emeralds, and suspicion hardened into certainty. Now, facing Ellen across the candlelit room, he saw the momentary panic flit across her face and he wondered if she would deny everything.

'No. Yes.' She put a hand to her head. 'So much has happened this evening, my thoughts are in chaos.' She took a breath, then another before saying slowly, 'If you have told me the truth, if we are truly married, then Jamie is your heir,

Max.' With an effort she forced herself to look at him. 'Will you take him from me?'

There was naked fear in her eyes as she whispered the words. If he truly wanted to punish her, he now had the means to do it and no one would blame him. He had every right to take the child. Why hesitate? Why not deliver the killer blow? Four years of pain repaid, in an instant.

He could not do it.

'That is up to you,' he said at last. 'The boy must join my household. You are his mother. And my wife. You may come, too. If you choose to do so.'

She closed her eyes, relief clearly visible in every line of her body.

'Thank you. Max, I am truly grateful.'

He said coldly, 'I do not want your thanks. If I do not divorce you, it is for the boy's sake, not yours.' With an expert flick he threw the cloak about his shoulders. 'We will discuss the details in the morning, but the boy will be joining my household as soon as I can arrange for it. With or without you.'

Max strode back to the Granby Hotel, barely noticing the chill wind that cut across from the Stray. Ellen had said her thoughts were in chaos, but they could be nothing to the turmoil raging within him. To discover his wife living as a widow in Harrogate was bad enough, but that she should be concealing his son was unforgivable.

He knew nothing about Furnell, the man she had taken as a husband. Had she married him as soon as she returned to England and palmed the child off as his? Max slowed his pace. Now his initial rage was dying down he realised the delicacy of the situation. There was no way to avoid a scandal. The news that he was married would shock the *ton*. It would be the topic of gossip in every drawing room in the land, although possibly not quite such a furore as would be caused by a divorce. And then there was Fred. What would his good friend say when he knew Max had been deceiving him for the past four years?

He stopped and looked up at the stars, exhaling softly. What did he really know about his wife? She appeared to be well respected here, but appearances could be deceptive. She had blown in and out of his life quicker than a desert storm. They had married after barely two weeks' acquaintance and a fortnight later she was gone. Perhaps he could have tried harder to find her, but he had shied away from telling anyone of his marriage or her desertion, so his enquiries had always been couched in the vaguest terms. Confound it, he should have overcome his shame and embarrassment and set his lawyers to discover what had become of her, then perhaps this whole sorry mess could have been avoided. Now he would need to tread carefully, if he was not to make a bad situation even worse.

A sudden gust of wind jerked him from his reverie. It was beginning to rain. He pulled his borrowed cloak about him and began to walk on. Fred and Georgie appeared to be upon good terms with Ellen, in the morning he would call upon them and find out all he could about the golden widow. Then he would be better prepared to act.

A sleepless night brought Max no comfort. Finding his wife again had been a blow, discovering he also had a son, an heir, had almost floored him. He would have preferred to think that Ellen had played him false, but not only was the boy the right age, one look at the white-blond hair and emerald-green eyes convinced Max the child was his. By morning he was reconciled to the fact that he had a family, but he must decide the best way to proceed.

He arrived at the Arncliffes' rented house in Low Harrogate to find his friends still at breakfast. He would have withdrawn again, but Frederick beckoned to him.

'Come in and sit down, Max. We have campaigned together too often to stand on ceremony. At least take a cup of coffee with us.'

'Yes, please do,' Georgie added her entreaty. 'Perhaps your being here will persuade Fred to eat a little more this morning.'

Max sat down at the table, his eyes wandering over the array of dishes.

'I know, I know,' said Frederick cheerfully, 'there is far too much here for Georgie and me to eat, but I cannot help it. Since Corunna I have always liked my table groaning with food. Not that it is wasted—what the servants don't eat is given to the poor. What we would have given to see such a breakfast when we were marching through the mountains of Galicia, eh?'

'Aye, those were hard times,' agreed Max.

'Let us not think of it,' said Georgie, shuddering. 'When I learned how you had suffered, chased halfway across Spain by the French, I cannot bear it!'

'Devil a bit, my love, that is the soldier's lot,' said Frederick. He reached across and took her hand. 'And Max here brought me home safe, even if there is a little more to me now.'

Max knew Fred was referring to the musket ball lodged near his lung, the reason for his current ill health. He said, 'I expected to find you at Sulphur Well this morning.'

There was a slight but definite pause, then Georgie said quietly, 'He was too weak to walk that far this morning.'

'Nothing serious,' said Fred quickly, when Max frowned. 'I have been trotting too hard, that is all.'

'When we arrived back last night he could hardly manage the stairs to bed,' Georgie told Max. 'He was no better this morning so I summoned Dr Ingram. He has promised to visit us later.'

Frederick gave a huff of impatience. 'And he will tell you what we already know, that I must expect to be up and down.' He glanced at Max. 'Georgie blames herself for keeping me out so late last night, but dash it all, Max, I do not want to sit at home like an invalid, waiting to die.'

'But perhaps you should have left a little earlier,' Max suggested.

'When everyone was having such a good time? Never. It does me good to be amongst my friends. I was particularly glad to see you and Ellen Furnell getting on so well. I have to admit you made a very handsome couple on the dance floor. She's a dashed fine woman, ain't she? And Georgie's closest friend, you know.'

'Indeed?'

'Our children are almost the same age so we have much in common,' Georgie explained.

'That is good, because I wanted to ask you about her.'

'What's this?' Frederick looked up from the sliver of ham that he was pushing around his plate. 'Are you interested in the beautiful Mrs Furnell? I vow I shall take it very ill if you throw over m'sister for the golden widow!'

Max could not smile. He knew his friend was funning, but the words flicked him on the raw. How was he to tell his friend he was married and had been for four years? Thankfully, he was saved from replying by the news that Dr Ingram had arrived.

'So the old sawbones is here, is he?' Frederick wiped his mouth and put down his napkin. 'I'll see him in the sitting room. No sense in climbing all those stairs again. No, no, stay there, Max. Georgie will be back to keep you company in a moment.'

Max watched as Georgie hurried to help her husband to his feet. He noticed how heavily Fred leaned on her shoulder as they went slowly from the room and when she returned a few minutes later there was an anxious crease in her brow.

He said bluntly, 'He has grown much weaker, even in the few days I have been in Harrogate.'

'Yes.' She sat down at the table and poured herself another cup of coffee. Her hands were trembling slightly, but she spoke calmly enough. 'The bullet has shifted; he cannot breathe so well now. Dr Ingram thinks it will move again, and next time it might be...be fatal.'

'Is there nothing that can be done? If it is a question of money—'

She shook her head. 'Thank you, Your Grace, but, no, that would not help. If Fred could be induced to lie in bed and never move then his life might be prolonged, but he says that would be worse than anything. He is getting progressively weaker. Dr Ingram thinks it cannot go on more than a few weeks.' She hunted for her handkerchief. 'For myself I am resigned to it, but I hate to think of little Charlotte growing up without her father.'

'Oh, Georgie, I am so sorry.'

'Your Grace is too kind.'

'It is Max,' he said, grief adding a touch of impatience to his voice. 'You know how much I hate formality.'

She gave a watery chuckle. 'I shall try to remember. I wanted to thank you for coming to Harrogate. It has cheered Fred a great deal to have your company. He won't ask you himself, but I know he would like you to be here until... until the end.' She wiped her eyes and smiled bravely. 'That is why I was so pleased you came to the ball last night. You seemed very taken with Ellen Furnell and I hoped she might encourage you to prolong your stay.'

He felt a frown gathering. 'If I remain in Harrogate, it will be for Fred's sake and yours. But I did want to ask you about Mrs Furnell.' He saw the sudden lift of her brows and said quickly, 'Please—ask me no questions, Georgie, not yet. Just tell me what you know of her.'

'I cannot tell you a great deal. She was here when Frederick and I arrived and has been in Harrogate a number of years, I believe. We became acquainted almost immediately, because of the children.' She smiled. 'I like her very much, she has been so kind to Fred and me. Oh, I know they call her the golden widow, which sounds so very frivolous, but she is very well respected. Truly, she is admired by everyone and gives generously to good causes.'

'A paragon, then.'

'You sound disapproving, but I assure you I have never seen any evidence of artifice or ill breeding in her. Since we have been in Harrogate, Ellen has been a very good friend and heaven knows I have needed one.'

'Yes of course, I beg your pardon,' said Max. 'Do you know anything of her husband?'

'Ellen was already a widow when she first came here, I believe, and her little boy was born here. He is a little older than my Charlotte and will be four in the autumn.'

Her little boy. *His* son. Something unfamiliar slammed into Max's gut, surprising him with its violence.

'Your Grace? Is anything wrong?'

Max saw the innocent enquiry in Georgie's eyes and knew it was time to tell the truth.

Ellen waved away the freshly baked muffins that Snow was offering to her. She had no appetite for breakfast, having spent a sleepless night trying to find a solution to the horrors that pressed upon her. Max's arrival had turned her world upside down. She would set her lawyers to look again at the army records, but in her heart she had no doubt that what Max had told her was true and he was as unhappy as she about the situation.

She felt physically sick with regret. If she had trusted him, they might now be living very happily together, but it was too late for that. She had killed his love, she must face up to the fact and to the future. It did not look very bright, but many couples entered into loveless marriages. She would survive. And at least he was not going to take Jamie away from her—that must be her consolation.

Ellen glanced at the clock. He would be here soon and then she would learn her fate. Most likely she and Jamie would be whisked away to one of his estates, where they would live in seclusion while the shocking news was announced. It would cause uproar, she had no doubt. At some point she must be presented at Court as the new Duchess of Rossenhall and she would have to face the sly remarks and tittle-tattle, but she knew enough of her world to be sure that her story would eventually be eclipsed by another scandal and she would be able to get on with her life.

But what life? Max had been her first, her only love. There had been so many suitors, most of them concerned only with her fortune, but none had ever touched her heart. She had grown up hedged about by warnings that gentlemen would court her for her fortune and she had never found it difficult to keep them at bay. She had developed a protective shell, always laughing, always smiling, until she had fallen in love with Major

Max Colnebrooke and let down her defences. She had thought he loved her for herself. She had not told him of her immense fortune, and, although he had said he was the younger brother of a duke, their respective backgrounds had seemed unimportant, a world away from the reality of love under a desert sky. Ellen loved Max from the first moment she saw him and married him without a second thought. If the marriage was legal then everything she owned now belonged to her husband. Even her son. She must make her peace with the Duke, for Jamie's sake.

She heard the thud of the knocker and carefully put down her half-empty coffee cup. It was time. Snow had instructions to show the Duke into the drawing room and she went there to join him, pausing momentarily outside the door to smooth down her gown and take a deep, steadying breath.

Max was standing before the fireplace when she went in. He was staring moodily at the carpet and when he looked up his expression did not change. Formality and good manners dictated how she should behave. She sank into a deep curtsy.

'Your Grace.' Silence. 'Will you not sit down?' Ellen perched on the edge of a chair and folded her hands in her lap, trying to look composed.

'I must tell you how much I…regret…the misunderstandings that have occurred between us.'

'Ha! Regret, you call it? Treachery, more like.'

She ignored this. 'I wish to be plain with you,
Your Grace. To tell you the truth.'

'No doubt that will be a novelty for you,
madam.'

Ellen winced at his sarcasm.

'I never lied to you and I will not do so now,'
she said quietly. 'There never was a Mr Furnell. I
never married. When I discovered I was carrying
your—*our*—child, I decided to pose as a widow.'

He looked at her hands. 'Where is the ring I
bought you—did you discard it, sell it, perhaps?'

'No. It is in my jewel box.'

Ellen thought of the heavy gold ring he had
given her, engraved with Arabic characters she
could not read but that he had told her said *'I love
you'*. Crossing the Mediterranean in the French
frigate she had more than once wanted to throw
the ring into the sea, but she had kept it, clinging
on to the hope that when she was back in England
she might be able to prove he had not lied to her,
that he really was the man he purported to be.
By the time her enquiries were concluded, and
her lawyers had told her that Major Max Colnebrooke could not have been in Egypt that winter, she knew she was pregnant and she had put

the ring carefully away. It was the only token she had of the child's father. Now she glanced at the plain gold band on her finger.

'I thought this was more in keeping for a re-spectable English widow.'

'A very rich English widow.' Her eyes flew to his face and he continued. 'You say you never lied to me, but you will admit you omitted to tell me the extent of your fortune. I only discovered it once I set about looking for you in England.'

She could not resist saying bitterly, 'Yet for all my wealth I am not considered a suitable consort for a duke.'

'A man wants a wife he can trust!'

She winced at that and said quietly, 'I hurt you very badly, did I not, Max?'

'More than you can ever know, madam.'

She bowed her head and for a moment there was only silence.

'And your family,' he said at last, 'are they complicit in this subterfuge?'

'My step-mama knows of it, but she is sworn to secrecy.'

'She is married to an Arrandale, so no doubt she is accustomed to scandal and intrigue.'

Ellen's head went up at that. 'You forget, sir, that until yesterday I thought you had tricked me, that my child would be born out of wedlock. Lady Phyllida understood immediately that I would wish to make a new life for myself. As for my father's family, when they learned of my disgrace, they immediately cut all connection with me.'

'Yes, I sent my people to the Tathams in an attempt to find you and they were met with nothing but silence. Of course, they did not know the Duke of Rossenhall was behind the enquiry.'

'It would have made no difference. I have never told them where to find me.'

'And is that why you chose Harrogate, to be as far away as possible from everyone you know?'

'In part. You will recall I was travelling with a companion, Mrs Ackroyd. By the time we returned to England she was very ill. The climate in the east had taken its toll of her health and she was advised to take the waters. We both have too many acquaintances at Bath and Tonbridge Wells, so we hit upon Harrogate. We set up home together and she was with me for twelve happy months.'

Ellen ended on a sigh, wishing her dear friend was with her now. She badly needed support.

'I remember Mrs Ackroyd very well,' said the Duke. 'She was an intelligent and educated woman.' He hesitated. 'Please accept my condolences on your loss, ma'am.'

'What? Oh, no.' Even in her present situation Ellen could not help smiling a little. 'She is not *dead*, sir. She has gone travelling again. Greece and Turkey, this time.'

She saw his lips twitch. So he had not completely lost his sense of humour. But his next words set her on her guard again.

'You live here unattended, unchaperoned.'

'I do not need a chaperon.'

'No, it would sadly curtail your freedom, would it not?'

'I live here with my servants and my son,' she retorted, bristling. 'If I was to behave indecorously, it would be all over the town within days.' She rose. 'Now, if that is all you have to say, I beg you will excuse me. You will no doubt wish us to remove from here as soon as possible and I have much to do.'

'There has been a change of plan.'

Ellen froze. He was going to take Jamie. He had decided to divorce her, to drag her name through the courts, expose her to ridicule and shame before banishing her from her son's life for ever.

'We cannot leave Harrogate immediately.' Giddy with relief, Ellen sank back on to her chair and as she did so Max continued. 'It is necessary to remain here for a few more weeks yet.

You will continue to live in this house and I shall stay at the Granby. We will be obliged to meet, of course—'

'Wait.' Ellen stopped him. 'I do not understand. Last night you were impatient to quit Harrogate.'

'I had not then thought it through.' He walked to the window and stared out. His large frame blocked the light and cast a shadow over Ellen. 'Frederick Arncliffe is dying. I have given my word that I will remain here with him until the end.'

She nodded slowly. 'I understand that, Your Grace, but once our situation is known, life here will be very difficult.'

'Our *situation* as you call it must remain a secret.'

'What?'

He turned on his heel. With the light behind him, she could not see his face, but his voice was hard and cold as steel.

'We must pretend we are merely acquaintances.'

'No! Do you think I can meet you now in company with equanimity?'

'You can, madam, and you will.'

'I will not.' Ellen was on her feet now. 'The news of our marriage must come out, that can-

not be helped. I am prepared for our situation to
be made public, for us to be ridiculed in broad-
sheets and pamphlets, but think of the uproar if it
is discovered we are pretending to be strangers.
I will not remain here to be humiliated.'

'There need be no humiliation if you play your
part.'

Her lip curled. 'Do you think the truth can be
concealed? One slip, one wrong word and the
gossips will begin to poke and pry. No, Your
Grace, you claim that we are man and wife, well,
so be it. We shall tell the truth and shame the
devil, but I will not play your games.'

She turned away, but in two strides he crossed
the room and caught her arm, roughly pulling her
back to face him.

'Believe me, it is no game, madam.'

The words were more of a growl and they
sent a shiver running through Ellen. He was so
close, towering over her, and awareness crack-
led between them. The blood pounded through
her veins, she felt the power of him, his ability
to send all coherent thoughts out of her head. No.
She would not allow him to dominate her again.
Sheer effort of will allowed her to meet his eyes.

'I see no reason for the secrecy,' she told him.
'It would be intolerable to live such a lie.'

'I am trying to protect a dying man!'

* * *

Max had not meant to tell her that, but she had goaded him too far. He saw her eyes widen in surprise and the combative fire in their blue depths was replaced by a puzzled look and something softer, something that reminded him of the warm, generous woman he had known in the desert. He *thought* he had known. Abruptly he released her and walked back to the window, staring out across the Stray. People were promenading, wrapped up and battling against the wind that never seemed to ease up, even in summer.

'What has my remaining in Harrogate to do with Frederick Arncliffe?' she asked quietly.

He knew if he wanted her help he would have to tell her something or the truth.

'Fred and I have been friends since childhood. We joined up together, fought together. We were in the Peninsula, retreating towards Corunna when Fred was hit by the musket ball that he still carries in his lung. There was no time to find a surgeon so I patched him up as best I could and somehow we got him on to one of the ships for England. I had to do my best for him. *It was my fault* he took that bullet.'

He thought of his life for the past four years. Every moment since Ellen had left him was full of grief, guilt and inescapable duty.

'But I do not understand,' she said. 'What has this to do with me?'

'When my brother died in a riding accident last year and I became the Duke, my family and friends threw themselves with enthusiasm into finding me a wife.' He turned to face her. 'I never told them about our marriage, you see. My pride would not let me. I felt such a fool, marrying a woman I knew nothing about, only to have her leave me and throw in her lot with the enemy.

'I endured their hints and jests, the constant parading of eligible young ladies. I ignored it all, politely but firmly declined to show interest in any woman. Then Fred got it fixed in his head that his little sister Clare was the bride for me. He thought it a perfect solution, since I seemed so set against marriage. It would stop the match-makers pursuing me, while making sure his sister and widowed mother were provided for, when he is gone. I should have killed the idea from the start, but that would have meant telling him the truth and I could not bring myself to do that. How could I explain to my best friend, a man who is closer to me than my own brother, that I had married and never told him of it?' He read the concern in her eyes and added quickly, 'Clare herself was never in any danger of believing the nonsense, nor her mother or Georgie. We all thought that, with Fred being so ill, it was best not to upset him. But as time has gone on the idea has become more and more fixed in Fred's brain. I have promised him that I shall look after Clare and I will, but not as a husband.'

'I quite see that it is a difficult situation,' said Ellen. 'However, I am sure, when everything is explained—'

'No.' Max shook his head. 'Fred must never know that I am married.'

She bit her lip. 'I have been living a lie for nearly four years, Your Grace, I do not wish to compound it with more deceit. I beg you will let me take Jamie away. We could live at one of your properties while you remain in Harrogate. There would be no need then for anything to be said to distress your friend.'

'Do you think I have not considered that?' Max responded, impatience feathering his voice. 'It will not do. I called upon the Arncliffes this morning and know full well that you and Georgie are engaged to meet at least three times in the coming week. She is your best friend; Frederick would expect you to tell her if you were leaving town. He is not a fool, he has already remarked how well we danced together last night. He might well guess at something near the truth.'

She gave an impatient tut. 'He is even more likely to do so if he sees us trying to act as strangers. I am no actress, I cannot, will not be part of such a ridiculous charade.' She walked across the room and tugged at the bell-pull. 'Jamie and I will leave Harrogate tomorrow. I can say urgent business has called us away. What you tell your friends here is up to you, but let us be clear. I *will not* stay.'

'You are my wife, madam, you must do as I bid you.'

'Must I?' Blue eyes locked with green. Max saw the stubborn tilt to that dainty chin and knew she would defy him. She continued in a steely voice, 'You may be a duke now, Your Grace, but unless you have the marriage certificate about you, the magistrate would have only your word against mine and the matter would not be resolved without a messy and very public brawl, which is exactly what you wish to avoid.' Her eyes shifted to the door as the butler came in. 'Snow will show you out. At present I have no idea where I shall go, but be assured I will keep you fully informed.'

With the butler looking on Max was unable to reply. With no more than a nod he left her, acknowledging that she had won the first round of what was going to be a prolonged battle.

* * *

Ellen did not move as he left the room. She remained on her feet until she heard the soft thud of the front door. Only then did she collapse on to the nearest chair. She was shaking and wanted very much to burst into tears, but there was no time to succumb to such a weakness. There was much to do. A tiny, rebellious voice whispered that she could run away, set up home for herself and Jamie in another town, under another name, but Ellen knew that Max would hunt her down, not for her sake, but for Jamie's, and if she pushed him too far he might well remove the boy from her care altogether.

She rose and shook out her skirts with hands that were not quite steady. She would take Jamie somewhere they were not known and there she would await the Duke's instructions.

A little over an hour later Ellen was in the morning room, writing yet another note regretfully cancelling an engagement, when Snow announced Mrs Arncliffe. Her heart sank when Georgie came in and dropped into a low curtsy.

Ellen said bleakly, 'He has told you.'

'Yes, Your Grace.'

'Pray, do not call me that. We are friends, or we were, until now.' Ellen clasped her hands together. 'You must think very ill of me, if Max told you how I deserted him.'

There was nothing but sympathy in Georgie's eyes when she replied, 'He told me only there was a misunderstanding.'

'Did he?' said Ellen, surprised. 'That is true, but I begin to think it was all on my part.'

'I am sure you had good reason.'

'I thought so, at the time.' Ellen took a deep breath. 'I thought Max had tricked me—that he was an imposter and the marriage was a sham. So I hid my disgrace, took another name and came here to live amongst you as a widow. It was wrong of me to deceive you so and I beg your pardon for it.'

'I think I might have done the same, in your place.'

Ellen managed a smile. 'Bless you for saying so. Will you not sit down?'

'Thank you.'

Ellen was gratified that Georgie chose to sit close, as she had always done. As if their friendship had not changed.

'I had to come,' Georgie said quietly. 'Max told me that you were planning to leave immediately.'

'I think I must.' Ellen glanced at the little writing table. 'I was going to pen a note to you, crying off from our walk this afternoon. I am sure you will appreciate there is a great deal to be done.'

Georgie's hand fluttered. 'I have come to ask you. To *beg* you, not to go.' Her eyes, heavy with sadness, flickered to Ellen's face. 'I have no right to ask it of you, but you said yourself we are friends and it is as a friend that I am here. Max came to see me, to warn me.' She sighed. 'You know what Harrogate is, Ellen. Your dancing with the Duke last night is already the talk of the town. If you leave Harrogate now, within days of your return, there is bound to be speculation. People will gossip, the resemblance between Jamie and the Duke will be remarked upon—it will be impossible to keep it all from Frederick and if he asks Max direct—' She broke off, biting her lip. 'Fred loves the Duke like a brother. He would be deeply shocked and distressed that Max kept *such* a secret from him.' She hunted for her handkerchief. 'I am very much afraid that he will take it very badly and any upset now lays him low.'

Ellen stretched out and touched her arm. 'Oh, my dear.'

'It was wrong to let Frederick think that Max would marry Clare, but you see, it gave him such comfort to think that his little sister would be established when he was no longer here to look out for her. We none of us thought it could do any harm, to humour a dying man. And he *is* dying, Ellen. You saw how tired and drawn he looked last night.' Georgie wiped a tear from her cheek. 'Dr Ingram called today and says it cannot continue much longer.'

'I am so very sorry, Georgie, but—'

'Please, Ellen, let me give you my reasons for asking you to stay. Believe me, I do not ask it lightly. Frederick is very fond of you and would take your leaving us now very hard. He worries about me, you see, and says often and often that he is glad I have such a friend as yourself to help me through the dark times that lie ahead. Also, Max is afraid that if Frederick found that he had been deceiving him all these years it would break his heart. It would certainly spoil their friendship, which would be very sad, for there is no time to rebuild the trust that has always existed between them. And, finally, if you were to remain here as Mrs Furnell, and to meet with the Duke, Fred might see for himself that Max and Clare will not make a match of it. He would not expect them to marry if the Duke's affections are engaged elsewhere. He only suggested it in the first place because he knew Max had set his face against marriage.' She stopped, taking a moment to collect herself. 'Ellen, I know as well as you that Harrogate will be scandalised when the truth comes out and I quite understand that you do not wish to live a lie, but you have been deceiving us these past four years, have you not? Would it be so very hard to continue the charade for just a little longer?'

Ellen looked into the anxious eyes fixed so beseechingly upon her and she felt her resolve weakening. She gazed down at her clasped hands, gazing at the plain gold ring, the symbol of her own lies.

'Very well,' she said at last. 'You and Frederick have been such good friends to me that I cannot refuse.' Ellen raised her head. 'I gave you my word I would be here when you needed me, did I not? I will honour that promise.'

She could almost see the weight lifting from Georgie's shoulders.

'Oh, Ellen, *thank you*. I was so very much afraid you would despise me, knowing what we had done.'

'Despise you?' Ellen shook her head. 'How can I blame you and the Duke for humouring your husband, when I have been guilty of a much greater deceit? No, no, we must do this for Frederick's sake, I quite see that.' She reached out and took Georgie's hands in her own. 'Now, go you home. It is getting late, so I think perhaps we should cancel our walk this afternoon, but tomorrow morning you must send Charlotte to play with Jamie, as usual.'

'Of course, and you must take tea with me later in the day, as we do every Sunday.' As they both rose Georgie put her arms about Ellen. 'How shall I ever thank you?'

'By remaining my good friend,' said Ellen, returning the embrace. 'I fear I shall be in need of your support. Perhaps, too, you would tell Max of my decision?' She gave a rueful smile. 'I confess my pride rebels against informing him of this *volte face*.'

Chapter Four

When Georgie had gone, Ellen tore up the pile of letters she had written. They were unnecessary, now she had decided to stay. She wondered how Max would take the news and how she would react when they next met. Last night it had been as much as she could do not to faint when she first saw him and it had been no easier this morning. While she had thought him a rogue her anger had helped her to maintain her composure, but the realisation that he had been telling the truth had filled her with shame and remorse that she had ever doubted him. Added to that was the fact that she thought him even more handsome now than when they had first met. The way her pulse leapt at the sight of him was proof that the attraction was still there, on her side at least. She dashed away a tear.

'Well, it is too late for that now,' she said to

the empty room. 'You had your chance and made a mull of it.'

The past could not be changed, so there was no point worrying about it. Ellen squared her shoulders and glanced at the clock; there was still time to take Jamie for an airing before dinner. She ordered her carriage, then went upstairs to change into her walking dress while Matlock took out Jamie's warm coat to cover his blue suit.

'I'd be happier if you would put up the head rather than sitting in an open carriage,' opined the maid. 'That wind is cutting, for all that we are at the end of May. And you should take a hot brick for your feet.'

'Nonsense, Matty, it is only a fresh breeze,' said Ellen. 'We shall come to no harm if we are wrapped up.'

But she did not stop her old nurse from following them to the travelling barouche and tucking a rug about their legs, nor did she point out that her son would kick off the rug within minutes of their setting off.

Jamie loved riding in an open carriage and as they drove along the edge of the Stray she pointed out the various animals grazing there before they turned away from the open ground and headed for Low Harrogate. The roads were busy at this time of day, when many of the visitors took a walk or a drive before dinner. For herself, Ellen would have preferred to travel out of Harrogate but the noisy, bustling traffic provided entertainment for her son.

They had not gone far when she saw Max's familiar figure striding along the flag way. He spotted their carriage and raised his cane to attract her attention. Ellen's first impulse was to pretend she had not seen him, but she berated herself for such a cowardly thought and gave word to her driver to pull up.

'I was on my way to see you,' he said without preamble.

Conscious that her son was listening, and also of the crowds, and her servants sitting on the box, Ellen responded brightly.

'As you see, Jamie and I are going for a drive and, alas, after dinner I am engaged to take tea with Lady Bilbrough. Perhaps you could call tomorrow.'

'Thank you, I shall join you now.' He glanced at Jamie. 'After all, the sooner I become acquainted with this young man the better.'

She watched in horror as he opened the carriage door.

'But there is no room,' she said desperately.

'Nonsense, there will be plenty of room if

Master James will consent to sit on my knee. What do you say, young sir? You will be able to see much more if you are a little higher.'

Ellen had always been proud that Jamie was such a friendly, confident child, but now she found herself regretting the sunny nature that had Jamie climbing on to Max's lap as if they had known each other for ever.

This is my son.

The words rang around in Max's head as he helped the little boy on to his knee. He had known it from the first moment he had clapped eyes on the child and he had felt strangely relieved when Ellen had told him she had never married again. She had not tried to replace him in her life, or their son's.

Their son. His heart lifted. This child would not be confined to the nursery as he had been. He would not be a cold, distant figure like his own father, but someone the boy could talk to, confide in. He found himself looking forward to the new role and it should start immediately.

'Well, ma'am, I think you should introduce us,' said Max, as they moved off.

Ellen narrowed her eyes at him. He knew she was put out by the way the boy had taken to him and could not deny a feeling of triumph. Ignoble, perhaps, but very satisfying.

'May I present my son James to you, Your Grace? James, this is the Duke of Rossenhall.'

'Duke,' repeated James.

'That's right,' Max smiled, surprised at the pride he felt to have this little fellow sitting on his knee. He glanced at Ellen and said quietly, 'I wanted to thank you, for agreeing to stay.'

She was sitting very upright and gazing resolutely ahead. She said coldly, 'Mr and Mrs Arncliffe are my friends. I am doing this for their sake.'

'Mrs Arncliffe is Lottie's mama,' Jamie informed him. 'Lottie is my friend.'

'Is she?' said Max. 'Well, Lottie's papa is my friend, too. We have known each other since I was your age. We were soldiers together.'

Jamie fixed him with his steady gaze.

'I want to be a soldier when I grow up. I want to wear a red coat and bang the drum.'

'Really? Perhaps I should buy you a toy drum, so you can practise.'

'Not until we live in a much larger house. One with very thick walls.'

Max laughed at Ellen's interjection. 'Mayhap you are right.' He hesitated. 'Is my presence upsetting you, ma'am?'

'Not at all,' she said politely. 'What is it you wish to say to me, Your Grace?'

'Why, nothing of moment.'

She bridled at that. 'I thought you wished to talk to me. Anyone watching will think that I—that you—'

He could not resist teasing her.

'They will conclude I am, er, smitten by your radiance, ma'am.'

Ellen glared. Max could see she was about to make a blistering retort, but as she opened her mouth little James piped up.

'What is smitten, Mama?'

'I think you had best ask the Duke, Jamie, since he used the word.'

'Witch.' He mouthed the word at her over the boy's head and received a very false smile in return. 'Well now, let me see. Smitten means enamoured, besotted.' He heard Ellen's scornful laugh and added gruffly, 'Not that *that* is the case, of course.' He saw that the boy was looking confused and felt compelled to explain. 'People will think I consider your mama very beautiful.'

'Mama *is* very beautiful,' stated Jamie.

Max's good mood was evaporating rapidly. He had thought her beautiful once, before he had known her true character.

'In looks, undoubtedly,' he said. 'But beautiful objects are not always what they seem.'

Ellen caught her under-lip firmly between her teeth. Would he be throwing these barbs at her for ever, and at times like this when she was least able to defend herself? She called to the coachman to drive to the Granby, then turned to address Jamie.

'It is time we were going home, my love. We will set the Duke down at his hotel.'

There was a challenge in her voice, but Max made no demur. He talked cheerfully to Jamie until they drew up outside the Granby Hotel, then he eased the boy from his knee and jumped down from the carriage.

'I am very glad to have made your acquaintance, Master James. I hope we shall meet again very soon.'

'Yes, please. And will you bring me a drum, Duke?'

Max reached out and ruffled the little boy's hair. 'Not *quite* yet, but one day, sir, I promise.' Then, with a brief touch of his hat to Ellen, he turned on his heel and was gone.

Ellen sank back against the seat as the carriage set off again, realising how tense she had been in the Duke's company. The charm she remembered from their first meeting in Egypt was still very evident, but it had been aimed at Jamie rather than herself and to good effect. She was grateful for it, because she wanted Max to get on well with his son, but it threw into sharp relief the Duke's icy politeness towards herself. She reached out and pulled Jamie closer, hugging him tightly. The little boy laughed and squirmed out of her hold.

'What is that for, Mama?'

'Because you have been such a very good boy.'

Ellen blinked away a tear. She must cope with Max's coldness towards her, as long as he did not part her from Jamie.

Ellen had been so absorbed with Max being in her carriage that she gave no thought to the consequences until she met General Dingwall at church the following morning and he quizzed her on her new conquest.

'There are none of us will stand a chance with you now we have a duke in our midst,' he told her with a fat chuckle.

Ellen laughed it off and did the same with several other acquaintances who mentioned that they had seen His Grace of Rossenhall riding in her carriage, and she was aware that at least two matrons with daughters of marriageable age gave her no more than a cold nod in greeting.

'Everyone is convinced I have set my cap at Max,' she told Georgie when she went to drink tea with her later that day.

Her friend merely laughed. 'And why not? He is a duke and, in the eyes of the world, a great catch.'

Ellen sighed. 'It appears the world and his wife were on the streets of High and Low Harrogate yesterday and saw I had taken him up. Not that I had much choice,' she added bitterly. 'He climbed into my carriage without so much as a by your leave.'

'But it was an excellent opportunity for him to get to know Jamie.'

'Yes, they hit it off very well. Max was surprisingly at his ease.'

'He is a great favourite with Charlotte,' said Georgie. She paused, then added daringly, 'I think he will make a very good father.'

Ellen's hand fluttered. She did not want to think of that just yet. She said, 'Tell me about Frederick. How does he go on?'

Immediately Georgie's sunny countenance clouded. 'He tells me he is well, but just walking to the Sulphur Well this morning exhausted him.'

'So, he is resting now?'

Georgie shook her head. 'I wanted him to do so, but he was determined to go with Max to visit an old friend in Knaresborough.'

'Oh, I beg your pardon if my coming prevented you from going with them. You should have told me and we could have rearranged our meeting.'

'No, no, they are gone to see another military man, so I am very happy to leave them to their soldiers' talk. They will relive old battles and no doubt reminisce about their campaign days. I am much happier to be taking tea with you. It does Frederick good, to be out of my company sometimes. His mind is as active as ever and he feels very well, as long as he can sit and do nothing. He loves to watch and listen, but the slightest exertion now tires him.'

Ellen saw the sadness shadowing Georgie's face, but it was gone in an instant and she was asking Ellen if she planned to attend the ball at the Dragon the following night.

'Tongues will wag even more if you give up your usual habits,' Georgie warned her. 'Frederick wishes to attend, but we must wait until tomorrow to see how he goes on.'

'Do you know if the Duke is going?' asked Ellen, idly pulling at a thread in her skirt.

'He said would be there, yes.'

'Send me word tomorrow if you are going, Georgie, and I will attend. Otherwise I shall not go.' Ellen glanced around to make sure the door was closed. 'I have no heart for parties and I see no point in playing out this charade if Frederick is not present.'

'Of course not, my dear. I shall bring Charlotte to Paradise Row tomorrow to play with Jamie and I should be able to give you an answer then.'

'Thank you.' Ellen bit her lip, then said impulsively, 'I am glad that you know the truth, Georgie. It is a relief to be able to speak of it to someone.'

'You could talk to Max.'

Ellen shuddered. 'I do not think so.'

'It is natural that you are a little awkward in each other's company, but that will pass, in time. If it is any consolation, Ellen, I am not aware that he has ever looked at any other woman. That is why Fred was so convinced he had set his face against marriage.'

'And I am very much afraid he does not want this one,' said Ellen sadly.

'Oh, I am sure that is not the case.' Georgie touched her arm. 'The Duke will be bringing Frederick home soon and stopping to dine, perhaps you would like to join us?'

'I would rather not see him at all.' Ellen heard the rumble of male voices in the hall and rose quickly from her seat. 'I must go.'

The gentlemen came in, Frederick leaning heavily upon the Duke's arm. Ellen felt an unaccustomed awkwardness when Max nodded to her. Her cheeks grew hot and her pulse jumped erratically. She knew not where to look. Even as a girl she had never felt so uncomfortable in a man's presence. She bade everyone a hasty *adieu*.

'Perhaps the Duke will escort you home,' suggested Georgie as she helped her husband into a chair.

Ellen sent her friend an indignant look at this blatant attempt at matchmaking.

'There is not the least need, I assure you. Besides, the carriage is gone now and it would make His Grace late for your dinner to escort me on foot.'

'Oh, we can easily set that back by an hour,' said Georgiana. 'Is that not so, Fred?'

'What? Oh, yes, and that will give me more chance to recover. I am so dashed weak now, you see, Mrs Furnell.'

Ellen realised that her friend was right; Frederick's brain was indeed as sharp as ever, for he had effectively made it impossible for her to refuse Max's escort. A glance at the Duke told her nothing. She could not read in that inscrutable countenance, nor from his polite tone, whether he was pleased or not by the appropriation of his time.

'I am only too delighted to walk you home, ma'am.'

'Then it is settled.' Looking like a cat who had just lapped the cream, Georgiana kissed Ellen's cheek. 'Goodbye, my dear friend. Lottie and I will call upon you tomorrow.'

'I have the distinct impression we have been outmanoeuvred,' stated Max, as he escorted Ellen out of the house.

'I hope you do not think *I* wanted this,' she said crossly. 'It was bad enough that you were seen in my carriage yesterday. I dread to think how tongues will wag now!'

'Well, I am not going back, if that is what you want,' he retorted. 'I cannot approve of my wife wandering about the town without even her maid in attendance.'

'Oh, come, sir, that attitude is very outmoded. Many widows and married women walk about the town unaccompanied.'

'But they are none of them so dangerously beautiful.'

Ellen missed her step. She felt as if all the air

had been knocked out of her. There was nothing complimentary in Max's tone, indeed, she had never heard him sound so irascible, but his words hit a nerve and stirred a memory. She was transported immediately to a distant time and place: Egypt and one particularly star-filled night.

They had been dining with their Mameluke hosts before Max led her outside, ostensibly to enjoy a little fresh air, but really so he might take her in his arms and kiss her. Even now the memory of his deep, searching kiss made her tremble. It had drawn a heartfelt response from her and when it ended she had been momentarily bereft, even though his arms remained firm, holding her against him so that she could feel the thud of his heart through the *abayeh*, the long loose robe he wore. They kissed and talked and kissed again. Max took her face in her hands and turned it up to study it by the light of the stars, then he began to kiss her brow, her eyelids, her cheek.

'You have a dangerous beauty, my love,' he murmured between kisses. 'You drive a man to madness.' His seeking lips found her mouth and she melted into him once more, her bones liquefying and heat pooling deep in her core. 'Marry me, Ellen,' he whispered against her skin. 'Marry me here, now.'

She had clung to him then, knowing this was

foolish, reckless, but not caring. He continued to cover her face and neck with kisses and in between his soft, seductive voice flowed over her like honey.

'My men are camped not twenty miles from here. There is an army chaplain with them. He would marry us. What do you say?'

His mouth captured hers again and her heightened senses reeled with the sheer pleasure of the moment. She tasted wine and warm spices in his kiss, breathed in the dark, woody scent of agarwood from his skin and when he broke off to demand her answer, she succumbed to the midnight madness to whisper a reply.

'Yes, Max. Yes, I will marry you.'

The vision of that enchanted night faded. Instead of a hot dry desert wind, gritty with sand and perfumed with spices, she felt the chill rain-laden breeze of an English summer on her face, and with it came the more prosaic smell from the cows in the nearby fields.

Beside her, Max gave a low growl. 'And here is another of your admirers coming now.'

Ellen had already seen the portly figure of Mr Rudby approaching on the opposite path. She hoped they might pass unnoticed, but the gentleman was already picking his way across the road, waving his cane to slow the approach of a lumbering ox-cart. Moments later he stood before them, beaming and smiling as he removed his hat and swept a low bow. They were obliged to stop. Formal greetings were exchanged, but since Max was particularly uncommunicative it was Ellen who responded to Mr Rudby's friendly overtures, agreeing that last Friday's ball had been vastly enjoyable and that Monday's ball at the Dragon would have to work hard to match it.

'Although if *you* are there, Mrs Furnell, it cannot be other than a success.' Mr Rudby beamed at her. 'Perhaps, ma'am, I should take this opportunity to reserve the first two dances with you for tomorrow night. I felt dashed put out when General Dingwall stole the march on me on Friday.' His twinkling eyes shifted from Ellen to the Duke. 'If you are not already engaged, that is.'

'Yes, she is already engaged,' barked Max.

Ellen bridled. 'I have not yet made up my mind to go.'

Max bared his teeth and said smoothly, 'But if you do, you are already promised to me, are you not?'

Anger flashed through Ellen. Her chin came up and she glared at the Duke.

Mr Rudby laughed. 'Ah, I see how it is and I

shall withdraw from the lists. But only tempo-
rarily,' he said gaily. 'Let me warn you, Your
Grace, that Mrs Furnell is the reigning queen of
our little society and has any number of admirers ready to do battle for her favours.'

'I am aware,' replied Max, at his most urbane.
'But I am confident I shall prevail. You see, I
have a distinct advantage over my rivals.'

Mr Rudby looked nonplussed at the Duke's
smiling reply, but he recovered quickly and gave
another laugh.

'Well, well, we shall see.' He touched his hat.
'I shall not keep you standing any longer in this
chill wind, although you will permit me to say,
Mrs Furnell, that it has brought an added sparkle
to your eyes. Would you not agree, Your Grace?'

'Has it?' Max swept an indifferent glance over
her. 'I had not noticed. Good day to you, sir.'

Thus dismissed, Mr Rudby went on his way.
Max offered Ellen his arm again, but she resolutely ignored it and set off at a brisk pace, her
dainty figure rigid with indignation. He waited,
knowing she would not remain silent for long.

'You were very uncivil to poor Mr Rudby.'

Max shrugged. 'He considers himself a rival.'

'And why should he not? Are you so puffed
up in your own conceit that you think you only

have to walk into a room and every man will give way to you?'

'What has really upset you?' he retorted. 'Is it the fact that I saw off your admirer or that I refused to endorse his fulsome compliments?'

'Compliments mean nothing to me. Especially yours!'

Even as she spoke she was schooling her face into a smile to greet a passing acquaintance. Then another couple stopped to speak. Max recognised them from the ball at the Granby and nodded to them, then waited impatiently for Ellen to exchange pleasantries.

'Are you friends with everyone in this dashed town?' he muttered as they moved on again.

'A great many of its inhabitants, certainly, which is why I take such exception to your possessiveness.'

'Let us be clear,' he growled. 'I will not have you flirting with all and sundry.'

'I do not flirt.' She paused. 'Anyone would think you were jealous.'

'Ha, what a nonsensical idea.'

Quite ridiculous, thought Max. He was not the jealous type. Even in those early days, when he had thought himself hopelessly in love with Ellen Tatham. He remembered those first two weeks they had been together in the desert. The son of one of the Mameluke beys had been very taken with Ellen and had done his best to woo her with gifts and promises of riches. If Max was going to be jealous of anyone it should have been that handsome devil, but it had not given him a moment's uneasiness.

Because he had thought then that Ellen was in love with him.

He heard her sigh. 'Pray let us not argue. This charade is not easy for me. Your riding in my carriage yesterday did not go unnoticed. I was quizzed upon it at church this morning and now your escorting me through the streets will add fuel to the flames of gossip.'

'It is nothing to what will be said when they learn that you are my wife. The flames will become an inferno.'

'But I shall not be here then to feel the heat.'

There was something in her voice he had not heard before—a note of defeat that disturbed him. This was not the laughing, fearless girl he had known. Nothing had daunted her, not even being in a foreign land and surrounded by warring tribes. For almost four years he had thought only of his own loss and never considered that she, too, might be suffering. He had been angry at her betrayal and imagined her living a happy and carefree existence somewhere, possibly under the protection of a rich lover. He knew now that was not the case, that she had truly believed he had deceived her.

And she had every reason to think that. At that time all the evidence pointed to it.

He pushed aside the uncomfortable feelings of sympathy. He would admit she had some reason to feel aggrieved, but the damage was done. He would not allow her dominion over him again.

'I agree arguing will not help,' he conceded. 'But it is necessary for us to spend time together. I hope we can manage that without ripping up at one another each time we meet.'

'I hope so, too,' said Ellen, but she sounded doubtful.

They had reached Paradise Row, where the road was busy with carriages and the pavement full of walkers enjoying an early evening stroll. A few more yards brought them to her house. The door opened immediately, as if the servants had been looking out for her. Max acknowledged, albeit grudgingly, that she was well regarded by her staff, as well as by her acquaintances.

She had regained her composure and now said in a cool, friendly manner, 'I will not invite you in, Your Grace, for I know you are anxious to return to your friends.'

Max was well aware that many eyes were

upon them, including the butler's seemingly indifferent gaze, as he lifted her hand to his lips.
He would leave them in no doubt that he was
making the golden widow the object of his attention.

Chapter Five

No one watching Ellen go about her morning tasks the following day would have thought anything amiss, but as she discussed menus with the housekeeper, tackled her accounts and spent an hour at her correspondence she was constantly on the alert, expecting Snow to come in at any moment and announce that the Duke of Rossenhall had arrived to see her. Yet when there was no such announcement, she felt a prickle of dissatisfaction. Despite his determination to keep her as his wife he was showing very little interest in her. Since that first, fraught interview he had not asked her how she had lived for the past few years, nor explained his plans for their future.

She voiced her concern to Georgiana, when she brought Lottie to play with Jamie that afternoon. Since it was a fine day they took the children for a walk on the common and as the little ones ran about them, Ellen broached the subject of the Duke's reticence.

'I would like to know what he intends to do with us,' she said, a frown knitting her brow. 'It is a very delicate situation, his family must be informed and that should perhaps be done before anything else.'

'What of your own family?' Georgiana countered.

Ellen smiled. 'My stepmother will be delighted to know I am reconciled with Jamie's father. Oh, she will want to know if I am happy, and James, of course, but that will be her only concern. As for my Tatham relatives, I have no doubt that as soon as they hear the news, all their previous animosity will be forgotten in a positive flurry of obsequious attentions that will be embarrassing to behold. Max's family, on the other hand, are likely to be appalled.'

'Well, you need not worry too much about them,' Georgie reassured her. 'From what Fred has told me Max's family consists of aged aunts and uncles who never cared a jot about him.'

'Ah, how sad,' exclaimed Ellen.

'Fred says that to the old Duke the boys were nothing more than a commodity. Thankfully Max was army-mad and he made that his life.'

'Until he became Duke.'

'A very reluctant one. The brothers were not close, but I think Max had always hoped there was time to change that. Fred says he always spoke of Hugo with respect and affection. He was devastated when Hugo died and I do not believe he wanted to return to his childhood home after that. It was only when the old steward died at the end of last year that Max began to take an interest in his inheritance. Until then he had left everything in the hands of his widowed sister-in-law, who still lives at Rossenhall.'

'Do you mean the Duchess would have dealt with everything after her husband's death, even the correspondence?'

'She is the *Dowager* Duchess now that you are here,' Georgie corrected her, smiling. 'But, yes, very possibly. Why do you ask?'

'Oh, no matter. I wonder what she will say when Max tells her about me?' murmured Ellen.

'Well, it is a very romantic story,' said Georgie. 'Star-crossed lovers, losing one another in the confusion of war.'

Ellen kept silent. That was the story Max had told his close friends, but she could not be sure it was what he intended to tell his family. She needed to talk to him, to prepare herself for the inevitable gossip.

'How is Frederick?' she asked. 'Will you be attending the ball tonight?'

'He is very well recovered from his excursion yesterday and determined to go. He took a chair to the Sulphur Well this morning, saying he wanted to save his energies for this evening.'

'Would you not prefer him to stay at home?' said Ellen, catching the anxious note in Georgiana's voice. 'I am sure his friends would happily visit.'

'*I* would prefer it, but Fred so enjoys going out. Dr Ingram sees no harm in it, indeed he is in favour of Frederick getting about as much as possible, while he can. We know there will come a time when he will not be able to do so. I only pray when it happens that he will not linger, for he will hate it.'

'Oh, Georgie.' Ellen squeezed her arm in silent sympathy.

'Yes, well, that time has not yet come and Fred is anxious to see what you will wear tonight. He wants it to be another of your London gowns that will put the rest of the ladies in the shade!'

Ellen laughed, glad to discuss something as frivolous as fashion and forget more serious matters for a while.

The Dragon was not quite as prestigious a venue as the Granby and stood a little way out of High Harrogate on the Skipton road, but its balls were equally well attended. The dancing had already commenced by the time Ellen arrived. She found Frederick sitting on the benches at the far side of the room, watching Georgie and Max on the dance floor. His foot was tapping in time to the music and he greeted Ellen with a cheerful wave as he moved up and made room for her to sit down.

'Have you ever seen such an infernal crush?' he asked, trying and failing to look indignant. 'As soon as it is known we have a duke in our midst then everyone turns out in the hope of meeting him. And all those matchmaking mothers are throwing their daughters in his way! Not that any one of 'em has a chance,' he added, with satisfaction. 'Determined bachelor, is Max. Dashed uncomfortable for the poor fellow, though, to have every eligible female on the catch for him. Thank goodness he has you and Georgie to dance with tonight, that will keep him out of their clutches.'

'You are not afraid that Max might *want* to dance with an eligible young lady?' Ellen ventured. 'Confirmed bachelors have been known to change their minds, you know.'

'Not Max!' Fred was adamant. 'He has had the prettiest women in the land throwing themselves in his way and never shown the slightest interest. If the diamonds of London society cannot tempt him then I do not think Harrogate will have anything to offer.' He realised this was not very complimentary to his companion and added quickly, 'I include you amongst the diamonds, naturally, ma'am, but I know from Georgie that *you* ain't in the market for a husband, any more than Max wants a wife. Oh, Lord, have I offended you?'

Ellen laughed and patted his arm.

'Not at all, sir. How could I be affronted when it is no more than the truth? But do, pray, tell me a little more about your friend. Has he always shunned society?'

'Well, he was never one for balls and the like. When we were boys all he wanted to do was to be a soldier.'

'And was he a good soldier?'

'Lord, yes. Max's family had no use for him and they were very happy for him to risk his life and add a little more glory to the family name. You look shocked, ma'am, but it is the truth. His father was a cold, proud man who cared more for his rank than his children. Hugo was very much the same, a cold devil, only Max cannot be brought to see it.'

'Was he very attached to his brother?' she asked him.

'More so than Hugo deserved,' said Fred darkly. 'My mother has lived in Rossenhall all her life and she has always maintained that Max was the best of the family. She wrote to me when he became Duke, saying she hoped he might turn the Rossenhall fortunes about. Things have been in decline for years, apparently, and never a push made to do anything about it.'

Ellen thought of the laughing carefree man she had known in the desert. 'He has spent his life as a soldier. This must be a big change for him.'

'Aye, and it's not what he wanted, that's for sure, but he will do his duty and I have to say I am glad he has quit the army. He was always a reckless fellow. To tell the truth I am surprised he came through it all without a scratch. He was an excellent officer, but quite careless of his own safety. He was involved in some special mission in Egypt and Nubia a few years ago, trying to curry favour with the locals against the French. It's my belief the army thought his being a duke's son would give him more standing with the local chieftains, but it came to nought.' He paused for a moment, then shook his head. 'Max has never talked of it, but I think it must have been a bloody business, for he was never the same after that. He began to volunteer for everything—the more dangerous it was, the better he liked it. It was as if he had a death wish. But he was a dashed good commander and the men loved him. They would have followed him anywhere and he always did his best to look after them. Why, you only have to look at me. He rescued me from the jaws of hell and brought me home against all the odds.'

He grinned at Ellen and she smiled even as Max's words echoed in her brain.

It was my fault he took that bullet.

She turned to watch the dancing, content to sit and think over all she had heard, but it seemed that now Fred had started talking he did not want to stop.

'I believe he took his brother's death very hard. It was so unexpected, you see. Hugo never had a day's illness in his life. His wife had lost a couple of babes at birth, but it was thought there was plenty of time yet to produce an heir, so when he broke his neck in a riding accident the family was deeply shocked.' He added grimly, 'They would rather it had been Max. They had always considered him expendable.'

'Oh, do not say so!' exclaimed Ellen, unable to keep silent any longer.

'I heard 'em say so, many a time.'

'That is quite dreadful.'

'Aye, ain't it? But Max was the younger son and in the army, too. I suppose it was only natural that they should think he was the more likely one to die. But he survived, against the odds.

Sometimes in war it is like that, those who ain't afraid of dying seem to have a charmed life, and there's no denying that Max put his life in danger to save me, when the dratted Frenchie made me the present of his musket ball. Max came back for me and carried me to shelter, even though we was under fire from all sides. It was solely down to his efforts that I managed to get back to England. And I am very grateful to have had these past two years with Georgie and little Lottie.' He straightened in his seat as the music ended. 'Not that it would do any good to tell him as much, ma'am. Much better to tease him.' He looked up as Max approached with Georgie on his arm. 'Well, sir, have you finished romancing my wife?'

'She won't have me,' replied Max promptly. 'She prefers you, which I think shows a distinct lack of judgement.'

He was still smiling when he turned to Ellen to ask her to dance, but the laughter had gone from his eyes and Ellen felt the chill.

'Aye, madam,' cried Fred gaily. 'Dance with him, an you will, that I may have my wife to myself for a while.'

Ellen accompanied Max to the dance floor, her mind going over everything Frederick had told her. Had her desertion made Max so careless of his own safety? And then to lose his brother. The thought filled her with a profound regret that she had not been there to comfort him. She shivered.

Max's gloved fingers tightened on her own. 'Are you cold, madam?'

His question brought Ellen back to the present. She realised with a little jolt of surprise that they had gone half the dance without exchanging a word or a smile.

'I am a little tired,' she confessed. 'Would you object greatly, Your Grace, if we were sit out the second dance?'

He inclined his head and when the music ended he took her hand to lead her from the floor. When he would have escorted her towards Frederick and Georgie she held back.

'I should like to talk to you, if we could find a quiet spot.'

His brows rose and he looked at her, then gave a little shrug. 'As you wish.'

A couple had just vacated a sofa in a convenient alcove and he led her to it, saying as he sat down with her, 'This should suit, we can be seen from the main room but no one can overhear us without coming very close. So, madam, what do you wish to talk about?'

His tone was politely indifferent and the impulsive apology withered on her lips. It was far too late for expressions of sympathy or regret; he did not want them. He did not want *her*. Very well, she would ask him about his future plans.

'I am anxious to know what is going to happen, when this charade is ended.'

'I shall take you and the boy to Rossenhall.'

'Have you informed your sister-in-law?'

'Not yet. As soon as I do, word will be all over the country within weeks. Dorcas is an inveterate letter writer.' He added, his lip curling, 'She covers sheet after sheet with gossip for her cronies.'

'And what story will you give her, Your Grace?'

'It must be as near to the truth as possible,' he said. 'We met and married in Egypt, but lost each other in the confusion that followed the British withdrawal from Alexandria.'

'For four years? Why did we not seek out one another sooner?'

'We did, but decided to keep our marriage a secret while I was in the army. Your going off to explore the Orient with only your old teacher as companion has given you a reputation for eccentricity.' She gave a gasp of outrage and he stopped, his brows rising in enquiry. 'Well, ma'am, do you deny it?'

'I went travelling because it was preferable to the alternative,' she said in a low, angry voice.

'Which was?'

'To marry and hand over responsibility for my fortune and my life to a man. You cannot know how it feels to be always pursued for one's fortune. To have ambitious parents for ever extolling the virtues of their offspring. To know that every word, every look will be closely scrutinised, dissected and discussed.'

'Oh, I do, ma'am,' he said grimly. 'I have lived under just such a burden since becoming a duke.'

She felt a quick stab of sympathy, but it was ousted by his next words.

'People will wonder why I did not install you immediately as my Duchess, but I shall make it known that you refused to give up your life of pleasure here.'

An angry retort rose to her lips, but he put up his hand. 'Be careful, Ellen, remember everyone can see us, even if they cannot hear what we are saying. You must try to appear composed. To use your own words, every look will be recalled, scrutinised, dissected and discussed, once it is known you are my wife.'

Ellen fanned herself, saying in a low voice, 'You would have everyone believe I was enjoying myself too much in Harrogate to know my duty!'

'You have it exactly, madam. That is why I have come to fetch you.' Ellen closed her fan with a snap and turned to him, about to protest, but he continued coldly, 'The world will think you selfish and capricious, my dear, but you will live with that. You may console yourself with the advantages you will have as my wife.'

She sat up very straight. 'Do you mean you will divorce me if I do not go along with this story?'

'Precisely.'

All thoughts of sympathy or regret were gone now. She eyed him resentfully and after a moment he laughed, mocking her.

'You will be well served for your deceit, will you not, *Mrs Furnell*?' He rose and put out his hand. 'Come, the next dance is about to begin and your beaux will be looking for you.'

He pulled her to her feet and stood looking down at her. He had his back to the room, shielding her from the company and no longer needing to keep his contempt hidden.

'Note I do not say your *other* beaux. Do not consider me amongst your conquests.'

His eyes, green as a cat's, taunted her. She thought wildly that this was how a trapped mouse must feel, at the mercy of a predator. But her courage rose and with it her anger. She would never allow Max to see her distress.

She said lightly, 'I never did consider you a

conquest, Your Grace. The fact that I was so ready to believe you had deceived me shows that I had very little opinion of you at all.'

His eyes narrowed. 'You loved me once.'

'Did I?' Ellen achieved a careless laugh. 'I really do not think so.'

Then, disengaging her hand, she stepped around him and sailed back into the main room.

Max watched her glide away from him, head held high. Within minutes she was surrounded by admirers and she walked off amidst them, giving them her glorious smile, turning aside their compliments with a witty rejoinder. A hard knot of bitterness was lodged somewhere beneath his ribs. So she had thought it all a game. She thought he was the sort of scoundrel who would trick a virgin with a sham marriage.

Perhaps he should not have been surprised. Her behaviour had never been that of a shy ingénue. Even on their wedding night she had returned his kisses with passion, a little wild and inexperienced, to be sure, but there had not been anything shy or retiring about her responses. Max frowned. He knew how to please a woman—he had been taught by the finest courtesans in London, his father had seen to that!—and the passion he had roused in Ellen had been real, he would swear to it. But just because she liked his love-making did not mean she believed it was more than a diversion. She had told him herself that she was accustomed to being courted and flattered for her fortune as well as her beauty. She said she had never taken any of her suitors seriously, what a fool he was to believe she had thought of him any differently.

His hands clenched into fists at his side. She was a heartless jade and had only been amusing herself. If it wasn't for the boy, he would begin the divorce procedure immediately. Whatever the scandal and humiliation he did not want such a woman in his life. He frowned. She was the mother of his son and from everything he had seen she was a good mother, too. It did not make any sense. But their liaison had been conducted with the threat of war hanging over them and he knew from experience that in wartime very little made sense. He went off to the card room, prepared to lose a great deal of money if it helped him forget about golden-haired sirens for a while, but such was the fickleness of Fate that even without trying he won a small fortune in a very short space of time.

Ellen had left the Dragon before the dancing had ended and did not see Max again. The following night she was engaged to join Lady Bilbrough at the theatre and she almost cried off, but her pride rebelled at giving up the treat of a play just because Max might be there. She dressed with care, choosing a demure high-necked gown of bronze satin with a matching turban that set off her gold curls. She arrived at the theatre just as her party were taking their seats for the performance. Almost immediately she spotted Max. He was in a box on the far side of the theatre with Georgiana, but a third chair was empty. Ellen fretted, impatient for the first play to end so she could ask Georgie if Frederick's health was worse. She was too anxious about her friend to be deterred by Max's presence and at the interval she went to their box to enquire. Thankfully, Max excused himself immediately and left the two ladies alone.

'Frederick is at home,' said Georgie, when Ellen sat down beside her. 'Last night's ball exhausted him. I have left him and Lottie in Gregson's care. She is an excellent servant and has been with us for years, and since Fred vows he is quite terrified of her I hope she will prevail upon him to rest. I have told him if he does not do so I shall not allow him to attend tomorrow night's ball at the Crown.'

'Is he so determined to go, then?' asked Ellen.

'Oh, yes, although he has agreed to take a

chair, even though it is so very near us.' Georgie sighed. 'He is so unutterably stubborn! I have suggested that we should stay home and invite friends to call, but he thinks that would be giving in to his weakness, as he calls it.'

'And what is Dr Ingram's opinion?'

'That Frederick should enjoy himself for as long as he can.' Georgie looked down at her fingers, twisting together anxiously in her lap. 'He believes it will not be long now.'

Ellen squeezed her friend's hands, wishing there was more she could do. She heard the door open and knew without looking that Max had returned. She could feel his presence, it enveloped her, like a cloak.

'I thought we should have some wine,' he said, holding out a brimming glass to each of the ladies. When Georgie would have refused he pressed the glass into her hand, saying sternly, 'I insist. It will put heart into you. You know I cannot abide lachrymose females.'

'You are right, there is nothing worse,' Georgie acknowledged, doing her best to smile. 'Thank you, you have been such a support to me, Your Grace.'

'How many times must I tell you to call me Max?' he said, sitting down beside her. 'We have been friends too long for such formality.'

Ellen turned away and concentrated fiercely on looking at the crowd as she sipped her wine. The kindness in his voice was like a caress when he spoke to Georgie and it brought back all the old longing. But his next words were for her and there was no softness now, only cold formality.

'Did you enjoy the play, Mrs Furnell?' She turned to face him and realised with some alarm that Georgie had slipped away and the Duke had now moved to the seat beside her.

She said carefully, 'It was very good.'

'That is not what I asked you.'

'*Othello* has never been a favourite of mine.'

'No? You do not like all that treachery and deceit?'

'I do not.'

'Yet deception is very much a part of life.'

'Desdemona deceived no one. She is innocent.'

He held her eyes. 'But you are not, are you? *Your* deception was deliberate.'

She looked into his face, all hard planes and uncompromising lines.

'I made a mistake,' she admitted. 'For which I shall pay dear.'

'We will both pay dear,' he bit out.

Ellen put out her hand. 'Max, I—'

He rose quickly, but whether it was because

Georgie had come back into the box or he was avoiding her touch Ellen could not be sure.

'Ah, well timed, Georgiana,' he said cheerfully. 'The dancers are about to perform and Mrs Furnell is anxious to return to her own party.'

She was dismissed. He did not want her apology. Ellen rose to take her leave and Max opened the door for her, smiling in a way that made her long to hit him.

'Perhaps you would you like me to escort you, madam?'

Ellen thrust her empty glass into his outstretched hand and fled. She wanted to go home, to scream and rant and cry her eyes out, but that was not possible. The musicians were already striking up for the dancing and comic songs that preceded the farce. She had time only to pause and compose herself before she re-joined Lady Bilbrough's party.

They were all agog to know what the Duke had said to her and ignored the dancers.

'He gave you wine,' breathed Miss Houseman, an elderly lady of exquisite sensibilities.

Even in her agitated state Ellen had to laugh.

'And why not, since he was bringing a glass for Mrs Arncliffe?' She felt obliged to concede that it was very kind of him.

'But to bring it himself, to have a *duke* wait

upon one. How…how *intimate*.' Miss Houseman fanned herself vigorously at the thought.

'And he talked to you for a good ten minutes.' Lady Bilbrough gave an arch laugh as she looked around at her friends. 'I think the Duke of Rossenhall is very taken with our golden widow.'

To her annoyance Ellen felt a blush rising. She smiled, as if to suggest it was a ridiculous idea, but she was very grateful that the audience was settling down for the next entertainment and she could turn her attention to the stage.

Chapter Six

The next evening Ellen was in a quandary. She knew that her friends would be disappointed if she did not appear at the Crown in another of the new gowns she had brought back from town, yet Lady Bilbrough's comment last night gave her pause. It would look as though she was trying to attract the Duke.

Ellen sat down at her dressing table, bridling at the thought. She had never needed any arts to attract admirers. She could not remember a time when she had not been pursued by rogues and gentlemen alike. That was the reason she had been so happy to join Mrs Ackroyd in her travels, to get away from the stifling society that decreed marriage was the only respectable choice for a woman. Even her future stepfather, Richard Arrandale, had set out to woo her for her fortune, until he had fallen head over heels in love with

Phyllida and become a reformed character. Ellen rested her chin on her hand and gazed unseeing into the glass, thinking of her step-parents.

The eleven-year-old Ellen had been quite prepared to hate her new step-mama, but instead she had loved her and with only seven years between them they had grown close, more like sisters than mother and daughter. The marriage had been successful and full of affection, but when Papa had died, Ellen had decided that her still youthful step-mama should marry again and done all she could to promote the attraction she saw growing between Phyllida and Richard, who was not at all the hardened rake he wanted to appear. Theirs was the sort of love Ellen had always wanted, but never found. At least, not until she met Max Colnebrooke. From the first moment she looked into his eyes and heard that amused, mellifluous voice, smooth and dark as chocolate, she knew she had met her match.

'All for love and the world well lost indeed,' she muttered, thinking of Mr Dryden's play.

But the free-spirited adventurer who had wooed her in Egypt was very different from the cold nobleman who now claimed her as his wife. She had not yet heard back from her lawyers about the legitimacy of their marriage, but she had no doubt it was true. Max had made it abundantly clear that he would have disowned her if he could do so. As it was they were bound together and she must make the best of it, for Jamie's sake. And the situation was made even more complicated because Max had misled his best friend. No more than Max did Ellen want to cause Frederick distress when he was so ill, so they would play out this charade for as long as it was necessary.

'And as long as I am Mrs Ellen Furnell then I should act like her,' Ellen told her reflection. She put up her chin and added defiantly, 'I shall wear my new sapphire silk and there's an end to it!'

Max dined with the Arncliffes and insisted they use his coach to make the very short journey to the Crown Inn for the Wednesday evening ball. Frederick knew this was for his benefit and, as he was helped into the sumptuous carriage, he objected vociferously to being treated like an invalid.

'But Max came here in his carriage and will require it to go back to the Granby afterwards,' Georgie pointed out.

Max was more blunt.

'Stop complaining, Fred. You should be grateful. This is infinitely preferable to hiring a chair for you while Georgie and I walk alongside and get our feet dirty.'

They were even then drawing up at the Crown Inn. Max helped Frederick indoors and to the benches before leading Georgie out to join one of the sets that was forming.

'It is a pity Ellen is not here or you might have partnered her for the first two dances,' murmured Georgie. 'Your attentions to her at the theatre last night have caused quite a stir. I heard no end of remarks in the Promenade Rooms today.'

Max bit down his retort. He bitterly regretted his actions at the theatre, detaining Ellen at the front of the box in full view of Harrogate society, but she had been so cool and aloof and he had wanted her to look at him, to talk to him. And then, when he had goaded her into responding and seen the remorse in her eyes, he had shied away before she could apologise, afraid he would succumb to her soft words. In his heart he accepted there was some justification for her deserting him. The mission to Egypt had been such a secret that not even his family had known of it. How could he expect her to believe him, in the face of all the evidence to the contrary? But the consequences of her actions had been devastating. He could not forget that. And therefore he could not forgive her.

'Even Frederick heard of it,' Georgie continued as they made their bows and the dance started. 'He found it quite amusing.'

Well, that was something, he thought. At least it might reconcile Fred to the idea that he would not be marrying his little sister.

The first two dances had just ended when a bustle at the door announced a late arrival. Max looked across in time to see Ellen sweep into the room.

'Oh, doesn't she look wonderful? That gown is the exact colour of her eyes,' Georgie exclaimed. 'She is so beautiful, do you not think so, Max?'

He turned away to escort her from the floor. 'A veritable diamond.'

His partner gave a gusty sigh and whispered, 'I think your story is so romantic.'

Max's lip curled and he led her as fast as he could through the crowd towards Frederick, but there was no relief to be found there. Fred held out one hand to his wife and waved Max away with the other.

'You had best make haste and claim your dance with Ellen Furnell, my friend. The other fellows won't hesitate to cut you out, duke or no duke!'

'I'm dashed if I will pander to her vanity.'

It sounded truculent even to his own ears and

had the effect of making both Fred and Georgie laugh at him. He went off, half-inclined to disappear into the card room, but in the end he joined the throng about Ellen, waiting for his turn to beg her hand for a dance.

Ellen watched him approach, but not by so much as a flicker of an eyelid did she show her unease. She had seen his scowl as he left Fred and Georgie, observed how he assumed a look of slightly bored amusement when he drew nearer and wondered what barbs he had for her tonight. As if she wasn't already suffering from his attentions. Their tête-à-tête at the theatre had given rise to any number of comments, from the barely concealed jealousy of her ardent admirers to outright disapproval from more than one fond mama with a daughter to marry off.

He bowed and requested the pleasure of dancing with her. Ellen dropped into a curtsy.

'I regret, Your Grace, that I am promised for every one now, except the last dance of the evening.'

'Then I shall count myself fortunate to have that,' he replied with another bow.

She was annoyed to see how her admirers had drifted away when confronted with the ducal presence. Was everyone so in awe of him? That put her on her mettle and she fixed him with a dazzling smile.

'I hope, Your Grace, that you do not mean to spend the rest of your time in the card room this evening, as you did at the Dragon. That would be very cruel, when there are any number of ladies here without partners.'

'So you were following my movements, were you?'

Ellen had no intention of admitting anything of the kind. She threw him a pitying look.

'It was remarked upon, Your Grace. And several ladies were disappointed.'

He looked taken aback by that and as she went off with her first dancing partner, Ellen felt a little spurt of satisfaction to know he was not so uncaring as he tried to make out.

By the time Ellen went in to supper with General Dingwall her satisfaction was completely routed. She had had the dubious pleasure of seeing Max dance every dance with a different lady. He was at his most charming as he circled the room for a country dance with a shy debutante, participated with great enthusiasm in a Scotch reel with a dashing matron and flirted outrageously with his pretty partner during the cotillion. She watched him give his arm to Frederick as they went into the supper room and he remained with the Arncliffes until an ambitious matron dragged her blushing daughter forward to remind him that the dancing was about to begin again. At that point he jumped up with alacrity, not even sparing a glance for Ellen as he passed her table.

She tried to concentrate on the general's anecdotes, but she had heard them before and they did not hold her attention. She was bored, the evening was so dull that she wanted nothing more than to go home but that was impossible, Mr Rudby was already coming up to claim her for his partner. She went back to the ballroom, hoping the exercise would drive off these unaccustomed megrims.

The evening moved inexorably to its conclusion. The final dance was the lively Boulanger, performed in a circle and with little opportunity for private conversation. That at least was a relief, thought Ellen, a smile pinned firmly in place as Max led her out. Her nerves were stretched to the limit, she felt angry and ill at ease and blamed it all on her partner. It was his fault she had had to remain on the dance floor, smiling like a ninny when all she wanted to do was to go home and shut out the world. The dancing seemed to go on for ever, but at last the musicians fell silent and her ordeal was over.

'I am taking the Arncliffes back to their house,' said Max, making his bow to her. 'Perhaps you would like to take your leave of them?'

'I would, thank you.'

Her reply was as studiously polite as his question. She would infinitely have preferred to walk away in the opposite direction but she could not leave the Crown without saying goodbye to Georgie and Frederick, so she bore the Duke's escort with as much grace as she could. However, they soon saw that the benches were empty.

'Perhaps they are waiting for you at the door,' she suggested, but when they went downstairs there was no sign of Fred or Georgie in the throng of guests waiting for their carriages.

A servant came up and bowed low to Max.

'Your Grace, I have a message for you from Mrs Arncliffe,' said the footman in a loud, carrying voice. 'She has taken her husband home in your carriage, Your Grace. Mrs Arncliffe regrets the inconvenience to yourself and very much hopes that Mrs Furnell will be able to take you up as far as your hotel.'

'Impossible,' Ellen said at once.

'Out of the question,' Max declared.

The servant looked a little startled at their

response, but at that moment the cry went up that Mrs Furnell's carriage was at the door, so he bowed again and stepped back to allow them to pass. Ellen stood, irresolute, but Max took her arm and ushered her out to the waiting barouche.

'At least a dozen people heard that message,' he muttered. 'We would look no-how if we refused to comply.'

Silently Ellen climbed into her travelling barouche and huddled in the corner, as far away as possible from her companion. She wished now that she had brought a cloak, so that she might wrap herself in its comforting folds, instead of having only her thin stole of Norwich silk. Not that she was cold, the summer night was remarkably warm, but the Duke's powerful presence made her skin tingle. She was so aware of him it was like a tangible bond; invisible, silken threads drawing them together. He was sitting on the edge of the seat, facing her, and that added to her unease.

She said pettishly, 'If you had not insisted upon dancing with me, you could have left with your friends.'

'If you had kept an earlier dance free we would not be in this fix. As it is I had to waste the evening doing my duty by all and sundry.'

'Hah, an exceedingly pretty all and sundry! You appeared to be enjoying yourself.'

His countenance was illuminated by the glow of the numerous street lamps shining in through the glass and his contempt was all too clear.

He said, 'Perhaps you would have liked me to spend the evening leaning against the wall and gazing soulfully at you, like those idiots who fawn upon you?'

'I cannot help it if that is what they do. I do not encourage them.'

'No, madam? That low-cut confection you are wearing tonight had every red-blooded male lusting after you, which I do not doubt was your intention.'

Ellen raged at his sneering tone. He had as good as called her a doxy! She lunged at him, but he was ready for her, catching her wrist in a vice-like grip.

'Oh, no, Ellen, you will strike me only when I allow it.'

They were so close now that with every ragged breath the lace of her corsage brushed his waistcoat. And they were both breathing heavily.

'I hate you,' she ground out, each syllable heavy with loathing.

He bared his teeth. 'What you think of me doesn't really matter, does it?'

Even as she opened her mouth to protest he swept her into his arms and kissed her savagely. With her nerves already stretched to breaking, Ellen had no defences. She was flying, falling, drowning under the onslaught. His kiss conveyed a mixture of angry frustration and desire. She knew it immediately, because she felt the same, but it was desire that swept her up, calling to the fierce yearning she had buried for so long. Her bones turned to water, she felt hollow inside, wanting him to fill her, to possess her, just as she longed to consume him. She trembled, gathering herself to respond.

No! Even while her body was screaming out to give in she remembered the pain of losing him. She could not bear that again; she could only survive if she remained in control. Ellen struggled in his arms, but they only tightened, holding her against him. She was desperately fighting her own desires as well as his and she knew she was losing. Her body was ignoring reason and succumbing to an overwhelming passion. Only the sudden slowing of the carriage saved her. They came to a rocking halt and the bluff, cheerful tones of her footman announced that they had arrived at the Granby Hotel.

Ellen pushed Max away and hastily drew back into the shadowed corner as the carriage door opened. In one fluid move he scooped his hat from the floor and jumped out, walking off to the lighted entrance of the Granby without a backwards glance. She pulled the thin shawl about her shoulders and felt the tears burning her eyes. Despite everything, despite knowing it could only bring more heartache, she knew nothing had changed. It was Max's strong arms she wanted around her.

There was no time for weeping. Ellen spent the short journey to Paradise Row composing herself and it was with tolerable equanimity that she went into her house, even finding a smile for her butler as he opened the door.

'A letter has arrived for you, ma'am,' he greeted her. 'Express from London.'

'Ah, that will be from my lawyer. Thank you, Snow.'

She carried the missive into the drawing room and waited until the door was closed upon her before breaking the seal. The neatly written, carefully worded missive contained no surprises. Her lawyer informed her that his enquiries confirmed that it was all as His Grace the Duke of Rossenhall had explained to her. The army records were now complete, including the Chaplains' Returns, and he had seen the marriage entry with his own eyes.

*I hope you will allow me to congratulate
you upon your elevation, Your Grace, and
to assure you that I am, as ever... etc., etc.*

She choked back a sob and scrunched the
paper between her hands. So she had proof, if
proof were needed, that she was Max's lawful
wife. Four years ago she would have given anything for that news. Now, the thought filled her
with dread.

Ellen remained at home the following day,
crying off from several engagements with the excuse that she was not well. Word spread quickly
and by dinner time she had received several messages of sympathy as well as a small nosegay
from General Dingwall. There was also a terse
note from Max informing her that if she did not
appear at tomorrow's ball at the Granby he would
personally come to Paradise Row to fetch her.

Damn him.

Knowing there was no escape, Ellen prepared
for Friday's ball as if for a battle. She made sub-
tle use of the rouge pot on her wan cheeks and
allowed Matlock to spend more time than usual
arranging her hair in artless curls. Even the silk
gown with its white lace trim was scarlet as a sol-

dier's coat. She delayed setting off for the Granby as long as she dared and half-expected to find Max glowering in the doorway when she arrived. He was not, but she immediately spotted his tall, commanding figure on the far side of the room. He was deep in conversation with a group of gentlemen, but not so engrossed that he missed her arrival. He glanced up and for a brief moment their eyes met, glances clashing with all the cold fury of duelling swords.

A cotillion had already started and Ellen was relieved the necessity of dancing immediately. She made her way around the room, gratified by the warmth of her reception as friends were quick to ask if she was fully recovered from her malaise. Ellen made sure that no one seeing the golden widow that evening would think anything amiss: her smile was brighter than ever, she laughed at the mildest joke and greeted every acquaintance with warmth and kind words.

At last she reached the benches where the Arncliffes were sitting. Ellen quickly put out her hand to stop Fred trying to struggle to his feet but his wife had already jumped up and was looking at her nervously.

'Georgie, my dear.' Ellen pulled her close and kissed her cheek, feeling a little shudder of relief run through her friend.

'Oh, Ellen. When I heard you were ill yesterday I thought it might have something to do with the trick we played on you Wednesday night.'

'Heavens, no, of course not.' The laughing lie tripped off Ellen's tongue with shocking ease. 'Why on earth should you think that?'

Georgie smiled in relief and linked arms with Ellen, moving a little further away so Fred could not overhear them.

'It was all Fred's notion and of course he does not know the truth about you and Max. He thought you were getting on so well that it would be a great thing to throw the two of you together, which, of course, is what we want, but I knew you would not like it.'

Somehow Ellen kept her smile in place, but she could not help saying, 'I wish you had dissuaded him.'

Georgie looked a little guilty. 'I confess I did not try too hard. Fred is not nearly so fixed now upon Max marrying his sister. That is surely a good thing.'

'Then, perhaps, might we tell him the truth?' suggested Ellen.

'Oh, no, I fear the shock would be too great. He and Max have been friends for so long, you see. To discover that Max had been married all these years and never told him would be such a blow. Please, Ellen, let us continue as we are. It cannot be for much longer.'

Ellen looked at Fred. He was watching the dancing with every semblance of enjoyment, but Ellen thought he looked thinner and more frail than ever. No wonder Georgie was worried. Fred's sudden smile and the way Georgie released her arm gave Ellen warning of Max's approach. She turned, perfectly composed and a friendly smile in place.

Fred waved his stick at him. 'Max, you old dog, you haven't said a word to me yet. Are you come to sit with me?'

'No, I have come to dance with Mrs Furnell, if she will do me the honour of standing up with me.' He was holding out his hand, a smile as false as her own curving his mouth.

Ellen's deep curtsy was perfectly judged. A model of respect and obeisance. A model of pretence. 'The honour will be all mine, Your Grace.'

Ellen did not miss the triumphant glance that Fred sent his wife. He thought himself a matchmaker, so surely the knowledge that she and Max were already married would not kill him.

But the knowledge of his best friend's deceit might.

Ellen's thoughts raced as they worked their way down the set. And what of Max? It would be an exquisite punishment to ruin his friendship with Frederick Arncliffe, to destroy the trust between the two men, but it would be too cruel a trick and she knew she could not do it.

'Come along, ma'am, I think we must have some conversation while we wait our turn to dance again.'

The Duke's soft drawl caught her wandering attention.

'To talk as well as dance with you?' she said through her smile. 'A double penance.'

'But one you must learn to endure.'

'For the present,' she flashed back, smiling even more. 'I am not doing this to save your face, but to spare my friend a shock that might well end his life.'

It was time to dance again; he reached for her hand, murmuring as he closed with her, 'And you will continue to do it, madam, if you wish to remain as my Duchess.'

She had the oddest fancy that twin devils danced in his green eyes. Her head came up. She would not give him the satisfaction of seeing her discomfiture.

The dance turned into a duel. Every barbed comment was parried and their smiles were icy as they vied for the advantage with furiously sharp wit and glittering ripostes. Even the clasp of their gloved hands was full of menace, shards of heat racing through Ellen's arm at each touch. Her heightened senses imagined the sparks flying around them, yet through it all they performed the steps with perfect precision. It was at once exhausting and exhilarating. Ellen's blood raced through her body and she felt gloriously alive as they battled for supremacy, neither giving an inch. When the dance ended she accompanied Max off the floor with her head held high.

Honours even, I think.

Mr Rudby was waiting to claim the next dance and the Duke relinquished her without any noticeable reluctance. He did not approach her again that evening, but Ellen saw the smouldering fire in his eyes whenever they rested on her. She recognised that look: despite all that had occurred he still wanted her. The thought sent a small, triumphant thrill skittering through her body, but she suppressed it angrily. Yes, he desired her, just as she still longed for his caresses, but that had nothing to do with tenderness, or trust. Or love.

By the time she left the Granby that night Ellen was exhausted. Her cheeks ached from smiling and there was an angry tightness in her chest. She was unusually silent as Matty helped her into her nightgown and brushed out her curls, but although she told herself it was tiredness, when at last she fell into bed it was to toss and turn restlessly, unable to forget the devils dancing in Max's hard-as-emerald eyes.

She fell asleep eventually, but even in dreams she could not escape. It was their wedding night. She felt again the gentle rocking of the *dahabiya* as she lay naked on the bed, waiting for Max to come to her. Then he was before her, his muscled body gleaming in the near darkness. She trembled, shivered in anticipation as he stretched himself out beside her, cupped her breast in his hand and gently stroked it with his thumb, circling the nub until it was hard and aching. She slipped her arms around his neck, pulling him close while her body arched and her thighs parted instinctively, inviting more intimate caresses. She moaned softly, her skin longing for his touch as desire pooled, curled and unfurled, rippling through her in ever-growing waves. Her senses swam with the sweet, heady scents of an Egyptian night, she breathed in the delicate, woody fragrance on Max's skin as she clung to him and he carried her towards the final climax. And even as she was falling into oblivion she heard his voice murmuring softly. 'With my body, I thee worship.'

* * *

A knock on the door roused Ellen. She stirred, remnants of the dream so fresh in her mind she thought it was real and she almost purred with the feeling of sensual well-being. Until Matlock's brisk good morning brought her back to the cold reality of an English morning.

Ellen was at breakfast when her butler announced the Duke. Her hand shook as she put down her cup, spilling coffee into the saucer.

'I have shown him into the morning room, ma'am,' said Snow, observing her reaction with interest.

Ellen forced herself to finish her breakfast, silently berating herself for betraying her agitation. Speculation would no doubt be rife below stairs. Then she gave a mental shrug. This was nothing to what would ensue once it was known she was a duchess.

Ten minutes later she went into the morning room, her stomach swooping when she saw the Duke and memories of her dream returned with shocking clarity. She had to remind herself sternly that it *was* only a dream and he knew nothing about it. Nevertheless, his superbly fitting coat and skin-tight pantaloons only enhanced the athletic body she remembered so well.

Her mouth dried and she was unable to utter a word. Thankfully he did not seem to notice.

He coughed, as if ill at ease. 'I have brought something for James.'

Ellen looked at him, bemused. He gestured beside him and she dragged her gaze down to the small hobby horse propped against a chair.

'Oh. Th—thank you. That is very kind.' She struggled to marshal her thoughts, to put aside her own concerns and think only of her son. 'Would you like to come and see him?' His hesitation disarmed her and she said gently, 'I am sure he would like to receive it from you.'

'Very well.'

He followed her up the stairs to the nursery. It wasn't until her fingers were on the door handle that Ellen wondered if she should have summoned Matlock to bring Jamie downstairs. Heaven knew what chaos they might find. Resolutely she turned the handle. Whatever rules might prevail in a ducal nursery, Max should see his son as she saw him every morning.

They entered into an atmosphere of cheerful busyness. Hannah, the young chambermaid appointed to help in the nursery, was clearing the breakfast dishes while Matlock held Jamie on her knees as she eased him into his little blue coat. When Hannah spied their visitor her eyes widened and she hastily bobbed a curtsy before scurrying away. Matlock was made of sterner stuff. Unhurriedly she fastened the last of the coat buttons and set the boy on his feet, then she rose from her chair.

'It is the Duke,' said Jamie, recognising his companion from the recent carriage ride.

Ellen ignored the inquisitive gleam in her old nurse's eyes and said brightly, 'Yes, Jamie. His Grace has come to see you.'

Max dropped down to the little boy's level. 'I have a present for you.'

He held out the hobby horse and with a delighted cry Jamie ran forward to take it.

'Say thank you, Master Jamie.'

Matlock's reminder brought the boy up short. He stopped in front of Max, his little face creasing with effort as he made a bow. Ellen's heart swelled with pride and she wondered if Max appreciated this show of manners in one so young.

'I know you would prefer a drum,' Max was saying gravely, 'but every soldier should learn to ride, you know. Here, try it now.'

Ellen watched Max hand over the toy. He was smiling at Jamie and the resemblance between father and son was so strong that she pressed her clasped hands against her breast, trying to ease the sudden ache that assailed her.

Looking up, she realised that she was not the only one to notice the likeness. Matlock was staring hard at the Duke, realisation dawning in her sharp eyes. Ellen had not taken her maid to Egypt and upon her return she had told Matty only that her lover had died before they could be married. She saw now that before the day was out she would have to tell her faithful servant the truth. But not now. Not yet.

For a moment they all stood and watched Jamie gallop around the room.

'Have you had him on a horse yet?' Max asked Ellen. 'No? Well, we will remedy that when we get to Rossenhall.'

Matlock drew in a long hissing breath. 'Rossenhall, ma'am?'

Ellen ignored her maid and said, 'We must not delay His Grace any longer, Jamie. Say good day to the Duke.'

The little boy brought his trusty steed to a halt before Max and gave him a sunny smile.

'Goodbye, Duke. Thank you for my horse.'

'You are very welcome,' said Max solemnly, then with a nod to Jamie and Matlock he walked to the door and held it open, waiting for Ellen to pass out before him.

She felt the change as soon as the nursery door was closed and a glance at the Duke's face showed that the cold mask was back in place. They went downstairs and walked silently to the front door. There was no sign of Snow, but Max's hat and gloves were resting on the narrow side table.

She said, as he picked them up, 'It was very kind of you to bring a gift for James.'

The green eyes swept over her, cool and indifferent.

'Whatever I may think of you, madam, the boy is an innocent victim. I would not have him suffer.'

With that he was gone, letting himself out of the house and closing the door firmly behind him.

Whatever I may think of you...

He could not have made it plainer that he regretted his hasty marriage.

Max strode away from the house, seething with anger and frustration. If only she had trusted him. If only she had given him a chance to explain himself once he returned to England, instead of hiding away. *Hiding his son away.* Jamie seemed a delightful boy, but Max knew nothing of children. Confound it, he had no idea what he was supposed to do!

His experience of family life was limited. He

and Hugo had rarely seen their parents. Their early life had been spent at Rossenhall with an army of servants to attend them, but none of the warmth and love Ellen lavished upon her son. On the rare occasions when the Duke and Duchess were at home the children had been presented to them for no more than an hour each day, washed and dressed and paraded before any guests who might happen to be staying. Once the boys went to school they saw even less of their parents, and with three years' difference in their ages the brothers grew apart. As the future Duke, Hugo was welcomed home to learn what was required of him and Max was packed off to the army. It could not have been made more clear that he was not needed or wanted at Rossenhall. Max did not want that for his children.

Children! He stopped suddenly, earning a sharp reprimand from a gentleman walking behind who almost cannoned into him. A muttered apology, a touch of his hat and Max set off again, more slowly. More children would mean taking Ellen to his bed again. He had eschewed all women since she had left him. In truth, he had never found one to compare, so it had not been a hardship, and the thought of taking temporary comfort in the arms of some lightskirt repelled him. That had been his father's way and his mother, too, had had her lovers and never made any secret of it. In Ellen Max thought he had found a life partner. That was why it had been such a bitter blow when she had left him. But seeing her again he knew he still wanted her.

He recalled that kiss in the dark, jolting confines of her carriage. If she had not pushed him away, if they had not arrived at his hotel, he would have taken her then and there. The attraction was as strong as ever, although she had left him, although she had kept his son hidden from him. He could not help himself. Even dancing with her had been like some erotic mating ritual, each glance, each touch a tiny pinprick of desire until his whole body was on fire and it was as much as he could do not to drag her from the dance floor and sate his lust with her against the wall of the nearest alley. He closed his eyes and shook his head. By heaven, her hold over him was as strong as ever. How was he going to live with her as his Duchess?

Chapter Seven

Church on Sunday morning was a welcome return to something like normality for Ellen. She was relieved that Max was not present amongst the crowd filling the little chapel, but even so he haunted her as she greeted friends and acquaintances after the service. She could almost feel his presence hovering about her, ready to carry her off and leave the congregation a prey to gossip and speculation. As she moved through the crowd, smiling as if she had not a care in the world, she wondered how many more times would she be here to greet her friends and acquaintances? What would they say when it was learned she was Duchess of Rossenhall?

It had been difficult enough explaining the truth to Matty, who loved her like a mother. Ellen had expected the old retainer to censure her strongly for her behaviour, but so far she had been uncharacteristically reticent, for which Ellen was very thankful. She could not expect her friends and acquaintances in Harrogate to be so understanding. Well, it could not be helped. And at least she had one good friend who was privy to her secret. After visiting the nursery to give Jamie his luncheon, Ellen went off to take tea with Georgiana Arncliffe. As it was a warm day she decided to walk down to Low Harrogate, hoping the exercise and fresh air would help her to throw off her increasingly dismal thoughts.

She arrived to find the house in uproar.

'Fred collapsed this morning,' Georgie explained as soon as Ellen had stepped into the hall. 'Dr Ingram is with him now.'

'I can tell from your face you think it is serious.'

Georgie nodded. 'The bullet has shifted. Poor Fred, we put him to bed immediately, but he is coughing up blood and his breathing is difficult.'

Ellen caught her hands. 'Tell me what you want me to do.'

'Would you take Lottie home with you, as we discussed? I need Gregson to help me, so there will be no one here to look after her.' Georgie wiped away a tear. 'Fred has already kissed her goodbye.'

'Yes, yes, of course I will take her, but is there nothing I can do for you here?'

'Thank you, but, no. I have sent for the Duke, and if you will look after Charlotte that would relieve Fred's mind greatly.' She smiled through her tears. 'He does not want her to see him in distress and this is such a small house there can be no avoiding it. Lottie knows you, I am sure she will go happily.'

Ellen blinked back her own tears as Georgiana said goodbye to her daughter. Lottie went off happily, chattering all the way. As they had expected, Jamie was delighted to see his friend, and Matlock was only too pleased to take the little girl under her wing.

Ellen took the children to feed the ducks on the pond outside the hotel, but when the children settled down to their supper in the nursery under Matlock's watchful eye, she hurried back to Low Harrogate. She arrived just as Max was showing Dr Ingram out. The doctor tipped his hat to Ellen, but did not stop, and she looked up at the Duke.

'Frederick?' she asked, their disagreements forgotten.

'Very restless.' He stood back for her to enter the house. 'Georgie is with him now. Ingram does not think he will last until morning.'

Ellen stripped off her gloves and closed her eyes for a moment before asking if she might go up to the sickroom.

'Of course. Perhaps you can persuade Georgiana to take a little dinner, she has eaten nothing since yesterday.'

Max followed her up the stairs to the main bedroom. Frederick was lying almost flat in the bed, eyes closed and his breathing laboured. Georgiana sat beside him, wiping his brow with a cloth soaked in lavender water. As they went in Frederick's eyes opened and a smile flickered across his dry lips.

'Max. Come to see me off?'

'Not a bit of it,' he replied cheerfully. 'You will plague us for some time yet.'

'Liar,' murmured Frederick, without heat. His gaze shifted. 'Ellen. How is Lottie?'

'I left her and Jamie falling asleep over their supper,' said Ellen, coming forward. 'They have been out of doors all afternoon and I hope they will both sleep soundly.'

'Good.' For a few moments everything was silent, save the rattle of Frederick's breathing, then he gently pushed Georgie's hand away from his brow. 'Let me have a few words alone with Max, my love.'

Georgie looked distressed and Ellen went to her.

'I saw that your table is laid for dinner,' she said softly. 'You must eat, my dear, so let us go now and leave the gentlemen to talk.'

Max thought Georgie would refuse, but when Ellen murmured that a little food would sustain her through the long night she rose and went towards the door, stopping on the way to clutch at his hand.

'You will call me, if there is any change?'

'You have my word.' He waited until the ladies were out of the room before he crossed to the bed and sat down beside it. Frederick's breath rasped out and Max frowned. 'Should you not be sitting up?'

'Doctor said to keep me lying flat. Damned musket ball, he's afraid if it moves again it will be the end, but I'm done for anyway.'

'Never say that, Fred.'

'Aye, you kept me alive at Corunna, did you not? Against all the odds.'

'And we'll do it again, my friend.'

'Not this time. I'm finished, Max, I know it. And truth to tell I don't want to live if it means being a damned invalid for years, a burden on everyone.' He put out his hand and Max grasped it. 'You'll look out for Georgie, Max, won't you?'

'Of course, Fred. You've no need to ask that.'

'No, I know. And Clare? I know she still has Mama, but there'll be no man in the family, once I am gone.'

'I will look out for her,' said Max. 'You have my word on that, Fred, but—'

'I know.' The claw-like fingers clutched at his hand. 'I talked of you taking Clare as a wife. I won't hold you to that, my friend. I thought it would be a solution, because I knew you would need a duchess, however much you had set your face against the idea. But recently you've been showing more interest in the fair sex.' Fred gave a short laugh which ended in a gasp of pain. 'Ellen Furnell. She'd suit you, old friend, although I am not sure you'll succeed there. She's had her fair share of admirers.'

'I am sure she has,' muttered Max grimly.

'Never shown the least interest in any of 'em.' Frederick stopped, his breath coming in long, laboured wheezes. 'Either she loved her husband so much that no one else can match up. Or...' another gasping breath '...some scoundrel hurt her so badly she won't risk having her heart broken again.'

'Or she has no heart.'

'Like you, then.' The words brought Max's eyes to his friend's ashen face. Fred gave a twisted smile. 'I blame that damned cold family of yours. They made you afraid to love, afraid to reach out to anyone, lest they reject you. It doesn't have to be that way, my friend. Look at me.'

Max gave a wry smile. 'What you and Georgie have is very special, Fred. I do not deserve such a love.'

But Fred's eyes were closing and he did not reply.

Ellen had insisted her friend eat at least a small supper and take a glass of wine. She remained at the dining table while Georgiana picked at her food. Ellen had already sent her carriage away, determined to keep vigil with her friend through the long night. She soon discovered that Max had formed the same intention and they agreed to share the night watch and rest on the sofa in the little sitting room between shifts. Georgiana protested, but they would not be swayed.

'You will wish to be with Fred all night,' Ellen told her. 'Someone must be with you and it will be better if Gregson sleeps now, for you will need her later.'

Ellen and Max took it in turns to sit with Georgie at the bedside while Fred slipped in and out of consciousness. Evening turned to night and gradually the sounds from the streets died away to no more than an occasional shout or the rumble of a cart. When Max came upstairs to relieve Ellen just before dawn, Georgie was slumped over the bed, sleeping, her hand holding Fred's on top the coverlet. Silently Ellen withdrew and fell into an exhausted slumber on the sofa. She was awoken some time later by urgent footsteps on the boards above her head, the sound of voices and an anguished cry. Ellen flew up the stairs, knowing what she would find.

By the time the first rays of the sun were gilding the eastern sky it was all over and Ellen's carriage was at the door, ready to take her home. She went into the sitting room to collect her bonnet and gloves and found Max standing there, head bowed, staring at the floor.

He said, without raising his head, 'How is Georgie?'

'She is sleeping. Gregson is with her and can do all that is necessary now. I shall keep Charlotte with me until her mama is ready for her to come home.' She hesitated. 'Can I take you back to the Granby?'

'Thank you, no. I have commissions to carry out for Georgiana. The minister, the undertaker...'

'Ah, yes, of course.'

Max had his back to her, but there was an almost imperceptible droop to his shoulders. Ellen's heart ached for him; he had lost his closest friend. He and Frederick had known one another since childhood and, following so close upon the death of his brother, she guessed this new loss had hit him hard.

She picked up her bonnet. It was not her concern. He had made it very clear he did not want her sympathy. She had no right to comfort him. The bonnet hovered a few inches off the table, then she put it down again and crossed the room. She slipped her arms about him, pressing her cheek against the solid wall that was his back. He trembled slightly, possibly with revulsion that she should dare to intrude upon his grief. Silently Ellen drew away. Blinking back a tear, she scooped up her gloves and bonnet and left the house.

Max heard the soft thud of the door, felt the shadows lift as the carriage moved away from the window. He drew himself up, trying to shake off the black fog that clouded his mind. After so many years of soldiering he should be accustomed to death, but this was different somehow. Grief at his brother's demise still gnawed at him and now Frederick's death had torn the wound open again. At least he had eased his conscience by telling Fred about his marriage. He was not sure how much his old friend had heard or understood, but when Max had finished and begged forgiveness for keeping such a secret, he had felt the faint but definite pressure of Fred's fingers on his hand. It had been the last communication of any sort.

Summoning every ounce of determination, Max swung about, jammed his hat on his head and strode out of the house. The black fog hung about him, heavy and impenetrable as he performed his various duties. But through the blackness there were two small, wavering flickers of comfort, fragile as candle flame. The first was that he had made his confession to Fred and the other was the memory of Ellen's arms clasped around him.

The rituals of death filled the next week. Georgie had no family and Frederick's mother was too frail to make the long journey north for the funeral so it fell to Ellen and Max to support the grieving widow. They were obliged to meet often, but any conversation between them was brief and to the point, and often they exchanged nothing more than a nod of acknowledgement.

The Arncliffes were liked and respected in both Low and High Harrogate and St John's Chapel was packed for the funeral service, which Ellen hoped would be of some comfort to Georgie.

Sad as the week was, Ellen did not want it to end, because the following Monday Max was carrying her off to Rossenhall. On the Sunday she took Jamie to visit Georgie and Charlotte, and while the two children played in the nursery under Gregson's watchful eye, Ellen explained the arrangements Max had put in place for their journey.

'We shall be quite a cavalcade,' she said, trying to sound cheerful. 'It is a journey of nigh on two hundred miles and will take us several days to reach Rossenhall. The Duke has sent Mr Flynn, his valet, ahead to arrange our accommodation en route.' She drew a breath, thinking of the journey ahead, of being in close proximity with Max for days, nights on end. 'I vow I am a little nervous.'

Georgie shuddered. 'As I would be, if I suddenly discovered I had several large properties under my command.'

Ellen did not wish to correct her misunderstanding, so she said merely, 'No, that does not worry me. I helped my step-mama look after Papa's houses, and at the Academy Mrs Ackroyd was very keen that we should understand household matters. All her pupils were from wealthy families, you see, and we were expected to know how to run any establishment, from the humblest cottage to a palace.'

'And what will you do with your house in Paradise Row?' asked Georgie.

'It will be sold. Snow has already informed me that he is going to retire, but Max has agreed that I may find the rest of the staff positions in one or other of his houses, if they do not wish to stay here.'

'And have you explained the situation to Jamie yet?'

'I have told him that Max is his papa, but he insists upon calling him "Duke". I do not think he really understands what is going on at present.'

'Poor little man, it is very hard for him, but once you are settled at Rossenhall I am sure it will be easier. And I shall be following you very soon. Frederick's mother has written to offer me and Lottie a home with her in the village. I believe Max may have suggested it to her, because he has insisted upon sending his carriage to convey us to Rossenhall when the time comes. Did he discuss it with you?'

Ellen shook her head. 'We have not had much opportunity to converse.'

The truth was that Max had so far preferred to communicate via written messages. He was avoiding her company, Ellen knew it and was thankful for the respite while she put her own feelings for him into perspective. They could not hope to return to their former intimacy, but perhaps in time they might achieve an amicable partnership. She found herself praying that it might be so.

The summer sun was beaming down as an impressive line of carriages drew up at Paradise Row. Knowing that the truth could not long be kept a secret, they had agreed that both households should be informed of the situation before Max carried Ellen away from Harrogate, and she knew as she stepped out of her house that she was being scrutinised by the Duke's retinue. She was subjected to particularly close inspection from the groom, who was holding the heads of the glossy bays harnessed to the low-slung curricle standing at her door. Since the Duke intended to drive himself, Ellen had invited Jamie and Matlock to accompany her in the travelling barouche.

As Ellen had anticipated, the journey to Buckinghamshire proved exhausting. She and Matty spent their days keeping Jamie amused in the carriage. When they stopped each night Matlock took charge of the boy while Ellen faced an even more daunting challenge: dinner with the Duke. She could not blame Flynn for arranging a private dining parlour for the Duke and Duchess each evening, but she would have much preferred to be in the public rooms. However, there was no help for it, so every evening she and Max were studiously polite to one another, talked of unexceptional subjects and retired early to their separate bedchambers before starting the procedure all over again the following morning.

Max was determined not to be alone with Ellen any more than was necessary. When they met at mealtimes he restricted his remarks to the mundane and said nothing to rouse her spirit. If she fired back at him, if he saw even a glimpse of the woman he had fallen in love with, then he was sure the defences he had put up would begin to crumble and he did not want that. He did not want to allow her back into his heart and if that meant driving two hundred miles over roads that varied from the good to the abominable in a vehicle designed for racing, then so be it.

On their final evening on the road Ellen appeared in the dining room in the sapphire silk

she had worn to the ball at the Crown. The night
he had kissed her. Just the thought of it brought
a familiar flare of desire. She must have noticed
something because she coloured a little and said
defensively, 'I feel a little overdressed.'

'You look delightful.'

He meant it, but the indifference he forced
into his tone made her wince. He regretted it,
but with the servants traipsing in and out of the
room it was impossible to retrieve the situation.
Ellen appeared to recover, but he knew she was
uneasy, Max could feel the tension building between them. He tried to diffuse it by asking her
how she had enjoyed the journey.

'It has been much better than I anticipated.'
She smiled for the benefit of the landlord and his
servants who were fussing around them, bringing dishes and pouring wine. 'I am grateful, Your
Grace, for your consideration, I am sure you
could have made the journey in half the time.'

As she helped herself to a little rice and
chicken he noticed the ring on her wedding finger, the ornate gold band with the Arabic inscrip-
tion he had given her to seal their union. Had it
cost her an effort to wear it again? Did it remind
her of the vows they had taken, vows she had
been so quick to break? He quashed the voice

in his head that whispered in her defence. She should have trusted him.

Her soft voice broke through his thoughts. 'I am surprised you did not travel on ahead, since you have your curricle.'

'I could have done so, I suppose.' He paused while the servants withdrew. 'But it would not look well for me to arrive at Rossenhall without my bride. I have instructed that you are to be received there tomorrow with all the honour that is due to your station.'

'Even though I do not deserve it.'

He could not bring himself to deny it, even though he knew it was unreasonable. Circumstances had decreed his presence in Egypt should be a secret, so how could he expect her to believe him, when the facts seemed to prove otherwise? But he could not undo the consequences of her desertion, the black depression that had enveloped him and led him to embark upon so many reckless raids. To risk so many lives besides his own.

That is your guilt, not hers. Why do you punish her?

The question slammed into his mind like a revelation, but it was too sudden, the pain too raw and he pushed it away again. He struggled to speak, his tongue tied by the torrent of emotion that flooded in and her words hung in the silence like an executioner's sword.

She said quietly, 'I shall do my best to be a good duchess. If you will let me.'

'I am sure you will.' He wanted to smile at her, but coughed instead and looked away, hating himself but disguising his feelings, as he had learned to do as a boy. 'Now where is the rascally landlord with our wine?'

Ellen bit back a sigh. For a moment she felt like throwing her plate at Max. That would provoke a reaction, but perhaps not the sort she desired. Instead she fixed on her society smile, complimented the landlord on the excellence of the food, and discussed the recent floods in Shropshire and the possibility of the King's recovery from his latest bout of madness. Nothing personal, nothing that might remind them of their previous time together, and as soon as the meal was finished she retired to her lonely bedchamber, where the exertions of the journey allowed her to slip away into blessed oblivion for a few hours.

Max was in the private parlour when Ellen came downstairs the next morning and when he asked after Jamie, she explained that Matty had already given him his breakfast and was now taking him for a walk.

'It is good for him to use up some of his high spirits before the journey,' she explained.

'Is he very hard work for you?'

She smiled at him, touched by his consideration.

'Why, no, not really. Matty and I take turns to keep him amused, tell him stories and sing songs. It has been a long journey and he has done very well for such a little boy.'

'Let us hope his good behaviour lasts for this final stage, then.'

No more was said, but when Max escorted Ellen to the waiting carriages they found Jamie engaged in a battle of wills with his nurse. He was clutching the hobby horse and glaring at Matty, a mulish set to his mouth.

'Now what the devil is going on here?' demanded Max.

'Master James wants to take his toy into the chaise with us, Your Grace,' Matlock explained. 'I've told him there's no room, but he won't listen. We shall be black and blue if we let him have his way.'

'We shall indeed,' Ellen agreed, wondering how best to resolve the impasse without tears.

Jamie's lip was already trembling as he declared he wanted to keep horsey with him. To Ellen's surprise Max stepped into the breach.

'Of course you do,' he said cheerfully. 'But the ladies wouldn't like that. What do you say to helping me with *my* horses?'

'Do you mean...sit up in the curricle with you?' demanded Ellen, shaken.

'Yes, of course.' Max smiled down at Jamie. 'A fellow can get very tired driving a team on his own all day.'

'B-but he is too little,' she objected. 'He might fall out and you will not be able to watch him all the time, if you are driving.'

'Then let his nurse come with him.' Ellen saw Matlock's look of horror at the idea. Max clearly noticed it, too, for he shrugged and said, 'Or you could come with us.'

For a few moments Ellen could think of nothing to say.

'I shall help you, Duke,' declared Jamie, his good humour restored. He held out the hobby horse to Matlock and kindly informed her she might put it away, then he ran to Ellen and took her hand. 'Come along, Mama.'

Ellen looked at Max. 'Are you sure you want to do this?'

'Do we have any choice now?'

A ragged laugh shook her. 'No, not unless we want a tantrum.'

Minutes later they were off, Jamie sitting proudly between the Duke and Duchess and waving goodbye to the grinning ostlers, who had witnessed the little scene.

Ellen kept one hand on the wide rail and an arm about Jamie, pinning him firmly to the seat as Max deftly negotiated the narrow roads. She heard a chuckle from the groom behind them.

'Don't you worry, Your Grace,' he addressed her cheerfully. 'The master ain't never overturned us yet. Not that we're used to driving females and young 'uns, of course.'

'That will do, Stevens,' said Max repressively.

He was looking quite severe and Ellen wondered if he was regretting his generosity. She tried to think of something to break the silence.

'Did your father teach you to drive?' she asked him at last.

His bark of laughter had a bitter note to it.

'He took no interest in anything I did. His only concern was that I should not disgrace the family name.'

'It is quite reprehensible,' she burst out, indignantly.

'Oh, he did what he thought was his duty,' said Max drily. 'My education was the best money could buy, in every field, including the bedroom.'

A *frisson* of excitement ran through Ellen as she recalled his skill as a lover, but she could not ignore the unhappiness in his voice and sought for some way to dispel it.

She said daringly, 'Then it was not all wasted.'

As she had hoped, the haunted look left his eyes and he laughed. 'No, not all of it.'

Jamie tugged at his sleeve. 'When can I hold the reins, Duke?'

'Very soon now. Once we are clear of the town you shall do so.'

Knowing Jamie would be impatient for his treat, Ellen distracted him, pointing out two little dogs scrapping over a bone and a pie-man balancing a tray of freshly baked pastries on his head. Five minutes later they had left the town behind and were bowling along the open road. They soon drew away from the other carriages and when they reached a straight stretch of empty road Max slowed his team.

'Now, Jamie, let us see how you can handle the ribbons.'

He lifted the boy on to his lap and showed him how to hold the reins in his little hands. Ellen watched anxiously, determined not to spoil Jamie's enjoyment by showing her concern. The groom leaned forward and murmured in her ear, 'No need to fret, ma'am. The master's covering him all right and tight.'

Ellen turned and gave Stevens a grateful smile. She had expected the Duke's staff to treat her with cold reserve, but those she had met so far had shown her a kindly respect, which was very encouraging.

It was not to be expected that such a small boy could sit still holding the reins for very long and after ten minutes Ellen judged he had had enough.

'You have done very well, Jamie,' she said. 'Perhaps the Duke will let you try again later.'

'Yes, of course,' Max nodded as Ellen lifted the boy on to the seat between them. 'But for now we must pick up the pace a little.'

Immediately Jamie's face lit up. 'Yes, let's race!'

'We shall do nothing so indecorous,' declared Ellen, trying to sound severe.

Max looked across and she met his eyes. It was a moment of understanding, of shared pleasure, and it warmed her.

With his wife and son beside him in the curricle, Max had not expected to enjoy the drive, but to his surprise the miles flew by and they soon reached their final stop. The Rising Sun was barely fifteen miles from Rossenhall and Max was well known there. He saw the speculation in the landlord's eyes as he regarded Ellen and Jamie, but they were escorted into the private parlour with many a low bow and assurances that they would receive every attention.

Max nodded, drawing off his gloves. 'The rest of the party are some way behind us, but we will take our refreshment immediately.'

'Yes, Your Grace. Immediately, Your Grace.'

'Your distinction has served us well on this journey,' remarked Ellen, as the landlord bustled away, shouting orders to his staff.

Max grimaced. 'I could do without all the bowing and scraping, but it does have its uses.' He looked down at Jamie, who was tugging urgently at Ellen's skirts. 'Now what is wrong?'

Ellen swung Jamie up into her arms. 'He needs the privy.'

He frowned. 'Can he not wait until his nurse arrives? Or let a servant take him.'

'Certainly not.'

Jamie stretched out his arms towards Max. 'Duke take me.'

But Ellen was already heading for the door, saying with a laugh in her voice, 'I do not think your papa is *quite* ready for that, Jamie!'

Then she was gone, but the memory of her irrepressible laughter remained with Max, causing a reluctant smile to tug at the corners of his mouth. He threw his hat and gloves on to a side table. This was not what he had intended at all. He wanted to keep his distance from Ellen, he wanted them to be politely civil to one another, but it was impossible when that little imp was present. There was no doubt the child had inherited his mother's engaging ways. Max had noticed during the journey south that Ellen had won the approval of his staff, even Stevens, his suspicious groom. Of course they none of them knew the truth, that she had left him within weeks of their marriage. He must harden his heart against her. She was the only woman he had ever loved and her desertion had almost destroyed him. He had no intention of falling in love with her all over again.

When Ellen brought Jamie back to the little parlour, Max was once more in control. He politely invited them to sit down and enjoy the selection of pies and cold meats provided for their refreshment. Ellen refused a glass of milk for Jamie and persuaded him to take a little herb tea.

'We still have an hour's journey ahead of us

and milk might upset his stomach,' she explained
to Max. 'I do not wish to introduce a bilious little
boy to your staff.' She glanced towards the window as she picked up her coffee cup. 'Here are
the rest of our party. Jamie and I will be able to
finish the journey in the barouche.'

Max pushed away his empty plate.

'That would be the most fitting way for you to
arrive,' he agreed. 'Or—' He stopped, fighting
with himself. Trying to resurrect his defences.

'Yes?'

She sounded a little breathless, but he dared
not raise his eyes to look at her.

'Or you could come with me.' Silence. He continued, 'I have no doubt the announcement that
I have a wife and son has given rise to a great
deal of gossip at Rossenhall. For us to arrive *en
famille* would do much to allay the speculation.'

'Th—thank you. You are very kind.'

Kind! Was that it? No, he *wanted* her beside
him, but he could hardly admit it, even to himself, so he said gruffly, 'I am repaying your kindness to *me*. When Fred died.'

Ellen fussed over Jamie, wiping the crumbs
from his mouth, cleaning his hands, resigning
herself to the fact that Max was paying what he
saw as a debt, and doubtless thinking of how it

would look to his household. It was not for her benefit at all. He was just being sensible and it was very silly of her to feel like crying.

Chapter Eight

Ellen hugged Jamie closer as the curricle slowed and turned on to the winding drive that led to Rossenhall, the Duke's principal seat. As a young girl she had been told many times that with her looks and her fortune she could marry into the peerage. Indeed, her admirers had included a marquess and more than one earl, but such a marriage had never interested her, even though the education she had received at Mrs Ackroyd's Academy had made her eminently qualified for such an exalted position. Ellen had decided at a very early age that she would only marry for love and she had found that love with Max. It had not mattered a jot to her whether he was a poor soldier or a prince. Now, she felt a certain irony that after years spent avoiding society, she was returning to it as a duchess.

When the house finally came into view she

began to wish she had chosen to travel in the elegant travelling barouche rather than arriving in an open carriage, with her face glowing from the fresh air and her hair windblown. It would have been a more fitting entrance for a duchess, but it was too late for regrets, so she turned her attention to her new home. The house stood proudly before them: a creamy grey Palladian mansion with two wings spreading out like open arms on either side of a central block, where two flights of curving stone steps ascended to the main entrance set beneath a pediment supported by four immense stone columns.

'It has been altered significantly over the years,' Max told her, as they approached. 'The old house was rebuilt in the last century and the east and west wings added to make it more a more suitable residence for a duke.'

Even as he spoke the servants began to file out on to one set of steps to greet them.

'I am glad the sun is shining,' remarked Max as he brought the curricle to a halt before the entrance. 'You are seeing the house at its best.'

There was no time for her to reply. Stevens had run to the horses' heads and Max was already walking around to help her alight.

'Give me the boy first.' Jamie went to him willingly and once Max had settled him comfortably on one arm he reached out his hand to Ellen. 'Welcome to your new home.'

Ellen accompanied the Duke up the curling steps, past the waiting servants who bowed or curtsied as they went by. With their son in his arms, Max was making it plain to everyone that this was his family and she was grateful. At the top of the steps stood a plump, rosy-cheeked woman in a spotless white cap and apron, whom he introduced as Mrs Greenwood, the housekeeper.

'She will make you acquainted with the rest of the staff at some stage, I am sure.' He turned to the black-coated figure standing beside the housekeeper. 'And this is Perkins.'

The butler bowed low to Ellen.

'Welcome to your new home, Your Grace.' He straightened and addressed the Duke. 'The Dowager Duchess is awaiting you in the drawing room. She asked that I show you in directly you arrived.'

'Thank you, Perkins, but that will not be possible. First I must take my son to the nursery.' He threw a glance at Ellen, his eyes glinting with amusement. 'You see, I have learned something of a parent's duties already. Come along.'

Some half an hour later Ellen and Jamie accompanied Max to the drawing room, where the

Dowager Duchess was waiting for them. She looked to be only a few years older than Ellen and her thin frame was clad in black, unrelieved by any touch of colour. Her fair hair was simply dressed about her head and covered with a black cap, adding to the severity of her demeanour. Her haughty expression did not soften as Max made the introductions.

Since the Duke was holding Jamie's hand, Ellen went forward and kissed the Dowager's cheek, saying in her friendly way, 'Please, call me Ellen, and I hope you will allow me to call you Dorcas.'

The Dowager stiffened at Ellen's embrace and quickly drew away, turning to address Max.

'And that is your son.' Her pale blue eyes rested upon Jamie. 'Your heir.'

'Yes,' Max smiled. 'Let me present to you James, the Marquess of Dern.'

Dorcas sat down and held out her hands. 'Well, James, have you a kiss for your aunt?'

Max chuckled as Jamie shrank against his leg. 'Go along, young sir, she won't bite you.'

Looking at Dorcas's cold eyes and thin smile, Ellen was not so sure. She picked up her son and sat down with him on her knee.

'I am afraid he is a little shy of strangers,' she said, holding him close.

The Dowager ignored her.

'When do you go to town, Maximilian? It is usual for a new duchess to be presented within days of her marriage. I know your case is a little exceptional, but you would not wish to be backward in your attentions.'

'The Court has waited four years to see my Duchess,' he replied, 'another few months will not matter. We shall go to town in the spring.'

'Really?' Dorcas raised her fine brows. 'And what does my new sister-in-law say to that? Ah, but I am forgetting,' she continued swiftly, as Ellen opened her mouth to speak. 'No doubt you welcome the delay, since you preferred to hide away, rather than take your place here as Maximilian's wife.'

Ellen did not flinch from her cold stare. She knew Dorcas was trying to discompose her, but she would not allow that.

'I am here now,' she said quietly. 'And I mean to stay.'

'I dare say everything here will seem very strange to you,' remarked the Dowager with a condescending smile. 'Harrogate is so very far north and I understand you have been living in a very *small* way.'

'Yes, my whole house in Paradise Row would fit into this chamber,' said Ellen cheerfully. 'I do hope I shall not be expected to clean it all myself.'

Max stifled a laugh at the Dowager's shocked expression.

'My wife is teasing you, Dorcas,' he said, sending a frowning look at Ellen. 'She is no stranger to large residences. I have seen her family home and it is a very substantial property, I assure you.'

'But it is not a duke's seat,' Dorcas pointed out, clearly not amused.

The entry of Perkins caused a welcome distraction.

'I took the liberty of ordering tea to be served,' said Dorcas as the butler was followed by footmen carrying the elegant silver spirit kettle and trays full of porcelain. She added with a graciousness as false as her smile, 'I hope you will forgive me, I realise that this should be your task now, Your Grace.'

'Pray, call me Ellen. And there is nothing to forgive. There will be time enough for me to take up the reins.' Ellen glanced at Max and a sudden memory surfaced. 'However, I think His Grace might prefer coffee,' she murmured. 'Or, perhaps a tankard of ale after the journey?'

She saw his look of surprise.

'Yes, I would. Ale for me.'

Ellen nodded at the butler, who bowed low.

'It shall be done immediately, Your Grace, and if I may suggest, a cup of milk for the Marquess? It's as fresh as can be, Cook having sent for it as soon as she set eyes on the young master.'

Jamie had been leaning against her, but now he sat up.

'Milk? I would like that very much, if you please.'

He clasped his hands together and looked up so hopefully that the old retainer's stately manner deserted him and he gave Jamie a fatherly smile.

'Then you shall have one, my lord. His Grace was always partial to a cup of milk when he was a little boy.'

'That will be all, Perkins!' The Dowager Duchess's shrill tones cut across the room. The butler's countenance became an impassive mask once more and he withdrew silently. Dorcas shifted around to address Ellen. 'If I may give you a word of advice, dear sister, the boy needs to learn what is due to his station. Servants will take advantage if he shows them too much deference.'

'Nonsense,' said Max. 'The boy's manners are very good.' He glanced at Ellen, a reluctant grin tugging at his mouth. 'He will have them all eating out of his hand before the week is out.'

Ellen smiled, but said nothing. She could only hope that she would have a fraction of Jamie's success.

While she engaged in the ritual of tea drinking with her sister-in-law, Ellen considered her situation. It was clear that Dorcas resented her presence, but the fact that Max had defended Jamie against the Dowager Duchess's strictures was heartening. She did not feel quite so alone.

By the time they had finished their refreshments, the rest of their retinue had arrived and Ellen took Jamie back to the nursery, glad of the excuse to leave the stilted atmosphere of the drawing room. The milk had refreshed the little boy and Ellen left him telling Matlock about his journey in the curricle.

'...and the Duke even let me hold the reins, Matty!'

Ellen smiled as she closed the door upon them, knowing he at least was happy in his new home. As she moved away from the door she saw the housekeeper waiting for her at the top of the stairs.

'I've come to escort you over the house, Your Grace,' she announced, sinking into a curtsy. She saw Ellen's look of surprise and added, 'The Dowager Duchess sent me.'

Ellen smiled. 'Mrs Greenwood, is it not? I wonder, would you be very put out if we were to leave that until tomorrow? We have been travelling for days and I am sorely in need of a rest. The only room I really want to see now is my bedchamber.'

'Bless you, Your Grace, of course you do.' The older woman softened quickly in response to Ellen's friendly tone. 'I will take you there immediately, Your Grace. It was Her Grace who said it must be today.'

Ellen stopped and put her hand on the woman's arm. 'Mrs Greenwood, I fear it is going to be very confusing if you call both myself and the Dowager Duchess "Your Grace". I would very much prefer it if you called me ma'am.'

'But I couldn't do that, Your Grace,' declared the housekeeper, scandalised. 'That is not how we address a duchess.'

'It is how you will address *this* Duchess,' said Ellen firmly.

'But the Dowager Duchess—'

'You may continue to call the Dowager Duchess whatever she wishes.' Ellen saw that the woman was looking perturbed and she squeezed her arm, saying gently, 'I am mistress here now, Mrs Greenwood, and that is my wish.'

'Very well your—ma'am,' the housekeeper

sank into another curtsy. 'But what His Grace
will say about it I don't know.'

Ellen did not know, either, but she was determined to make her mark.

'That,' she said quietly, 'is my concern. Now,
shall we continue?'

'Well, Maximilian, are you going to tell me
the truth now?'

Max was looking at the door which had just
closed behind Ellen and Jamie, but his sister-in-
law's words brought his attention back into the
drawing room. Looking at Dorcas, he could not
help comparing her chilly manner with Ellen's
natural grace. Perhaps it was this house. Rossenhall was such a stark, cold place, he hoped
it would not rob his new Duchess of her warm
friendliness.

'The truth?' He raised his brows at her. 'You
had my letter, Dorcas. I met and married Ellen
in Egypt and since then she has been living incognito with my son.'

'A very peculiar arrangement.'

'Not really. I was out of the country and Ellen
did not want to come to Rossenhall alone.'

'And you have both kept the secret for four
years? Who will believe such a tale?'

'Everyone, unless you give them cause to

doubt it.' He fixed his eyes on his sister-in-law and said with deadly deliberation, 'I know how you like to gossip in your letters, Dorcas, but in this case you will say nothing about my marriage, other than what I have told you. Ellen is my wife and James my lawful heir. Any speculation on your part would reflect badly on the family.'

'But Ellen Tatham is a nobody.'

'A very rich nobody,' murmured Max.

Dorcas's lip curled. 'She is not your equal, Maximilian. Really, what will our friends say when they learn you have married a tradesman's daughter?'

'A wealthy East Indiaman's daughter, Dorcas,' he corrected her. He smiled grimly. 'They will say I did very well to capture such a prize. And from what Tony has reported to me in his letters, we need it.' He rose. 'Remember what I said, Dorcas. Whatever your private thoughts, you will show the world you are content with my marriage. Do you understand?'

Having received a very grudging assent Max left the room. Dorcas did not approve of his marriage and she could make trouble, with her poison pen and host of friends in high places. The gossip would not hurt him that much, but it could affect Ellen's comfort. Very few in his world would cut the acquaintance of the new Duchess, but there would be barbed comments and cruel jibes.

'It is no more than she deserves,' he muttered as he made his way downstairs to the steward's office. 'If she had remained in Portsmouth as I asked, none of this would have occurred. She brought it on herself.'

Somehow the words rang hollow. She had tried to find him, he had to concede that much, but as he reached the steward's door he stopped, the pain of her betrayal roaring through him.

'Not enough,' he muttered. 'She did not try hard enough.'

Shaking his head to clear the angry thoughts he opened the door, forcing a cheerful greeting for the man sitting at the desk.

'Well, Tony, how goes it?'

Anthony Grisham had been steward at Rossenhall for only six months. He had been in the Peninsula with Max, an excellent quartermaster until a cannonball had taken off his left arm and he had been sent home. When Atherwell, the old steward, had died, Max had offered Tony the position. Tony had demurred at first, because of his disability. Max had told him, 'You are the same age as me, Tony. With thirty years in your dish you are too young to let that brain of yours go to waste and it is your brain and administrative skills that I need to help me.'

So he had persuaded Tony to move to Rossenhall, where he had spent his time making himself familiar with Max's estates and his tenants and putting in order an office that had seen little change for forty years. Now Tony jumped to his feet and greeted Max with obvious delight.

'Welcome home, Your Grace. I did not think to see you today.'

'I had some time to spare.' He waved Tony back into his seat. 'Have I missed a letter from you while I was travelling, have you sold the carriage horses yet?'

'No, Your Grace.'

'Did you discuss with the Dowager which ones she wanted to keep for her barouche?'

'I mentioned it to her, yes.'

'Well?'

Tony looked a little sheepish. 'She burst into tears.'

'Ah.' Max pulled a chair towards the desk and sat down. 'I see how that might have spiked your guns.'

'It did, Your Grace. I...er...did not think I could proceed until I had discussed the matter with you.'

Max shrugged. 'A few more weeks won't

break us. I am more concerned about what you have found now you have had a chance to look more thoroughly into the accounts. You mentioned before I went away that you thought all might not be well with the Rossenhall finances.'

Tony pushed his hand through his thick brown hair and threw another glance at his employer.

'Are you sure you would not rather leave it until tomorrow?'

'No I would not,' said Max. 'Tell me now.'

It was more than an hour later that Max emerged from the office, a frown darkening his brow. When he met Perkins in the hall he said curtly, 'Is the Dowager Duchess still in the drawing room?'

'No, Your Grace, she has gone to her room to change for dinner.' The old man gave a gentle cough, clearly wishing to say something else, and Max gave him an enquiring look.

The butler stared straight ahead of him and said woodenly, 'The *new* Duchess has given instructions we are to address her as "ma'am", or "the mistress".'

'Has she, by Gad?'

Perkins nodded. 'Your Grace has no objection?'

'I? Why should I object?' Max's eyes narrowed. 'The Dowager Duchess does not approve?'

'When she heard of it, Her Grace said we must refer the matter to you. It *is* highly irregular,' the butler conceded, 'but not, if you will allow me to say so, disrespectful.'

'If it is what my wife wishes, then so be it.' Max laughed. 'It will make life a little less confusing for the rest of us.'

'That is precisely what the mistress said to Mrs Greenwood, Your Grace.'

Max was about to move on, but there was no one else in the hall and he paused. Perkins had been butler here since his father's time and Max knew no servant could be more loyal, so now he took the opportunity to ask, casually, 'And what does the housekeeper think of the new mistress?' He added, when the butler hesitated, 'Come along, out with it, man.'

'Well, it's early days yet, of course, but Mrs Greenwood thinks she will do very well. Very well indeed.'

With a bow the elderly retainer proceeded on his stately way, leaving Max standing in the hall. It was clear that Ellen had made a good impression upon the household, so that was a relief, and heaven knew there were plenty of other things to worry about. The interview with Tony had shown him that the financial situation was worse than he had suspected. He was tempted to summon Dorcas down to his study and have it out with her now, but that required a cool head, and he needed to think things through, first. The chime of a distant clock reminded him of the time. He had yet to change, so he headed for his room, taking the stairs two at a time.

When he entered the drawing room some forty minutes later he found Dorcas alone, idly flicking through the latest copy of the *Lady's Magazine*.

'Is the Duchess not with you?' she asked, putting aside the periodical. 'I made sure you would escort her, in case she should lose her way. After all, she will not be accustomed to living in such palatial surroundings.'

Max ignored this.

'I am glad to find you alone,' he said. 'There is something I want to say to you.'

'No doubt it is about money.' She plucked restlessly at her skirts. 'Are you going to scold me?'

'I would not be so impolite.' He rested one hand on the fireplace, looking down into the empty hearth. 'I have been going over the accounts with Tony. None of the economies I suggested have been put in place.'

'You left me in charge. I did as I thought fit.'

'You have blocked him at every turn, yet you know he was trying to carry out my wishes.'

She hunched a shoulder. 'Grisham is a soldier, as are you. What does either of you know of running a duke's estate? The changes you suggest are ludicrous.'

'They are necessary, if we are to survive.'

'Survive? What nonsense is this? There have been Colnebrookes at Rossenhall since the Conqueror.' Her lip curled. 'It was never intended that you should inherit the title. You do not understand what is due to your station. You were not brought up to it. We must maintain our standing in the community. Would you have us live on air?'

'Of course not, but neither would I have us living beyond our means.' He glanced at her. 'And it is not only the estates that are causing concern. You have been running up large bills, Dorcas.'

'Fiddle. A few little purchases here and there.'

His brows rose. 'And last month's bill from Tattersall's for a curricle and pair? That was for your brother, I suppose.'

'Giles must have something to drive.' Her expression softened to a genuine smile. 'He drove out to see me in it and he was so pleased—you are frowning, Maximilian. Would you begrudge the boy his happiness?'

'Not at all, but it must not be at my expense. Hugo provided a handsome jointure for you, Dorcas, and I am happy for you to live here, but I will not fund your brother's extravagance.'

She hunted for her handkerchief. 'Giles is all the family I have now.'

'But there is no reason I should pay his gambling debts.'

'It is but a few hundred pounds.'

'A few *thousand* pounds,' he corrected her.

'Giles went to Brighton and had a run of bad luck—that is all.'

'Do not try to fob me off. Tony has gone back through the books; this has become a regular occurrence.'

'You would take that… that *cripple's* word against mine!'

'He lost an arm fighting for his country, madam, but it has in no way affected his brain!' Max stopped, taking a deep breath while he regained his temper. He said more quietly, 'I tell you now, Dorcas, any future expenses for your brother must be paid from your own funds. And if you will take my advice you will tell Giles that he must make his own way in the world. It is doing him no good to be so reliant upon you.'

'He must live as befits his rank. Our father was a viscount—'

'Without two groats to rub together,' said Max brutally. 'As a younger son Giles should have found himself some profession. Since he prefers not to do so, he must learn to live within his means.'

She glared at him, angry spots of colour staining her cheeks.

'No doubt you have gleaned these miserly ways from your wife,' she said spitefully. 'Trade is in her blood, after all. I am sure the merchant in her is cock-a-hoop at catching such a prize as you.' She gave a savage laugh. 'You do not think for one moment I believed that farrago of lies you set about? You never *agreed* to her living incognito, Maximilian.' Her lip curled. 'Oh, you need not worry. I shall not give away your secrets, but within these walls let me tell you that the woman is nothing but a charming fortune hunter. You have been duped, sir! Have you never wondered why she should keep herself hidden from you all these years, only to reappear once you had become Duke? She allowed you to find her!'

'That is a lie.'

Max frowned. Ellen could not have known he was going to be in Harrogate. He had not known it himself until Georgie's last letter had arrived, but a glance at the Dowager's confident smile shook him. He cast a challenging glance at her.

'If that was the case, why did she not contact me as soon as I inherited the title?'

Her eyes slid away from him, but she replied with a thin smile, 'That would have looked very mercenary. How much better to let you think it was all your own doing, that she was reluctant to foist herself upon you?'

Before Max could reply there came a soft voice behind him.

'I beg your pardon. Am I very late?'

Max turned, the breath catching in his throat when he saw Ellen hesitating in the doorway. She was dressed in the red silk net she had worn the first time he had seen her in Harrogate, a matching ribbon threaded through the golden curls artlessly arranged about her head and a glitter of diamonds at her neck. In the ballroom she had looked ravishing, her cheeks flushed, eyes sparkling with laughter. Now she looked pale, a little apprehensive, but no less desirable, as his body was making very clear. Angrily he trampled those feelings, forced them deep. What he felt now was not love, merely lust for a beautiful woman. Four years of bitterness and pain had wiped out any affection he might feel. However, it was not his plan to show any discord before his sister-in-law, so he moved forward to greet Ellen, briefly carrying her hand to his lips.

'I trust you managed to rest,' he said politely.

'Yes, thank you. How did you spend your time?'

'I have been with my steward, Anthony Grisham.'

'Ah, yes, you mentioned him when we drove in. He lives in the lodge we passed, near the gates.'

Max nodded. 'Yes. He was sorry not to be here to greet you earlier, but you will meet him tomorrow.'

'I shall look forward to it.'

Max thought of the way old Perkins had unbent towards the new Duchess, the smile that lit up Mrs Greenwood's face when she talked of her new mistress. Doubtless Ellen would charm Anthony, just like the rest of his staff.

She would charm you, too, if you would let her.

He pushed the thought away. Once burned, twice shy. He would not trust her with his heart again.

'And how do you like your rooms, Your Grace?' Dorcas asked Ellen.

Max noted his wife's hesitation and said quickly, 'The Duke and Duchess's suites were refurbished by my brother, in a manner befitting his rank.'

His own bedchamber was a masterpiece of ostentation, the massive bed hung with heavy damask hangings decorated with strawberry leaves and each of the bedposts topped with a gilded coronet. The Duchess's room was similarly ornate, with no expense spared on gold leaf and rich embroidery. Max guessed it was not to Ellen's taste, but he did not wish her to voice her opinion. He might hate it, but he could never say so. It would seem like a criticism of Hugo.

After meeting his eye for a pregnant moment she replied with a smile.

'How could I be other than delighted with my apartment?'

The Dowager gave a thin smile and began to explain how she had designed the hangings herself.

'And the Indian wallpaper, too. Dear Hugo was determined on having the finest furnishings at Rossenhall and spared no expense.'

Dorcas trailed off and glanced nervously at Max. She was obviously recalling their earlier conversation, but he had no intention of referring to it again. That money was spent and there was no point in more recriminations.

Ellen felt the tension in the room, but for once it was not between her and Max, and she was thankful for that. Dorcas rose and shook out her skirts.

'Shall we go in to dinner?' She turned to Ellen.

'I hope you do not think it is too late an hour, anything earlier is considered quite provincial, you know. I have no idea what time you were wont to dine. Harrogate society has its own rules, I suppose.'

Ellen ignored the sneering tone and said she was perfectly ready to dine at any hour that suited her sister. The Duke escorted both ladies to the dining room, but as they entered Dorcas stopped and stared. She gave an outraged gasp.

'Did you order this, Maximilian?' she snapped.

'It was my doing, Dorcas,' said Ellen. 'I spoke to Perkins and asked him to put us both at this end of the table, near the Duke. When we are dining alone it is quite ridiculous that I should sit at the far end, where I would have difficulty both seeing and hearing what is going on.' She turned to Max. 'If Your Grace is opposed to it, I shall order it to be put back.'

He said shortly, 'As mistress here now, madam, you must order things as you wish.'

'Thank you.'

Ellen tried to meet his eyes, but he would not look at her. Nevertheless, she was grateful for his support.

Dinner was a quiet affair, the conversation polite but desultory until the covers were removed and the servants withdrew, leaving the diners to enjoy their sweet wine and the little dishes of bonbons. Dorcas sighed.

'Really, I do not know what they will be saying below stairs, to see us so crowded up in this way. Hugo would never have allowed such informality.'

'There are always changes with a new master,' said Ellen gently. 'I hope it will not be too distressing for you, Dorcas.'

'Oh, dear me, no,' replied the Dowager. 'I am not concerned for *myself*, dear, but for you. Living in a ducal household will be a great change for you.'

'I am sure it will,' agreed Ellen. 'No doubt I will grow accustomed to living in the grand style.'

'Not so very grand, if Maximilian has his way,' tittered Dorcas. 'He will have us all living on bread and water.'

'Oh?' Ellen turned to look at him. 'Did Mr Grisham have bad news for you this afternoon?'

'He did. We are not reduced to penury, but the estate is not paying its way and it has not done so for years.'

'I hope you are not blaming dear Hugo for the straits you now find yourself in,' said Dorcas sharply.

Ellen noticed Max's hesitation, as if he was loath to criticise his brother.

'You must admit he did nothing to help,' he said at last. 'Instead of improving the land and making the tenant farms more profitable, there were too many ambitious schemes and wild speculations, to say nothing of the lavish entertaining.'

Dorcas sat up very straight. 'And why should we not entertain?'

'No reason at all, but was it necessary to have the town house completely refurbished?'

'It is expected that the Duke of Rossenhall should live well.'

'To live well, yes, but not beyond our means.'

'Hugo's inheritance was severely diminished. It was your father's crisis of conscience that has put us in this position,' stated Dorcas. 'He was very foolish to sell the family's interests in the West Indies and free the slaves. Atherwell was against it and Hugo tried to tell him, but he would not be swayed.'

'That was ten years ago,' Max replied shortly. 'The finances should have recovered by now.'

'How would you know that?' Dorcas threw at him. 'You have rarely been here.'

'I know and I am beginning to regret it,' he replied. 'If I had spent more time at Rossenhall and seen for myself what state things were in rather than taking yours and Atherwell's word that everything was in order, at least I would have been better prepared for what I would find.'

'So now you are going to make life a misery with your cuts and economies,' snapped the Dowager. 'It will be so uncomfortable.'

'If you do not like my economies, Dorcas, then I suggest you remove to the dower house and live on your widow's jointure.'

'I am sure it will not be so very bad,' said Ellen pacifically. 'And perhaps we might increase our income with wise investments.'

Dorcas nodded eagerly. 'Max could buy back the West Indian properties.'

'No,' he said firmly. 'I will not do that.'

'Surely you do not think there is any risk in it?' Dorcas selected a sweetmeat from the dish in front of her. She said comfortably, 'Slavery will never be abolished. How can it be, how would we survive without slaves to work the plantations?'

Max set his glass down.

'Let me be plain with you, Dorcas. If I had been in England at the time I would have agreed with Father and supported the bill,' said Max steadily. 'I cannot condone slavery; I have seen too much of it.'

'There are other investments we could make,' put in Ellen. 'There are any number of possibilities in this country, the new canals, for instance, or coal and steel. Or perhaps the new manufactories that are growing in the north. It need not be speculation, but sound business sense. The returns could be used to improve your estates and make them profitable.'

Dorcas gave a little snort of derision. 'That smacks of trade.'

Ellen waved one hand. 'It is all trade, whether it is importing sugar or tea from the Indies or producing goods here.' She turned back to Max. 'Papa used to say a wise man would spread his investments to protect against a calamity in any one of the markets. I could put you in touch with his old friends in the city who could advise you. I am sure they would remember his name.'

'No doubt.' Dorcas sniggered. 'Especially now it is linked to the Duke of Rossenhall! Really, Max, it is not to be thought of. We would be besieged by toadying mushrooms.'

Ellen felt a little spurt of anger. She said quietly, 'Some of those *toadying mushrooms* could purchase the entire Rossenhall estates twice over.'

Max gave a bark of laughter. 'Very true.' He looked at Ellen. 'It is worth considering. It could do no harm to talk to your father's contacts.'

'Maximilian,' Dorcas said sharply, 'Cartwright and Busby have always handled the family's investments.'

'And they have done nothing for us for years,' he retorted. 'We will look into it. We could sell one or two of the smaller properties to fund it, perhaps.'

'That might not be necessary,' replied Ellen. 'I have capital that is not invested.'

The Dowager pounced on that. 'I would remind you, Duchess, that everything you own now belongs to your husband. He does not need your consent to use it as he wishes.'

'Yes, thank you, Dorcas.'

Ellen reeled at Dorcas's words and barely heard Max's impatient retort. Foolish of her to forget even for a moment that she and Max were not equals.

When they had married, in the heat of the pitiless Egyptian sun, she had trusted Max implicitly. Mrs Ackroyd had suggested that they should wait and have settlements drawn up, but Ellen had been too impatient, too in love with Max to consider such a thing necessary. In a moment of recklessness, at the age of two-and-twenty, she had given up her life and her fortune to a husband. Her step-mama had always maintained with some amusement that when Ellen finally fell in love, it would be very heavily indeed. How right she had been, but it was no laughing matter.

She glanced at Max now, as he frowned at his sister-in-law. Dorcas had only spoken the truth. Ellen had no doubt she could run the Duke's households, manage his staff and even stand up for herself against the Dowager, but the thought that everything, including her beloved child, could be taken away from her at the whim of the man sitting at the head of the table sent a chill running down her spine. Better not to think of that. She pushed back her chair.

'I think we should leave the Duke to his brandy,' she said quietly.

Dorcas followed Ellen back to the drawing room and at first she seemed intent upon making up for her previous ill humour. She drew Ellen into conversation, but it was soon clear that her only intention was to convey in the subtlest way that she thought the new Duchess wholly unsuited to her role. After listening silently for a good ten minutes to her strictures, Ellen had had enough and when the Dowager paused for breath she broke in, speaking quietly, but leaving her sister-in-law in no doubt of her displeasure.

'Let us be plain with one another, Dorcas. I know you do not want me here, you think me nothing better than a tradesman's chit.' The Dowager's eyes widened at that and she looked suddenly anxious. Ellen nodded. 'I am well aware you think my birth is far too lowly for this elevated position, but I am the Duke's lawful wife and I shall fulfil that role to the best of my ability. Max did not marry me for my money, but it is not unusual for a nobleman to choose a rich wife, regardless of her birth. In fact, at least half a dozen of my schoolfellows married titles and some of them came from far more dubious backgrounds than mine. So I have no fear of being ostracised by society when we go to town next spring.' Dorcas was looking quite furious and Ellen decided she had said enough for one evening. She rose and declared that she was going to bed. 'I hope we have cleared the air a little and can start afresh tomorrow.'

'What, go now?' said Dorcas, her thin eyebrows shooting up in surprise. 'Before the Duke has joined us?'

'It has been a long day and I am exhausted,' she replied, truthfully. 'I want to look in on little James and make sure he is sleeping and then I shall retire.'

'But you cannot go off without informing Maximilian. He might wish to talk to you.'

'Oh, I am sure you can tell him where I am.'

Ellen regarded her sister in law with a steady gaze. 'As you have been at pains to point out to me, this is the Duke's house. If he wants me he knows where to find me.'

With that she whisked herself out of the room.

Chapter Nine

Ellen sat before her looking glass, breathing deeply to let the anger seep away with every exhalation. She had a great deal of sympathy for her sister-in-law and was determined not to fall out with her. It was barely a year since Dorcas had lost not only her husband, but her position in society, although Ellen was not sure which of the two she had valued most. She thought of the rooms directly above her, the nursery. Mrs Greenwood had explained they had been fully refurbished by Dorcas when she had come to Rossenhall as a new bride. They included every convenience, every luxury, but had never been required, and Ellen suspected it was a severe trial for her sister-in-law to think of Jamie in the rooms she had hoped would be used by her own sons.

There was a knock at the door and the Duke

walked in. Ellen said nothing, reminding herself
that as her husband he had a perfect right to enter
her bedchamber. Her heart gave a little skip as she
studied him in the mirror and she thought how
well he looked in the dark evening coat and white
linen with the candlelight glinting on his fair hair.
She recalled that he had looked just as handsome
in the Oriental robes he had worn in the desert.
But they had both been so much happier then.

'Dorcas said you had gone to bed,' he said.
'Are you unwell?'

'No, I am fatigued, nothing more.'

'I have never before known you to be tired.'

She gave him a wry look in the mirror. 'I have
never before dined with the Dowager Duchess.'

She reached back to wrestle with the fasten-
ing of her diamond necklace.

'Here, let me do that.'

Ellen froze, trying not to tremble as his fingers brushed the skin at the back of her neck.
His hands stilled for a moment and she thought
wildly and with aching regret that once he would
have bent to kiss her neck. And he could do so
now, if he so wished. If he was not regretting
their marriage. If he loved her.

'Where is your maid?' he said, unclasping the
necklace and handing it to her before stepping
away. 'She should be helping you.'

'Matlock is in the nursery with Jamie. She will be here soon to help me into my nightgown.'

Her throat dried and she stared fixedly into the glass. It was impossible not to think that once such a comment would have made him grin and say that he would help her out of it again, but not now. Now he looked severe and stony-faced. He turned away and stood before the fireplace, idly playing with the ornaments on the mantelshelf.

'I wanted to talk to you. About your fortune.'

'I have no fortune. As Dorcas so kindly reminded me, everything I own is now yours.'

'We must change that,' he said. 'We must draw up a proper settlement, make sure there is a widow's jointure for you, should it be necessary. I shall write to the lawyers in the morning.'

'Thank you.'

He swung around, meeting her eyes in the looking glass. 'You sound surprised. Do you think I would do any less for you?'

She was uncomfortable with him towering over her, so she pushed herself up from the dressing stool. She still had to look up, but he was not quite so intimidating.

She said quietly, 'I am aware you think I wronged you, Max, but I truly believed we were not married.'

'So you have said.'

'Can you not believe me?'

'Oh, I believe you, madam. I believe you set your people to discover the truth, when you returned to England, but could you not have waited until you could ask *me*?'

'Max, I—'

He flung himself away from her outstretched hand.

'Do you understand what you did, madam? To desert me, to deprive me of my son, my heir? You might have thought me an imposter, a deserter who was merely calling himself Max Colnebrooke to impress you, but when Hugo died why did you not swallow your pride and enquire again, just to be sure, if only for your son's sake? But, oh, no. Not even a word of condolence for the loss of my only brother. I would never have thought you could be so heartless.'

'I *did* write, Max, I wrote twice—'

'Do not add lies to your offences!'

Ellen flinched. She said quietly, 'I never lied to you.'

But he was not listening. He was scowling at the floor as he paced back and forth, his anger barely contained.

'You judged me a villain and gave me no opportunity to explain myself.' He turned to her, snarling. 'Well, is that not so?'

Ellen met his angry gaze. What could she say that would not cause more pain?

'Could we not put the past behind us and start again?'

'What you ask is impossible.' His eyes rested on her in a dark, glowering look, then he sighed. 'We neither of us want this marriage, Ellen, but we are caught in it, for the sake of the boy.'

Long after he had left the room Ellen did not move. She stared at the closed door, feeling as if someone had wrenched out her heart.

Max closed the door behind him with great care. He prayed she had not heard the heavy thud of his heart, or seen the effort it cost him to appear polite and indifferent when in truth he wanted to drag her into his arms and lose himself in the desire that was as strong as ever. Walking away from her, saying those words, was the hardest thing he had ever done in his life.

It was necessary, he told himself as he went to his own bedchamber. He could not afford to go back to the loneliness, the black depression he had felt when he returned from Egypt to find she had disappeared. In Ellen he had thought he had found a soulmate. He had thrown caution to the winds and married her, a rash, foolish gesture and quite out of character. When he discovered how she had left Egypt he had not given up hope immediately, convincing himself that it had been expedient for her to put herself under the protection of the French. So he had come back to England, expecting to find her waiting for him, but there was nothing. Nothing but pain and guilt and intolerable grief in the years that followed.

Ellen woke to find the sun streaming into her bedchamber. She went to the window and stared out, feeling her spirits lift at the view. The terraced gardens were full of summer flowers and elegant statuary, and then the sloping lawns led the eye to a large lake. Beyond that, parkland stretched to the horizon.

'This is my home, now,' she murmured, hugging herself. 'For better or worse.'

She knew this was only one of the estates belonging to the Duke of Rossenhall. It was magnificent, but Ellen had a shrewd idea of the costs involved in running such a property, and from what Max had said last night the accounts were not in good order. She felt a little tremor of excitement run through her. There was much work to be done here and she could help. She was determined to help.

An hour later she made her way down to the breakfast room, getting lost only twice on the way. Max was alone at the table. He rose and moved to hold a chair out for her, one at some distance from his own, she noticed. Irritation prickled. Did he think she would throw herself at him in a fit of unseemly passion? Then she saw the strained look about his eyes, as though he, too, had not slept well.

She said, as a servant brought more freshly baked rolls to the table, 'Since the weather is fine I should like to drive about the grounds this afternoon.'

'The carriage will be at your disposal.'

'I thought perhaps you would like to escort me.' She peeped at him under her lashes, saw the faint hesitation before he refilled his coffee cup.

'Unfortunately that will not be possible. I am leaving at noon. I have business in town.'

'Today? But we have only just arrived.'

'It cannot be helped. My business is in the city, so there will be no social visits, else I should take you with me. Would you like more coffee?'

'No, thank you. Can your business not wait a few more days? I hoped you might show me Rossenhall.'

He did not meet her eyes. 'Dorcas and Mrs Greenwood will acquaint you with all you need to know.'

'I have already arranged for the housekeeper

to give me a tour of the house this morning, but your land here is extensive. With the park and the farms, there is so much to discover.'

'You want to know about the estate, too?'

'Of course,' she said. 'I am eager to learn everything I can.'

'Then ask Tony Grisham. I am sorry I have not had time to present him to you, but Dorcas will do that, if you ask her.' He put down his napkin and rose from the table. 'I shall be seeing my lawyer about drawing up the settlements for you. I also thought I might look up these friends of your father's to discuss...*our* investments. Perhaps when you have broken your fast you could write me any necessary letters of introduction.'

And with that he strode out of the room.

Ellen broke off another piece of bread and chewed it thoughtfully. He had almost run away from her. Did he hate her so much that he could not remain in her presence, or was it that he felt the attraction, the connection between them, as she did? The little flame of hope that refused to die flickered a little brighter.

Max was surprised to find a small party gathered in the hall for his departure. Ellen had brought Jamie downstairs, even though Max had made a point of visiting the nursery to say goodbye. Dorcas proffered her hand for his salute and then he was obliged to take leave of his wife. Even as he hesitated Ellen stepped forward and put her hand on his shoulder, reaching up to kiss his cheek. He kept his hands by his sides, fists clenched to stop himself reaching for her as he was enveloped in the faint but alluring scent she wore. He should say something, but even as he struggled for the words, little James caused a diversion by tugging at his coat-tails.

'Duke, Duke, will you bring me a drum from London? You promised, you know.'

The tension eased. Max heard Ellen's gurgle of laughter as she swept the boy up into her arms.

Typically, Dorcas gave a little tut of disapproval. 'Your papa has important business. He cannot be thinking of toys for you.'

'But I *did* promise.' Max flicked Jamie's cheek with one finger. 'I will see what I can do.'

Over the boy's head he met Ellen's eyes. She said softly, 'Thank you.'

It was too much. He did not want a family. He did not want this additional pull on his emotions. With a curt nod he turned on his heel and hurried away to the waiting chaise.

Ellen knew the gloom that settled over the house when Max had left was not wholly in her imagination. The cloud had rolled in and a fine drizzle put an end to her plans to take Jamie for a drive. Instead she left him playing happily in the nursery and set off to explore the nether regions of the house. Mrs Greenwood had taken her on an extensive tour of the main rooms and guest chambers, and they had even, on Ellen's request, ventured into the attics, next to the nursery, but there had been no time to visit the kitchens or the service rooms in the rustic.

When Ellen had mentioned it to Dorcas she had been dismissive.

'Why ever would you wish to go there?' she had said. 'The chef, Monsieur Tissot, has been presented to you and any other member of staff will be fetched upstairs, if you should wish to see them.' She added, with a touch of pride, 'I have never found it necessary to venture into the servants' quarters. It is not a duchess's province.'

Ellen had kept her counsel, but now, with hours to spare before she needed to change for dinner, she set off to explore. The kitchens were situated in a pavilion behind the east wing and a few tactful words in his own language to the tyrant who presided over them had Monsieur Tissot falling over himself to present every one of his minions to milady. After a tour of his domain she headed back to the rustic to look for the estate offices. As she turned on to a long passageway she almost bumped into a gentleman in riding dress coming in the other direction. He stopped and backed away, putting up his hand as he hastily begged her pardon.

'You must be Mr Grisham, the Duke's steward,' said Ellen. She smiled and shook her head when he clapped his hand over the empty left sleeve tucked into the pocket of his coat. 'It was not *that* I noticed first about you, Mr Grisham, it was your ink-stained fingers! There is no other person you could be.' She held out her hand. 'I am delighted to meet you, sir.'

With laughter shining in his own grey eyes, Tony Grisham wiped his one hand on his coat before touching Ellen's fingers and bowing over them.

'I am honoured, Your Grace. What can I do for you?'

'You could guide me around this warren of rooms and corridors, and the outbuildings,' she confided. 'I thought, while the Duke is away, I should learn as much about Rossenhall as I can. That is, unless you are very busy?'

'No, Your Grace, not at all. I have just put my ledgers away for the day.' He gave a wry smile as he glanced as his hand. 'Perhaps I should clean myself up first, though. I would not wish to offend you.'

'If a little ink is all that is the matter then there is not the least need,' she told him, twinkling. 'I am frequently in the company of my son when he is a great deal grubbier than *that*.'

He laughed. 'Very well then, Your Grace. Where would you like to begin?'

They started with a tour of the palatial stable block, where Tony said he would introduce her to the head groom.

'Would that be Stevens?' she asked him. 'He was with His Grace in Harrogate.'

'No, ma'am. His Grace brought Stevens with him from the military. Old Joshua Thirsk has been in charge here since the old Duke's time— the present Duke's father. There is a head coachman, too, of course, but it is Joshua who is firmly in charge of the stables.' He coughed, saying apologetically, 'He likes to do things his way, ma'am, so it's not as orderly as perhaps the Duke would like.'

He led her across the yard to a shaggy-haired individual in a worn leather waistcoat and wearing a ragged kerchief tied around his neck. The old man regarded her with a rheumy eye. She greeted him in her friendly style and waved one hand towards the stables behind her.

'Are any of these horses used on the farms?' she asked him. 'There seem to be far more than would be required by the family.'

'Ah, well,' he told her, 'when the Dowager Duchess went into mourning she purchased several teams of black horses to pull her carriages.'

'And the horses they were replacing, they were sold, I suppose?'

The groom shifted from one foot to the other and looked at Tony, who answered, 'No, ma'am. They are still here. Two teams for every carriage.'

Ellen met the steward's eyes and bit her lip upon the various exclamations that occurred to her. In the light of what Max had said about the finances she could see why he was concerned.

'Do we *need* so many horses?' she asked cautiously.

'His Grace plans to sell several of the teams,' said Tony.

Joshua rubbed his nose. 'If ever he's here long enough to make a decision.'

'Well, perhaps you should help him,' Ellen suggested. 'If you and Mr Grisham were to draw up a list of the horses you wish to keep; we can put it to His Grace when he returns.'

'Ah, but I wouldn't want to be doing anything rash,' objected the groom, looking anxious. 'His Grace said as how the Dowager was to be consulted, and besides that, the Dukes of Rossenhall has always kept the very best 'osses in their stables.'

'And that will not change,' said Ellen. She realised he was concerned that his little kingdom would be drastically reduced and she was at pains to reassure him. 'But I am sure you will agree that it is quite foolish to keep all these animals here if they are not being used.'

And with another smile, she swept on.

By the time Ellen parted from Tony Grisham they had reached an excellent understanding. Her genuine interest in Rossenhall matched his own and she soon realised that he was eager to impart his knowledge. The following morning he took her to the Home Farm and after that they went out each day to call upon the tenant farmers. Ellen included Jamie in these visits, knowing he would enjoy the drive, but she was also aware that having Max's son with her would break the ice with the families she was meeting.

It was a full week before Max returned to Rossenhall. He instructed his driver to take the chaise directly to the stables and when they came to a stand in the yard he jumped out. For a few moments he stood, looking about him, a faint crease between his brows. He saw Stevens coming out of one of the stalls and beckoned him over.

'What's going on here?' he demanded.

'Your Grace?'

'Don't act the fool with me,' growled Max. 'This yard's tidier than I've ever seen it. The broken barrels have been removed, doors and windows repaired—even the cobbles look as if they have been washed down. Have you taken charge now? You know I have told Old Joshua about it a dozen times—well, what are you grinning at?'

'It was the Duchess, Your Grace. She told Joshua how she liked to see everything clean and tidy, like.'

'The Duchess. *My* Duchess?'

Stevens grinned. 'Aye, Your Grace. Mr Grisham brought her around here. Let me see, it must've been the day you left for London. She met Old Joshua and then the very next day she comes again, bringing him a scarlet kerchief and a new tobacco pouch, and telling him how glad she is that the stables are in such good hands. Turned him up sweet, she did.' He glanced past the Duke and his grin widened still further. 'See for yourself.'

Max turned. His head groom was standing

in the archway, fists on his hips as he watched the stable-hands pull the carriage away. A laugh bubbled up inside him: Joshua's white hair had been brushed flat and he looked cleaner than he had ever seen him before in a fresh shirt and with his new red kerchief around his neck.

'Good day to you, Joshua,' he called and the man came slowly across. Max waved a hand around the yard. 'You have been busy here and about time, too.'

The old man scowled. 'Well, if we're to be having visitors again then we needs to smarten ourselves up, don't we?'

'Visitors?' Max queried.

'Aye. The new mistress says it'll be like the old days, with the family living here now.' The man's faded eyes gleamed. 'There'll be guests and the like, and they'll need stabling for their fine horses.'

Max folded his arms. 'We have fine horses of our own and you've never seen the need to clear up before.'

'No one's ever taken an interest before,' retorted the old man, looking his master boldly in the eye. 'The mistress says she wants to be proud of her stables. And she says I deserves to rest more, too, so I've agreed to let young fellow-me-lad here get on with running the place.'

He jerked a thumb at Stevens, who nodded.

'Aye, that's right, but I'll be coming to you for advice, Joshua, like Her Grace suggested.'

'Aye, well, mind you do,' barked the old man before turning his stern gaze back to Max. 'If that's all, Yer Grace, I'll be getting on. I promised the mistress I'd have the stables spick and span for her by the morning and if I don't watch they stable lads they'll be playing cards in the barn instead of cleaning the harnesses.'

'See what I mean, Your Grace?' murmured Stevens as the old man walked away. 'It's a transformation. Not that I mind at all, if it means he'll let me get this place in order.' The groom looked at him from under his bushy brows. 'We *will* be staying for a while, won't we, Your Grace? There's a deal of work to be done, but it will take time.'

'Then I think we must stay,' agreed Max. 'I have neglected my duties here for far too long.'

He strode off to the house, making his way to the small door in the rustic that led directly to the estate offices. He found Tony Grisham sitting at the big table, papers and maps spread before him. He waved the steward back into his seat and took a chair opposite him.

'I have driven direct from town,' he said, in response to Tony's greeting. 'And if there is any wine left in that decanter I would be glad to take a glass with you.'

'Of course, Your Grace.' Tony filled a wine glass and handed it over. 'Was your business there successful?'

'Yes, on the whole, although there is much more to be done. How go things here?'

'Very well,' said Tony, surprising him. 'The staffing matters have been resolved.'

'You have found a lady's maid for the Duchess?'

'I didn't, Your Grace. The Duchess has appointed Alice, one of the chambermaids and Mrs Greenwood's niece, at that. The girl is keen to advance and the mistress thinks she will do very well. That left a vacancy for another chambermaid and the mistress suggested we appoint Old Joshua's granddaughter to the post. And talking of Joshua…' Tony hunted around on his desk and handed Max a piece of paper. 'Here's the list of horses we plan to sell, with your approval. I have gone through it with Stevens and Joshua and they have agreed the best horses to keep.'

'And the Dowager is happy with this?' Max saw Tony hesitate and he barked, 'The truth, if you please.'

Tony said carefully, 'I believe she was a little tearful when the mistress explained it.' When

Max made a face he grinned. 'Mrs Greenwood told me she went off into hysterics and would have set the household by the ears if the Duchess had not stuck some burnt feathers under her nose. Apparently that brought her round pretty quickly.' He smothered his grin with an apologetic glance at the Duke. 'I beg your pardon, Your Grace, but you said you wanted the truth.'

'So the Duchess had a hand in this, too,' exclaimed Max, throwing the paper back on the table. 'Good heavens, I have only been away a week! What other havoc has my wife wreaked upon the household?'

Tony's brows went up. 'Why, none at all, Your Grace. She has acquainted herself with all the household staff and a good number of your tenants. And when she discovered the damp in the wash house was making one of the laundry maids wheezy, she moved her up to the nursery to help Matlock. That meant we could take in one of villagers' daughters to work in the laundry.' Tony shrugged. 'The new girl's simple-minded, but she works hard and the others look after her very well. And now the Duchess has taken charge of the household I have more time to go through the mountain of papers that has been building up since your father's time. If Your Grace will forgive me for saying so, I think the Duchess has made a pretty good start here.'

Max recalled Tony's words as he made his way through the house to his bedchamber. Everything was quiet and orderly, yet there was a different atmosphere, the gloominess had gone. Blinds had been put up, shutters opened and fragrant floral displays adorned the side tables. A particularly colourful arrangement had been placed on the drum table that stood in the centre of the cavernous entrance hall.

Like the old days.

Old Joshua's words came back to him. He had not seen flowers like this since his mother had been Duchess. She had died when he and Hugo were still at school and somehow the habit of bringing fresh flowers into the house had been lost. And much more had been lost, too, he thought as he ran up the main stairs. The laughter had gone from the house, as well as what little affection he and Hugo had ever known. Max had no illusions, his mother had been a selfish, frivolous woman, interested only in her own pleasures, but occasionally it pleased her to lavish affection upon her children. Those loving gestures, infrequent and carelessly given, had acted upon Max like rain in the desert. He had worshipped the laughing beautiful goddess that was his mother, lived for those small moments of tenderness, so different from the dutiful, false affection of the females the old Duke had purchased to initiate his sons into the ways of love.

Love! Max almost laughed at the memory. Ellen was the only woman whom he had ever loved and look what it had cost him.

Flynn, the Duke's manservant, was waiting in the bedchamber with a fresh set of clothes. Max put on the embroidered white-silk waistcoat and wandered over to the window as he buttoned it. Although they were not adjoining, his rooms were on the same side of the house as Ellen's and he wondered what she thought of the view. Would she love this place, as he had done, before his father had effectively banished him from Rossenhall by making it plain his presence here was unnecessary, unwelcome, even? Would Jamie like living here? Glancing down, he saw the Duchess was on one of the lower terraces. Jamie was with her and they were making their way towards the lake.

'Your coat, Your Grace.'

'What?'

Max turned to see Flynn holding up his coat of blue superfine. Quickly he thrust his arms into it, barely giving the valet time to brush the creases from the shoulders before hurrying away.

By the time he caught up with them they were at the water's edge, throwing pieces of bread on to the water for the ducks. He could hear Jamie's childish laughter as the birds fought noisily for the treats. Ellen was crouching beside him, one arm around her son to stop him toppling headlong into the lake as he launched each fresh crumb into the air.

'If you make them too fat, they will not be able to swim.'

His comment brought Ellen's head round quickly. She rose, keeping one hand on Jamie's shoulder, and smiled. There was a becoming colour in her cheek, but that would be from the fresh air. Max would not fool himself into thinking she was truly pleased to see him.

'If you had sent ahead, we should have been at the door to welcome you.'

'Unnecessary, I assure you. And Jamie would prefer to be here.' He had been standing with his hands behind his back, but now he brought forth the object he had been hiding. 'I thought you might like to try this.'

Jamie gave a delighted squeal. 'A boat! Look, Mama, a boat!'

'It is a yacht,' said Max, holding it out.

'You brought this from town for him?' asked Ellen.

'I have brought something very different for him from London,' said Max. 'No, this was in one of the attic cupboards. It is a replica of my grandfather's yacht. It was made for Hugo and me. Shall we see if it is still seaworthy, Jamie?'

'Ooh, yes, if you please, Duke!'

Max gently lowered the white-painted hull into the water, feeling inordinately pleased when the little yacht bobbed merrily on the water. The ducks paddled away, realising their feast was at an end.

Jamie jumped up and down impatiently beside him. 'May I hold the string? Please, Duke!'

'Very well.' Max handed over the cord and tied the end loosely around the boy's wrist. 'Hold on to that, Captain Jamie, and you will not lose your ship.'

Jamie slipped his free hand into Max's. 'Shall we take her around the lake?'

'If you wish.' After a heartbeat's pause he held out his arm to Ellen. 'Will you join us?'

He knew the invitation sounded grudging, his voice coldly polite, but after regarding him for a moment she smiled and put her hand into the crook of his arm. He glanced down at her. The rim of her chip straw bonnet concealed her face, but she did not appear to be in any way discomposed and that pleased him. He wanted to be able to meet like this, as friends.

His conscience kicked him: it was not what he wanted at all. He wanted to slide his arm about her waist and pull her close, to discard that ridiculous bonnet and cover her face with kisses and, when Jamie's nursemaid came to fetch him away, he wanted to take Ellen to some secluded spot and make love to her, to caress her until she was crying out in ecstasy...

'I beg your pardon, Your Grace. Did you speak?'

Her soft voice interrupted his thoughts. She had turned to look up at him, a quizzical lift to her delicate brows. His heart was pumping so fast it threatened to choke him. He could never give in to that desire, not without risking the defences he had been at such pains to build. He needed to think of more mundane matters.

'I wanted to ask you if you liked the view from your room.'

'Very much, Your Grace. The grounds here are beautiful.'

'I believe you have been busy in my absence. The changes to the staff, improvements in the stables. Flowers in the house.'

'I hope you do not think I have been too forward. I consulted Mr Grisham on everything.'

'But not the Dowager Duchess.'

'Not on *everything*. She does not like change. It oversets her.'

'But you are ready to restore her with the use of burnt feathers, I believe.'

He observed the faint, mischievous twitch to her lips.

'That was most unfortunate, but I could not allow such a fuss over how many horses we should keep. And once the situation was explained, Dorcas understood perfectly. Well, perhaps not quite that, but she is reconciled to the situation. And she will have four of the smartest horses to pull her barouche.'

They had reached a section of the lake where the rushes grew thick and close to the bank, making it impossible to pull the little yacht further, and they stopped.

'I think we have walked far enough today,' said Ellen as Max untangled the string from the reeds and lifted the boat from the water. 'It is time to go inside.'

There was a mutinous look on Jamie's face, but Max put a hand on his shoulder.

'Your mama is right, sir. A captain must always know when to rest his crew.'

Harmony restored, they walked to the house, where they found Matlock on the terrace. She gave a slight bob to acknowledge the Duke and Duchess, but turned her attention to the little boy.

'There you are, Master James. Eliza has prepared a bath for you; and by the looks of you it is very timely. Come along, young man.'

Max crouched down and held out the yacht. 'You may take it up to the nursery and keep it there, as long as you promise to take care of it.'

Jamie nodded solemnly and went off with his nurse, the little boat clutched reverently in his arms.

'That was very kind of you,' Ellen told him.

He shrugged. 'When I saw you going to the lake I remembered the yacht. Luckily it had not been moved for years so it was easy to find.' He escorted Ellen to the double doors leading from the terrace to the drawing room. He said lightly, 'Is that my parental duty done for today?'

'Why, no. Jamie will be brought down to join us for a little while before dinner. I want him to become better acquainted with his aunt. The Dowager is not used to children and finds half an hour of his company is quite sufficient.' She hesitated. 'Our arrival at Rossenhall has been quite an upheaval for Dorcas. It will take a little time for her to grow accustomed.'

'She can be difficult. You do not allow her to bully you?'

'I have never allowed anyone to bully me.'

'No,' he said. 'I pity anyone who might try.'

His sudden smile, the warmth in his voice, caught Ellen off guard. She felt breathless and unsure as they stood in the drawing room, the birds singing outside and the pretty little ormolu clock on the mantelpiece chiming the hour. She wanted him so badly it frightened her.

Max looked around, waved one hand towards the sideboard.

'Will you take a glass of wine with me?'

'I, no, I thank you. It… I must change. For dinner.'

She berated herself for a simpleton. He was offering her an olive branch and she should take it. But she felt too weak, too out of control. With a hasty gasp that he must excuse her, Ellen almost ran from the room.

Chapter Ten

No one could have been more serene and composed than the Duchess of Rossenhall when she entered the drawing room that evening. She greeted her sister-in-law calmly, agreed that Alice, her new maid, was very good at dressing her hair and turned to acknowledge the Duke. He was standing on the far side of the room and looking immaculate in a dark coat that was sculpted to his athletic figure. His fair hair was brushed back from his strong, handsome face with its lean cheeks and those sensuous lips that only had to smile to set her pulse racing.

She gave him a little nod, a slight smile, and took a seat beside Dorcas. She might be composed now, but her earlier agitation was not forgotten. One smile from the Duke and she had been ready to melt. He did not want that; he had told her as much. And neither did she. The love she had felt for him during those few weeks in the desert had been all-consuming. Too fierce, too hot. She had been exposed, vulnerable and to allow that to happen again could only lead to heartache, so she must hide behind cool smiles and not embarrass either of them with a show of affection that Max clearly did not want.

She had barely made herself comfortable when Matlock came in with Jamie, who was washed and scrubbed and dressed in a woollen suit the colour of cinnamon, which accentuated his fair hair and green eyes.

Dorcas drew in a sharp breath and looked quickly from Jamie to Max.

'Well,' she muttered, 'whatever gossip and scandal the news of your marriage might cause, Maximilian, that is clearly your son.'

'Did you ever doubt it?' said Ellen, with a flash of anger.

With a little push from Matlock, Jamie stepped forward and made a creditable bow to the ladies.

'Good evening, Aunt, Mama.' He turned and made a similar obeisance to Max. 'Good evening.' He screwed up his face as if trying to remember a difficult lesson. 'Papa.'

Dorcas nodded her approval 'I am glad to see the little Marquess is learning some manners at last. I was growing quite anxious about his wildness.'

'He is not yet four years old,' Max reminded her. 'Personally I should be sorry if he lost all his natural liveliness.'

That liveliness was evident now as the little boy hopped from one foot to the other, clearly bursting with news.

'I wanted to play for you, but Matty says no,' he told his mama.

Ellen looked at Matlock for enlightenment.

'Master Jamie has a drum, madam.' The nursemaid cast a darkling look at Max. 'It was a present from His Grace.'

'I made a promise,' said Max, when all eyes turned towards him.

'Well, that is very thoughtless of you, Maximilian.' Dorcas sniffed. 'You have no consideration for my delicate nerves, or for your staff. It is bad enough that the boy is careering around the house all day on his hobby horse in your absence—'

'That only happened once. A wet day when he could not go outside,' Ellen put in. 'And Eliza was with him to make sure he did no harm.' She added gently, 'You were in your room at the time, Dorcas, and knew nothing of it until Perkins mentioned at dinner how pleasant it was to have a child in the house again.'

'The point is that although riding a hobby horse might be done quietly, a drum is a very different matter.'

'I agree with you entirely,' said Ellen. 'Which is why Jamie will play with it out of doors, well away from the house.' She gave way to a mischievous impulse to add, 'And, since his papa was a soldier, perhaps *he* should teach him how to use it properly.'

Jamie had been following the conversation with knitted brows, but at this he turned a hopeful gaze upon Max.

'Oh, yes, please, Duke. Can you teach me?'

'I am sure we will find some time for that.'

'Tomorrow?'

'Perhaps. We shall see.' Over Jamie's head Max narrowed his eyes at Ellen, threatening retribution, but she merely smiled, knowing in this case he was not seriously displeased. It was a relief that Max was getting on so well with his son.

At the allotted time Matlock came to collect Jamie. As soon as the door was closed upon them Dorcas declared that the boy should go to school.

'And so he shall, in good time,' Ellen told her. 'Are you concerned that he has no friends here? I have begun to remedy that. We have already met some of the village children and soon he will have an old friend here to play with.' She turned to Max. 'I called upon Mrs Arncliffe while you were away and she tells me your carriage is to be sent to Harrogate to fetch Georgiana and Lottie. They should be with her in a week or so.'

Max heard this with some surprise. 'You went to see Frederick's mother? Dorcas went with you, I suppose?'

'I was not well,' said Dorcas, fidgeting in her chair. 'But I did insist that Ellen should go in the carriage, with two footmen up behind her.'

Ellen chuckled. 'And very grand I felt, too. I hope, once I am more acquainted with the area, that I shall be able to drive myself in the gig.'

Dorcas gave a disdainful sniff. 'A gig is hardly the equipage for a duchess.'

'You are right,' replied the Duchess, a martial light in her eye. 'I will take the Duke's curricle, then. Or perhaps I shall buy a phaeton.'

Max grinned. 'A high-perch phaeton, I suppose?'

'Naturally.'

The look she gave him was brimful of mischief, but Max resisted the urge to smile back. He had not intended to take her part and now tried to steer the conversation to safer waters.

'So you went to see Mrs Arncliffe,' he said.

'How is she? I know her health has not been good.'

'She is bearing up. And she is very much looking forward to Georgiana's arrival.'

'If you had waited, I would have come with you. I would not wish to be backward in my attentions to such an old friend.'

'Then we shall call again,' she replied equably. 'I wanted to tell her about the funeral, since she was too unwell to attend. I took her some funeral biscuits, which is why I could not leave the visit any longer, or they would have gone quite stale.'

Dorcas was looking mystified and Ellen explained, 'It is the custom in the north, you see, to provide biscuits and hot wine for the mourners. The biscuits are wrapped in paper and sealed in black wax for the mourners to take away to their families. I thought it important to assure Mrs Arncliffe that everything was done properly, according to custom.'

Perkins came in to announce dinner and the conversation ended, but it nagged at Max and when they were seated at the dining table he said abruptly, 'I beg your pardon. I should have been with you to make your first visits here.'

Dorcas tittered. 'I am sure no one was surprised to see your new Duchess out alone. After all, she is renowned for her independence.'

Max frowned, but Ellen replied cheerfully enough, 'There is much to be done here that will keep us both busy. I do not expect the Duke to live in my pocket. Perhaps you will tell us, Your Grace, how you fared in London?'

Max replied mechanically. He should be pleased she was reconciled to the fact they would be leading separate lives. Instead he was vaguely dissatisfied that she should accept the situation so readily.

Later, in the drawing room, Ellen was dispensing tea to her sister-in-law, when she remembered a matter she wanted to discuss with the Duke.

'Several people have asked me if we are holding the August ball. Is this something we should prepare for?'

'There can be no ball this year,' declared Dorcas.

'Why not?' asked Ellen.

The Dowager gave an exasperated huff.

'In the circumstances. Think how people will talk!'

'There will be talk whatever we do,' said Ellen. She turned to look at Max. 'What is this ball, Your Grace?'

'It originated during the time of the Sixth Duke, my grandfather. He wanted to honour my grandmother's birthday, which was late August, with a ball for all our local neighbours, villagers and tenants alike. When my father became Duke he continued with the ball and it became something of a tradition.'

'Although naturally, we did not hold one last year,' put in Dorcas. 'With poor Hugo so recently departed it would not have been seemly.'

'Then with the Duke's permission we shall revive it.' Ellen smiled at the Dowager. 'Perhaps you would advise me on the arrangements.'

Dorcas put up her hands as if to fend off the idea. 'No, no, it was always far too much for me. Why, everyone from the neighbourhood is invited, even the farmers! I have never approved of that. It would be better held in the assembly room above the Red Lion.' Her mouth twisted in distaste. 'No, I merely draw up a list of those I wish to invite and then only a few of my friends, for most could not be persuaded to share the ballroom with such people! The steward and housekeeper organise everything else.'

'Then they can help and advise me,' said Ellen, unperturbed.

The Dowager's thin mouth turned down even further. 'Mr Atherwell was as much Hugo's secretary as his steward, he wrote all his letters for him and was much the best person to compose the invitations, he had such lovely handwriting. One cannot expect Mr Grisham to do nearly so much, with his...disability.'

'Tony Grisham is a more efficient steward with one arm than many men with two!' flashed Max.

He looked as if he would say more and Ellen said quickly, 'I do not think we need trouble him with that side of the arrangements, Matlock writes a very fair hand.'

'A nursemaid!'

Ellen smiled at the Dowager, ignoring her remark.

'I shall need you to advise me on those we must invite, Dorcas, and of course the Duke shall give me a list of everyone he would like to come.'

'This has never been about the Colnebrookes,' said Max. 'It is a local ball, for local people. However, I have no objection to you inviting your own family, if you wish.'

'I would like to invite my step-mama and her husband, but no one else, not this year.'

Ellen thought of the letters she had received only that week from her Uncle Tatham. His response to the news that she was now a duchess was so gushing it was almost offensive, from a relative who had previously cast her off. She did not want to subject Max to such an obsequious meeting. Not yet.

'My dear Maximilian, you cannot have considered,' said the Dowager, frowning severely. 'There is barely a month to organise everything. It cannot be done. No one will come at such short notice.'

'The tenants and villagers will be able to come,' Ellen pointed out. 'And they are the ones for whom the ball is intended, are they not?'

Dorcas was not satisfied. 'But what of our acquaintances? A few close friends or family might stay here, of course, but the rest must be put up at the local inns, if they cannot stay with friends in the area. No, no, it is far too much to organise in the time and it will not do to put on a shabby affair.'

'I am sure we shall manage,' said Ellen, relishing the challenge, the opportunity to show Max what she could do.

'It is, of course, the Duke's decision,' said Dorcas in crushing accents that left no one in any doubt of her view.

Max looked at his wife. She was perched on the edge of her chair, her blue eyes sparkling and a becoming blush mantling her cheeks. Compared to the Dowager, reclining on the sofa, so pale and listless, Ellen exuded health and energy. She was looking at him hopefully and at last he nodded.

'Very well, if you think you can arrange it, we shall hold the Rossenhall Ball this year.'

'I shall begin work on it tomorrow,' said Ellen, smiling. 'And I promise you it will *not* be a shabby affair!'

True to her word, the following day Ellen began her preparations for the ball. Lists were drawn up, duties allocated and even the Dowager was persuaded to help, albeit reluctantly. Dorcas prophesied gloomily that it would be too much work for the new Duchess, but Ellen merely laughed and went about her business.

She had thrown herself into her new life with enthusiasm. She enjoyed making and receiving courtesy visits from the neighbouring families, she met daily with the housekeeper, planned menus with the chef and organised her time so that she could spend a good portion of each day with Jamie. Every day was busy, full of activity that sent her to bed each night too exhausted even to dream. And that was what Ellen wanted.

Over the next few weeks she saw very little of the Duke. It was for the best, she told herself. It was what Max wanted, but her heart ached every time she saw him riding out with Tony Grisham, or striding across the lawns to the stables. If she had taken that glass of wine he had offered her, the day he had returned from London, if she had stayed to talk, perhaps she could have told him how much she had missed him, how much she regretted those lost years. Instead she had run away from him, afraid her tears, her affection, would repel him. Panicked by the fear of being hurt again.

However, as the weeks went by and they became more comfortable on the brief occasions they met, Ellen felt a growing need to reach out to the Duke, to try to make amends for the years of separation. Her chance came when she went to his study to discuss an invitation for the forthcoming ball. The matter of the invitation having been resolved, she moved to the door and hesitated. Max was sitting at his desk, but he looked up, his brows raised, when she did not leave the room.

'Was there something else?'

He was so at ease, so approachable, that she decided to try once again to bury the past. Summoning up her courage, Ellen went back and sank on to the seat opposite him.

'I thought—I wondered, if we might not recover something of the happiness we knew in Egypt.' He froze and she said quickly. 'Not as lovers, neither of us wants that, but I thought, perhaps we could be friends. Max, you know I

was under a misapprehension when I left you.
I can only apologise now and admit that it was
wrong of me.' She leaned forward, putting her
hands on desk. 'We should put the past behind
us, for Jamie's sake if not our own.'

He said warningly, 'Let us not pursue this,
madam.'

'But, Max, can you not forgive—?' She
stopped, recoiling from the flash of anger in his
eyes. It was as if the restraints he had put on himself to act normally had finally snapped.

'No!' The word exploded from him. 'You can
have no idea of the disastrous consequences of
your actions.'

'Then will you not tell me?' she begged him.
'How can I atone if—?'

'There can be no atonement!' He left his
seat and began to pace the small room, anger
radiating from him. 'It was not merely my life
you destroyed when you left Alexandria under
Drovetti's protection. At first I could not believe
you would do such a thing. I thought there must
be some rational explanation, but in England I
could find no trace of you. I was forced to conclude that you had gone to France.' He stopped,
turning his head to look at her. 'You left no word.
You allowed me to believe you had deserted me
for the enemy.'

'Yes, I deserted you,' she admitted sadly. 'But not for the enemy. Not for any man. I want you to know, Max, there has never been anyone else—'

'It is too late for that, madam.'

Ellen saw the muscles of his jaw working, could feel his tension. Every tiny thread of hope she had woven was being cut as she listened to his icy words. She waited in silence, knowing he had not yet finished.

'The bullet that killed Frederick was meant for me. I have had that on my conscience, too, since Corunna. I needed to be doing something, anything to help me forget you. If I had not been so eaten up with grief, so careless of my own life, I would never have volunteered for every dangerous mission. Every forlorn hope. I would not have led so many men to their deaths. Your betrayal made me reckless, madam, and I have lived with the guilt of it ever since.' He stopped before her. *'That* is what I can never forget. Nor forgive.'

Ellen's final flicker of hope died. He blamed her for countless lives that had been lost and what defence did she have? Nothing that would weigh against a single man's life.

So he had done it. He had told Ellen exactly why he could never forgive her and had seen the pain and sadness fill her eyes. There was no

going back now. They could never be happy and
he knew it was no more than he deserved for having destroyed so many lives. He shut his mind
to the question of whether Ellen, too, deserved
such a penance.

Following their meeting, Max made even
greater efforts to keep himself busy and out of
the house. He could avoid his wife, but not the
changes that had taken place at Rossenhall. The
tomb-like atmosphere he had come to regard as
normal in the house had gone completely. Furni-
ture that had stood in the same spot for decades
was moved, cushions were tumbled, books lay
open on various tables throughout the building
and even toys were to be found abandoned in odd
corners. He expected his staff to object to the
disorder, but to his surprise Perkins showed no
signs of irritation whenever he directed a footman to gather up the young master's toy soldiers
from the morning room and Mrs Greenwood
only smiled when Max suggested Jamie should
be confined to the nursery.

'Lord love you, Your Grace, the young master
is as good as gold when he is in the public rooms.
He never does any damage, I assure you, and 'tis
a pleasure to see him running around.'

Even Hobbs, the aged gardener, who could
be relied upon to grumble if the Duke's hounds

should trample the flowerbeds, had set aside a small plot where Jamie might dig the soil and plant sticks to his heart's content.

He should have been overjoyed that his son and his wife had made such a difference, that they were accepted so readily at Rossenhall. He was glad of it, yes, for their sake, but the changes only highlighted what might have been. If only.

As soon as Ellen had word that Georgiana and little Charlotte had arrived to make their home with Mrs Arncliffe she lost no time in calling upon them, and a few days later Georgie and Lottie made their first visit to Rossenhall. They arrived in an open carriage and as it was a sunny day they spent their time out of doors. The children sailed the yacht on the lake, under the watchful eyes of Matlock and her young assistant, Eliza, while Georgie and Ellen sat in the shade of the giant beech trees. They discussed the rigours of travel, the news from Harrogate and how Georgie and her daughter were settling in.

'And how is Clare?' asked Ellen. 'I did not like to ask you in front of Mrs Arncliffe, but I hope she is not too disappointed to learn that the Duke is married.'

'No, no, not at all,' said Georgie, laughing. 'It was only a madcap notion of Fred's that his sister should marry Max. Clare is enjoying her final months at school and looking forward to her presentation next year.'

'And we shall sponsor her,' replied Ellen. 'Max wants to do what he can for the family, you know that.'

'I do and Mama-in-Law is as grateful as I am for it.' Georgie glanced at Ellen. 'You have yet to tell me how you go on here.'

'Very well. Dorcas was very ready to hand over the running of the household. Not that she did very much towards it. She prefers to sit in her room and write letters or to drive out in her barouche to visit the one or two families she considers sufficiently grand to be accepted as her friends.'

'And have *you* made friends here, Ellen? Mama-in-Law tells me you are highly regarded in the village.'

'I try to do my duty.'

'Your improvements to the village school have been welcomed and so has the plan for new houses on Market Street.'

'That is the Duke's initiative, not mine.'

'I heard it came about after you had visited old Mrs Betts and seen the rundown dwellings for yourself,' said Georgiana. 'Will you deny you had something to do with it?'

'I did mention it to the Duke, yes, but it was his idea that we should invest in new houses rather than repairing the old ones.'

'A demonstration of his affection for his bride, perhaps.'

'Perhaps.'

Georgie gave her a shrewd look. She said gently, 'Are you not yet fully reconciled?'

'I doubt we ever shall be that.'

Georgie sighed. 'I take it Max is still angry at you for hiding his son from him.'

Oh, it is so much worse than that!

Georgie was watching her and the temptation to confide in a sympathetic friend was very great, but Ellen could not bring herself to admit that Max thought her responsible for Fred's death, too.

'You know how it is with us,' she said lightly. 'Considering everything, we rub along very well.'

Ellen gazed towards the lake, where Jamie and Lottie were playing happily. She knew Max visited the nursery, but never when she was present. He was avoiding her, they met now only in the evenings when Dorcas was in attendance. The Duke was always polite and courteous, but he resisted all her attempts to engage in any meaningful conversation or argument. He had put up a barrier around himself, invisible but strong and impenetrable as steel.

Georgie reached across and touched her hand. 'But you tried to find him, Ellen, did you not? Does he know that?'

'Yes, but looking back, perhaps I could have done more.' Ellen waved her hand, as if to brush away the heavy shadow of regret. 'Pray do not look so anxious. I have no doubt we shall be as happy as many arranged marriages.'

Ellen prayed Georgiana would say no more. She knew her composure would not stand close scrutiny. Thankfully the next question was easier to answer.

'And how is Max getting along with his son?'

'They are firm friends now.' Ellen's smile became genuine. 'Even though Jamie continues to call him Duke rather than Papa! But Max does not seem to mind.'

As if conjured by their discussions, the Duke appeared, striding over the lawns towards them. He was wearing his riding jacket, buckskins and top boots, as if he had come directly from the stables, and walking with the loose, easy stride of an athlete. As always, Ellen's heart leapt at the sight of him.

'I heard you were come, Georgiana,' he said. 'How do you go on?'

Ellen watched him lift Georgie's hand to his lips, saw the way his smile warmed his eyes as he spoke and felt the knife twisting in her heart, although she was careful to betray no sign of it when she was drawn back into the conversation. Max remained with them until Georgiana declared it was time to take Lottie home and they all made their way to the waiting carriage.

As they approached, Tony Grisham came trotting along the drive on his bay mare. He would have ridden on if Max had not called him over to be introduced. As he brought his horse to a stand and jumped down, Ellen noted with pleasure that Georgiana showed no embarrassment at meeting the steward. Tony, too, was at his ease, dropping down to speak to Lottie, laughing as she patted his empty sleeve and explaining that he had been a soldier, like her father.

'Oh, did you know Frederick, Mr Grisham?' asked Georgie, her face lighting up.

'I did indeed.' Tony stood straight, smiling. 'He was a fine man. I was very sorry to hear he was so ill.'

Ellen watched them as they conversed, seeing the colour come and go from Georgie's smooth cheek, hearing the warmth in Tony's voice as he talked of his army days.

'I must not keep Mama-in-Law's horses standing any longer,' said Georgie at last. 'She will be wondering what has become of me.'

'And I must take my mare to the stables,' said Tony. 'I am delighted to make your acquaintance, Mrs Arncliffe.'

With a nod and a smile, he went off. Ellen watched him walk away, a thoughtful crease in her brow. A word from Max recalled her attention and she saw Georgie and Lottie were now seated in the carriage and ready to leave. Dutifully, Ellen stood with Max, Jamie jumping up and down between them as they waved goodbye to their guests.

We must look like the perfect little family.

The thought brought a sudden choking lump to Ellen's throat and for a moment her vision blurred. She blinked away a threatening tear. She must hold on to her smile for a few moments longer, until Max walked away. It could not be long.

But this time he did not leave. Ellen heard a cough behind her. Matlock was waiting to take Jamie upstairs to change out of his muddied nankeens.

As Ellen turned to follow them indoors Max said, 'Are you busy? Do you have time to come with me to the stables?'

'Of course.'

Hiding her surprise, she fell into step beside him. He walked with his hands clasped behind his back, keeping a distance between them.

'It is looking much better since you asked Joshua to tidy up,' remarked Max, nodding towards the stable block.

'I did not actually *ask* him.'

'No.' Max flashed her a quick grin. 'Stevens says you…er…turned him up sweet. Whatever you did I am grateful. The trouble is, Joshua put me on my first pony and therefore has never taken anything I say seriously. He merely nods when I tell him to do something, then ignores me. He knows perfectly well that I would never turn him off.'

'It is always the same with old retainers, I believe.'

They walked through the arched entrance and she saw Max's groom walking a very small, brown pony around the yard.

'Tony Grisham heard the Allendales' children had outgrown this little fellow and thought he might do for James,' said Max as Stevens brought the pony to a stand before them. 'We went to see him today and brought him back with us. For your approval. I promised Allendale an answer by the morning.'

The constriction returned to Ellen's throat, but

for a very different reason. She stepped forward and scratched the pony's head.

'He's as sweet-natured as you could want, ma'am,' offered Stevens. 'And used to carrying children, too.'

'He looks perfect for Jamie,' she managed, just the faintest tremor in her voice.

'It is agreed, then. We shall keep him. Tony is joining us for dinner this evening, I shall ask him to ride over and settle the account in the morning.'

'And when shall we show him to the young master, Your Grace?' Stevens grinned. 'He'll be as pleased as punch when he sees this 'un, I'm sure.'

'That is up to his mother,' said Max. 'Well, ma'am?'

She must not cry.

'After breakfast tomorrow, I think,' she managed at last. 'Jamie will want to ride him immediately and there is not really time for that today.'

A time was arranged and Ellen was turning to go back to the house when Max touched her arm.

'There is something else.'

As he led her into the stables she said, trying to laugh, 'Really, Your Grace, it is not necessary for me to see where the pony is going to live, I am sure it will be perfectly—oh!'

She stopped, her eyes widening when she saw the beautiful grey mare moving restlessly in the loose box. 'This is not one of your horses.'

'No. The mare is yours, if you want her. I have been looking out for a mount for you and she came up for sale at Beaconsfield. The last owner named her Belle, but of course you may call her what you wish.'

The mare put her nose over the door of the loosebox as if in welcome.

'Oh, Max, she is lovely. And the name Belle suits her perfectly.'

'Yes, well, we had nothing suitable for a lady in the stables and as I recall you are a good rider. Of camels as well as horses—'

He broke off and Ellen felt the memories rushing into the ensuing silence. Galloping neck and neck across the sands on Mameluke-trained horses, Mrs Ackroyd affectionately calling her a hoyden because she was riding astride, the cheers of the Mamelukes fading and replaced by nothing but the drumming hoofbeats and their own laughter when they reached the winning post, another of the innumerable ancient ruins that rose up from the desert. Max winning by a head and claiming his prize, their first kiss…

Ellen felt its magic even now. She wanted to

touch his sleeve, to ask him if he remembered, but already he was turning away from her.

'Take someone with you, if you want to ride outside the park,' he said brusquely. 'Now if you will excuse me, I have business that will not wait.'

There it was again, she thought sadly as he left her. The door closing upon any form of intimacy.

Hell and damnation.

Max strode away from the stables, battling the wave of desire that was surging through him. It happened every time she was near, the tug of attraction that was almost impossible to resist. He had hoped it would diminish as they saw more of one another, but it was quite the opposite. He was more wild for her now then he had been four years ago, the first time he had seen her, perched up on that camel and quite unafraid, despite being surrounded by a hoard of angry warriors. No hysterical outbursts, no maidenly swooning. She had met his eyes and smiled, as if in recognition of a kindred spirit. He had known at that moment that he would make her his wife.

He shook his head, trying to rid himself of the memory. Better to remember how she had repaid him. How she had disappeared from his life without a word, never told him he had a son. Aye, he thought as he took the stairs two at a time, better to think of the cost of her betrayal.

But it did not stop him wanting her.

Flynn was waiting for him when he reached his bedchamber, a look of pained reproach upon his face.

'I had the water brought up for your bath an hour ago, Your Grace, since you ordered that it should be ready when you returned from your ride. I shall have to send to the kitchens for more.'

'Don't bother,' barked Max, stripping off his coat. 'I'll bathe in it as it is. The cooler the better!'

By the time Max joined the company for dinner his body was once more under his control. He was glad to find both Dorcas and Anthony Grisham were there before him, it avoided any awkwardness with his wife. Not that Ellen showed any signs of discomfiture. As ever she greeted him with cool friendliness and they maintained their places on opposite sides of the room for the half-hour that Jamie was with them. When dinner was announced Ellen beckoned Tony to accompany her, leaving Max to escort Dorcas. As they crossed the hall to the dining room he listened to her chatting merrily to his steward.

The perfect society wife.

Ellen had ordered the four places to be set at one end of the table, explaining to Tony that she considered him family and hoping he was not offended by the informality.

'Not at all, ma'am. I am honoured by it.'

Max knew Dorcas would not approve and waited for her to utter some barbed comment, but she merely glowered silently. It was not until the covers had been removed that anything occurred to mar the enjoyment of their meal.

As the servants withdrew, Dorcas said, 'What is this I hear of you buying a horse for the Marquess, Maximilian?'

'It is a pony,' Ellen told her, smiling. 'The most beautiful little creature. I am sure Jamie will be thrilled when he sees him in the morning.'

'You are keeping him, then, Your Grace?' asked Tony.

'Yes. I would like you to ride over to see Allendale first thing tomorrow and give him the asking price.'

'I am surprised you would allow such frivolous expenditure,' declared Dorcas.

'Not frivolous at all,' Max replied calmly. 'The

expense was more than covered by the sale of the spare carriage horses.'

Tony turned to Ellen. 'And how do you like your mare, ma'am?'

'I have yet to try her out, but I think she will suit me very well. But I believe it was you, Mr Grisham, who found that beautiful little pony for Jamie. I am indebted to you, sir.'

'It was nothing,' replied Tony, waving away her thanks. 'I knew the Duke wanted a suitable mount for the Marquess and the pony seemed ideal.'

Max grinned. 'And if I know Jamie we will have him careering all over the park by the end of the summer!'

That brought a cry from his sister-in-law.

'How can you all be so thoughtless, Maximilian?' She whipped out a handkerchief and pressed it to her lips. 'W-would you have the boy break his neck, like his uncle?'

Max was stunned, but Ellen immediately reached for her sister-in-law's hand.

'Oh, my dear. I beg your pardon if our talk has upset you.'

'Hugo's death was unfortunate,' said Max, his jaw tense, 'but my son must learn to ride.'

He looked at Ellen, wondering if Dorcas's outburst had given her second thoughts about Jamie riding the creature, but she merely smiled at him.

'Of course he must,' she said. 'You must not blame the Duke, Dorcas. He left the final decision to me. It was I who agreed we should buy the pony for James. And Stevens is going to teach him to ride. I have no doubt he will take great care.' She pushed back her chair. 'Shall we leave the gentlemen to their brandy?'

When they had gone Max silently filled Tony's glass, then his own.

'Was I insensitive?' he asked. 'I know the Dowager declared she would never ride again after Hugo died, but I thought that was because she never particularly cared for being on horseback. I didn't realise she would be so upset.'

'It argues an admirable depth of feeling,' murmured Tony.

'It argues an excess of sensibility,' Max retorted. 'Damn it, man, one cannot live in the country and *not* ride.'

'The Duchess agrees with you, Your Grace. She would not say such a thing if it were not true.'

'Aye, there is that.' Max drained his glass and reached again for the decanter. 'Tell me, what do the staff say now of my new Duchess? She has been here for over a month and is certainly making her mark, but I would not expect them to say anything to me.'

'They adore her,' Tony said simply. He met Max's stare with a steady look. 'It is true, Your Grace. Some were a little sceptical at first, because we were given to understand that she might not be quite up to snuff—'

'That would be the Dowager's doing, I suppose.' Max gave a short laugh. 'That look tells me I am right! Go on.'

He pushed the decanter towards the steward, who refilled his glass and sat for a moment, his hand clasped around the crystal.

'Well,' he said thoughtfully, 'the Duchess has a knack of making people love her. Not that she tolerates insolence, or any slacking amongst the staff, you understand, and they respect her for that. She has taken over the household accounts now, which has relieved me of a significant amount of work. And her grasp of what is required on the land is excellent, too. She is a real asset here.'

'Good God has she no faults?' exclaimed Max, startled. He saw Tony's brows shoot up and added acidly, 'This all sounds far too good to be true.'

'Well, the Duchess told me at the start she has never run a household on this scale, but she is not afraid to ask questions and take advice.' Tony hesitated a moment, then said slowly, 'She is determined to make you a good duchess, Your Grace.'

'The devil she is.'

Max frowned into his glass. She was good for Rossenhall, he knew that.

She would be good for you, too, if you would let her.

But that was the problem. He dared not let his guard down, or those twin demons of guilt and regret that pursued him would rear up and destroy him.

When they had finished their brandy the men went through to the drawing room, where they found Ellen alone, working at her embroidery.

'The Dowager has retired with a headache,' she explained, putting aside her tambour frame. 'It is very close and I think there might be thunder in the air, I know some people are susceptible to such weather.'

'But not you, Duchess?' said Tony.

'Oh, no,' she said cheerfully. 'I enjoy very good health. Which reminds me, Mr Grisham. Alice tells me that Phelps, the carter's boy, has broken his leg and cannot work for a while. I know he supports his widowed mother and the younger children, but I do not know the family.

Would they be offended, do you think, if I took them a basket?'

'Not at all, ma'am, I am sure they would be grateful. Mrs Phelps does a little sewing, but her income will not be sufficient to keep them all while the boy is laid up.'

'Ah, then I shall take over a couple of gowns that need repairing, too, and pay her something in advance.'

Tony was right, thought Max, listening to their conversation. Ellen was an asset. It was likely that she already knew more about the people here than he did. When he rode over the estates the men were happy enough to talk to him about the animals and weather and crop yields, but they rarely offered information about their families unless he asked for it and even then they were loath to complain. He knew she often drove out with Tony in the gig—Max had offered her the use of his curricle, but she had declined and had adamantly refused to let him buy her a phaeton— and now she had her own horse they would be able to go further afield.

He shifted in his seat. It was not Tony who should be riding out with Ellen.

'I beg your pardon, Your Grace, I had not meant to monopolise our guest.' Ellen's soft, musical voice interrupted his thoughts. 'In fact, we should not be talking business here at all, when I am sure you have both had a surfeit of it during the day.'

'Not at all,' replied Max, sitting up. 'I am glad you take such an interest, my dear. Perhaps tomorrow you and I should ride together, it would give you a chance to try out your new mare.'

There was no mistaking the pleasure that flashed across Ellen's face at the prospect, or the tinge of colour that stole into her cheek when she accepted the invitation.

'An excellent plan, Your Grace,' Tony agreed. 'There are several things I have been meaning to bring to your attention, but you do not need me with you, the Duchess knows and can explain everything. I can have notes ready for you by the morning. In fact, if you will excuse me, I shall go and draw up a list now.'

Max and Ellen both protested at this, but Tony insisted it was what he wanted to do and Max found himself alone with Ellen. She picked up her tambour frame again and set a few stitches. The silence closed in, hot and uncomfortable, and she soon put it aside, exclaiming, 'Heavens, but it is very close in here.'

She went to one of the full-length windows, where she struggled with the lock. Max went across to her.

'Here, let me.'

As he reached past her to open the catch he could smell that elusive fragrance of jasmine and lily of the valley he remembered so well. Scorching desire sent his thoughts reeling wildly and by the time he had recovered she had pushed the long windows wide and stepped out on to the terrace. At once her delicate perfume was lost in the scent of garden flowers, thick and powerful on the heavy night air.

'Ah, that's better.' She put back her head and took a deep breath before glancing over her shoulder. 'Will you not come out and enjoy it with me?'

The evening sky was bruised with deep purple clouds but as he stepped out on to the terrace the sun made one final effort, appearing for one last, glorious blaze and painting the landscape in jewel-bright colours.

Max looked at Ellen. She was staring at the scene spread out before them, her cherry lips parted in delight. A slight breeze ruffled her curls, turning them to molten gold in the sunlight. It also pressed the fine muslin of her gown against her shapely form. As if nature was taunting him with his wife's beauty.

'It is quite magnificent, is it not, Max?'

She turned to him, her blue eyes glowing with

an inner fire, rivalling the sapphires at her throat. He swung away. She was the only woman he had ever wanted, but he must resist her. He had fought battles, suffered bullet and sword wounds, but none of the scars went as deep as her defection. He would remember that and not give in again. To lose himself in her, to find happiness in her arms, however fleeting, would be a betrayal of all the men who had died because of his recklessness. He sought for a distraction and his eyes fell on the roses clambering over the low terrace wall.

'The dead flowers need removing. I will have a word with Hobbs in the morning.'

He felt a gentle touch on his sleeve.

'Do not turn away from me, Max.'

When he did not move she came to stand before him, her eyes glistening with tears. He put a hand to her cheek and she turned her head to press a kiss into his palm. His defences crumbled. His hand slid around her neck and he pulled her close. She turned her face up and he kissed her savagely, hungrily.

With a little moan Ellen put her arms about his neck, returning his kiss with equal fervour, teasing his tongue with her own. Memories flooded in: the taste of her, the feel of her naked body pressed against him, pliant and eager as they moved together, hot skin rolling on cool cotton sheets. The kiss lasted as long as that final blaze of light. Even as the sun disappeared Max raised his head, dragging in a deep, ragged breath.

'No.' He held her away from him. 'You bewitched me once, Ellen, I will not allow you to do so again.' Her eyes were huge and luminous in the twilight, filled with sadness that twisted like a knife in his gut, but he dare not weaken. 'Goodnight, madam.'

He turned and walked away, his back straight, spine tingling with the knowledge that she was behind him. Would she run after him, beg him to stay, to make love to her? It took for ever to reach the door and each step tested his willpower to the limit. By heaven, he was only flesh and blood, it would take no more than a word, a touch to shatter his resolve. But there was nothing, only silence, and as he left the room and closed the door behind him he risked one quick look back. Ellen had not moved from the terrace, a still, black figure against the darkening sky.

Chapter Eleven

No rain had fallen overnight, but morning dawned heavy with the threat of a storm. Dark clouds were broken by periods of intense sunshine. Ellen ordered the windows of the house to be opened, but there was only a thick, sullen breeze that moved the air yet did little to freshen the rooms.

Ellen felt the oppression on her spirits as she made her way down to the great hall. The clock was just chiming ten and Max had sent a message to say he would meet her there to present Jamie with his pony. She was wearing her riding habit, although she had no idea if it was still his intention to ride out with her. Not that she blamed him. Last night she had asked him for friendship, but when he had caressed her cheek so tenderly she had been unable to prevent herself from responding like a wanton. A mistake, she knew that, to show how much she still desired him. He had rejected her and she had been rooted to the spot in shame and humiliation while he walked away from her. Well, she had her pride. She would never let him see how much he had hurt her.

As she came down the final flight of steps she heard voices and found Max already in the hall, talking to Jamie while Matty stood to one side, looking on. A band tightened around Ellen's heart when she saw father and son together. James was holding the toy yacht in his arms and saying if he couldn't play with the drum perhaps they might go to the lake.

'Later, if there is time,' said Max, gently removing the yacht from Jamie and putting it on a side table. 'Now your mother is here we have something else for you.' He took the little boy's hand in his own and straightened, glancing across at Ellen as she approached. 'If you are ready, ma'am?'

Polite, considerate. Ellen saw the old butler hovering by the door, the smile on his face telling her that he knew what was waiting on the drive and was eager to see the little boy's reaction. She stretched her mouth into a smile, playing along with the charade that they were a happy family. Perkins threw open the door and they stepped outside on to the balcony. Stevens was waiting at the bottom of the steps, the little pony standing patiently beside him. Jamie's mouth dropped open. He looked up at Max, who nodded.

'Yes, he is for you.'

'If it takes his mind off that toy drum it will be a mercy,' muttered Matlock.

Max lifted Jamie on to the saddle and Ellen watched, smiling as Stevens adjusted the stirrups to suit.

'Can I ride him now, Mama, can I ride him, *please*?'

'I will take him for his first lesson now, ma'am, and gladly,' said Stevens, 'unless, Your Grace, you want me to accompany you?' He cast an enquiring look at the Duke. 'Mr Grisham left instructions for Jupiter and Belle to be saddled up for you and the Duchess to ride out this morning.'

'What? Oh—' Max frowned and glanced at her, as if realising for the first time that she was dressed for riding. 'Perhaps Her Grace should remain with the boy for his first lesson.'

Ellen's heart sank. Max was reluctant to take her with him. She hid her disappointment and was about to concur, but she was outflanked by the servants.

Stevens said quickly, 'There's no need for you to stay, ma'am, I'll take good care of the boy, you may be sure of that.'

And Matlock, in her blunt way, declared that

Master James would get on much better without his mama fussing over him. Ellen bit her lip and looked towards Max, who gave the tiniest of shrugs.

'Shall we go, then, madam?'

They set off for the stables. Thick white clouds were bubbling up in the west, encroaching upon the deep blue of the sky.

'It could well rain,' said Max, following her glance. 'If it does, we will turn back.'

'We do not need to go at all,' she countered, chin up to belie her heavy heart.

'And how would that look? No, we must ride out now, madam.'

Even though it is the last thing you want to do.

Ellen kept her head up and her smile in place. They must at least look as if they were enjoying themselves.

The stable hands were watching out for them and when they walked through the arched entrance, Max's black hunter and the new grey mare were waiting in the yard. Ellen immediately instructed the groom to take Belle to the mounting block. Max would not wish to throw her into the saddle.

The mare was fresh and as they trotted away from the stables Ellen was glad to concentrate on controlling her, rather than worrying about the silent and brooding rider at her side. A gallop across the park gave her the opportunity to try the mare's paces. It also dispelled some of the tension between her and Max: she thanked him for buying her such a spirited creature, he responded with a compliment on her ability to handle the mare. From there they progressed to discussing the other horses in the stables and then the tenants they were to visit that day. Ellen knew harmony was restored, in part.

We are discussing rents and crop rotation and ways of improving the land. As long as we keep to impersonal topics such as this we can rub along very well.

It should be enough, she told herself, but she knew it was not.

They were out for most of the day and by the time they turned for home Max was beginning to understand why Tony Grisham was so full of praise for the new Duchess. Tenants who had been stiff with awe and respect towards him opened up to Ellen, whose relaxed and friendly style soon put them at their ease. She knew just the right thing to say to draw them out about their worries and concerns.

'I congratulate you,' he said with grudging

respect as he threw her up into the saddle at the last of their visits, a particularly rundown farm at the very edge of his estate. 'Tony has been trying for months to persuade old Martin to let us repair his roof.'

'The poor man was clearly afraid that this sudden interest in his home meant you intended to turn him out,' she explained. 'Once he was assured you do not mean to replace him, he was much happier.'

'You also persuaded him to accept Tom Croft's youngest boy as a farmhand.'

'You cannot deny that Mr Martin has a wealth of knowledge and experience, and Tom has already told Mr Grisham that his youngest is not interested in following his brother into the family trade as a blacksmith. It seemed a sensible solution.'

'Very sensible.' He scrambled up on to his own horse and gathered up the reins. 'I think you are making yourself indispensable here.'

Ellen threw him an enigmatic look.

'That is my intention, Your Grace.'

And with that she urged the mare on and galloped away.

The threatened storm held off, although by the time they returned to the stables the sky was growing ominously dark and the sun was completely obscured by a heavy blanket of cloud. Stevens was waiting for them in the yard, eager to report on Jamie's first riding lesson.

'Not a bit afraid,' he told Ellen, when she had dismounted. 'Bless him, he didn't want to go back indoors. But little and often is what I told him, so we'll put him in the saddle again tomorrow, if that's all right with you, ma'am?'

Ellen gave her assent and walked back to the house with Max. He made no move to take her arm, but she dared to hope there was a little less restraint between them and she was glad of it.

Despite the lack of sun, the air was very warm and it was a relief to step into the cool marble hall.

'I must have a word with Tony,' said Max, stripping off his gloves. 'Then it will be good to wash away the dust and dirt. We covered many miles today and made important progress, I think. Thank you for coming with me.'

'It was my pleasure,' she told him, noting the soft but definite glow in his eyes. It could only be gratitude, or appreciation, but it warmed her, nevertheless. 'I shall change as soon as I have seen Jamie.'

Perkins, who was crossing the hall at that moment, stopped and gave a little cough.

'If you will permit me, ma'am, I saw Eliza taking the young Marquess to the gardens. With his drum,' he added.

Ellen laughed. 'Then I shall go and find them. How the day has flown, it is nearly time for dinner. I shall take him upstairs and he can tell me about riding a real pony.'

Eliza was on the terrace, collecting up a number of toys, including the colourful little drum that Max had bought for Jamie.

'He went upstairs to collect his hobby horse,' she said, in answer to Ellen's question. She looked past the Duchess, as if expecting to see the little boy at the open windows.

'I have just come through the drawing room and did not see him there,' said Ellen. 'I expect he has been distracted and is playing in the nursery. I shall go up.'

But when she reached the nursery Matlock shook her head.

'He hasn't been here, ma'am. I haven't seen him since Eliza took him out to play. I will check the other rooms, though, just in case he has gone exploring. But he so loves being out of doors I cannot think he will be up here.'

'No, I believe you are right.' Ellen thought of the house with all its doors and windows thrown wide and she felt a tiny prickle of anxiety. 'I will go downstairs and look for him.'

The deepening gloom within the house reflected her worries, and a low rumble of thunder added to her sense of unease. Max was on the half-landing, talking to his valet, and she did not hesitate to interrupt them.

'Your Grace, have you seen Jamie?'

'No,' said Max. 'Have you seen him, Flynn?'

'No, Your Grace, but I heard him earlier. Playing his drum on the west lawn.'

Ellen nodded and continued down the stairs. Jamie loved to be out of doors and that is where she would find him. She knew it.

'Shall I prepare your bath, Your Grace?' she heard Flynn's question, echoing off the stone walls.

'Yes, yes, I shall be up directly.' Before she reached the hall Max was beside her. 'What is it, what has happened?'

Having someone to share her concerns was new for Ellen. For a moment she lost some of her self-assurance.

'Jamie is missing. No, no, it cannot be anything serious.' She turned as the nursemaid appeared, on her way to the nursery with her arms full of toys. 'He did not come back out to you, Eliza?'

'No, ma'am. Is he not with Mrs Matlock?'

Ellen shook her head, flinching as a clap of thunder rumbled around the house like a portent of doom.

'When did you last see him?' Max asked the nursemaid.

'Well, it's hard to say, Your Grace. It couldn't have been that long since he went indoors, no more than an hour.'

'An hour!' Ellen gripped her hands together to stop them shaking. 'He could be anywhere by now.'

'Go upstairs and look for him, Eliza,' said Max. 'Not just the nursery wing, but the whole of the top floor, do you understand?' As the maid hurried away he uttered a few brief instructions to the hovering footman, then touched Ellen's arm. 'Come, they will check the grounds and the stables while we look around here.'

Ellen followed Max from room to room. The thunder was growing louder and more frequent. Jamie did not like thunder. He would not stay out in a storm. He wouldn't. She hugged the thought to her as they checked the study, the library and the anteroom where they found Tony sorting through numerous boxes of paper. He abandoned his task immediately to go and search the offices and basement rooms.

In the morning room they found the Dowa-

ger dozing on a daybed, an open book on her lap
and a dish of marzipan at her side. Max spoke
quickly.

'Dorcas, have you seen Jamie?'

The Dowager sat up, straightening her cap and
tutting.

'I have seen no one, I have been resting,' she
told them peevishly. 'My room was so hot last
night I hardly had a wink of sleep. I do not know
how you have the energy to go riding all over the
place when the weather is so close—'

'Never mind that,' Max interrupted her. 'We
are looking for Jamie.'

She hunched one shoulder. 'How should I
know where he is? He was outside my window,
earlier, with that infernal drum.'

'When was that?' asked Ellen, resisting the
temptation to shake her sister-in-law.

'Oh, I do not know, I was not watching the
time. I had come in here to lie down after my
nuncheon and he began marching back and forth,
banging on his drum so loudly it brought on my
headache. I told him to go away and play quietly.'

'That will have been when he first came
downstairs,' said Max, as they returned to the
hall. 'Do not worry, I have every hope of finding him soon. Perhaps he went back to the stables.' He gave a hiss of exasperation. 'Ellen, I

am very sorry if my giving him the pony has brought this about.'

'No, no you cannot be blamed for—' She stopped, her eyes fixed on the side table. 'The yacht. We left it there when we went out this morning.'

Max barked a question to the butler, who shook his head.

'No, Your Grace. I gave no instructions for it to be moved.'

Ellen was already running. She raced through the drawing room and out on to the terrace, the straightest line to the lake. Max was beside her. As they descended the steps the first fat drops of rain fell and by the time they had reached the lawns leading to the lake the rain was pouring down and they were both drenched to the skin.

'He would not be out in this,' muttered Max as they reached the water's edge and stopped, looking left and right.

Ellen did not give voice to her fears, but began to walk along the bank. She stopped, pointing.

'What's that?'

The white sails of the little boat were visible amongst the reeds. It was a good six feet from the bank, the leading string floating like a thin snake on the water, just out of reach.

'What if he t-tried…?'

Panic took over. She began to run frantically back and forth along the bank, calling out, peering at the reeds and only stopping when Max gripped her shoulders.

'Ellen, he is not in the water. There is no sign of him here and no current to carry him away. He is not here. Trust me.'

The self-control she had exercised so effectively for weeks gave way to unreasoning dread. He was gone, her child. Her baby. Her only reason for living, since Max no longer loved her.

'I must keep looking, I must!' She began to shake uncontrollably. Max's grip tightened and she threw up her head, her eyes beseeching him. 'He is all I have, Max!'

'We will find him, I promise you.'

His calm certainty steadied her. She drew in another shuddering breath, drawing strength from his presence. She swiped a hand across her cheek and dashed away a mixture of rain and tears. She must think where next to look.

A shout. Tony Grisham was running towards them, waving frantically.

'Safe.' That was the first word she heard. 'He's safe, Your Grace.' Tony came to a stand before them, chest heaving, but grinning even as the rain plastered his hair to his head. 'He came in by way of the kitchens and the scullery maid took him straight up to the nursery.' He saw Ellen look back towards the lake. 'He *was* here, ma'am, but he says he let go of the string at the first thunderclap. He was coming in to get help to recover the yacht when apparently he saw a hen was loose, so he chased it back to the kitchen gardens. Then the next clap of thunder sent him scurrying into the kitchens. That's why we couldn't see him. He's so small he was screened from us by the hedges.'

'Oh, thank heaven.' Ellen's legs felt so weak she thought she might have collapsed if Max had not been holding her. She reached out and clasped Tony's hand in both her own. 'Thank you,' she said fervently.

Max kept his arm around Ellen and hurried her indoors. He knew she would not rest until she had seen for herself that the boy was safe so he took her directly upstairs, leaving a watery trail behind them. Jamie was in bed and already half-asleep when they reached the nursery. Max felt his chest tighten at the sight of the little boy tucked up snugly under the covers, the blond curls still slightly damp. His son.

Ellen fell to her knees beside the bed, stifling a sob.

'That will do now, Miss Ellen,' Matlock told her gruffly, worry causing her to revert to addressing her mistress in the old way. 'You are dripping water all over the boy, which will not do him any good.'

'No. No, of course. I wanted to be sure he was all right.' Ellen leaned closer to plant a gentle kiss on his head before she pushed herself to her feet. Outside the thunder was still rolling, but softly now, moving away.

Ellen tried to smile, but Max saw it fade. She swayed and would have fallen if he had not been ready to catch her.

'Shock,' said Matlock as he swept Ellen up into his arms. 'She needs to get dry and warm. And as quickly as possible.'

'I will see to it.'

He carried her from the nursery, holding her against his heart. Even in her sodden clothes she weighed almost nothing. Down the stairs and past the door to her bedchamber, he took her to his own dressing room. Flynn would already have a bath prepared for him and he knew that would be the quickest way to drive the chill from Ellen's body. She was stirring, but he made no effort to put her down. It was a struggle to open the door, but he managed it, stepping through and kicking it closed behind him. The warmth of the room enveloped them both. Flynn had pulled the curtains across the windows, shutting out the storm, and as Max had hoped, a fire blazed in the hearth and the candles burned in their sockets, casting a cosy glow over the room.

In front of the fire was the hip bath, perfumed steam rising lazily from the water and scenting the air. Flynn came in from the bedchamber and could not hide his surprise to see his master arrive with the Duchess in his arms, but Max was in no mood for explanations.

He said shortly, 'Leave us.'

'Shall I send in Her Grace's maid?'

'No. I will deal with this.'

Flynn went out, closing the door quietly behind him. Ellen stirred again and Max looked down at her.

'We must get you out of that wet gown.'

Gently he set her on her feet, but she was shivering too much to do much more than stand still while he swiftly helped her out of her clothes and into the bath. The wry thought flashed across his mind that the practice he had had over the years of undressing women was at last proving useful. His own skin was beginning to feel the chill of his sodden jacket and shirt so he stripped down to his breeches and threw more logs on to the already roaring fire before turning his attention back to Ellen. She had stopped shivering and was lying back in the warm water, eyes closed.

A touch of colour had returned to her cheeks and as he knelt beside the bath she opened her eyes.

'Thank you,' she whispered.

He wanted to lean across and kiss the corner of her mouth, where the first tremulous signs of a smile had appeared, but he resisted. She would think he wanted her gratitude and that was not it at all. Instead he reached out and gently moved a stray curl from her cheek.

'Are you feeling better now?'

'I am getting warmer.'

'Good. Then if you will permit me I shall finish drying myself.'

Ellen rested her head against the high side of the bath. The warmth of the water was soaking into her limbs, relaxing her. She felt no urgency to do anything save look at Max. He had his back to her, so she felt free to watch as he dragged the towel across his shoulders, enjoying the way the light played with the muscles as he moved, throwing up shadows, accentuating the strong lines. She felt less relaxed when he discarded his breeches. There was a definite pleasure in looking at the narrow hips and strong thighs. He moved with a lithe grace, exuding power, and a tiny *frisson* of anxiety went through her when he disappeared into the bedroom, but he was back almost immediately, wrapped in an exotic dressing gown. The disappointment she felt because she could no longer see his body made her smile.

It was at that moment Max chose to look at her and heat flooded through her, rising up to colour her cheeks. If he noticed her blush he gave no sign, but picked a large towel from the rack on the far side of the fire and approached the bath.

'The water will be growing cold. Come along.'

Obediently she rose. As she stepped out of the bath he wrapped her in the towel and in his arms, pulling her against him. Ellen closed her eyes and let the memories flood back as the thick material enveloped her, gentle and comforting against her skin.

'I have not felt towelling as soft as this since my wedding day,' she murmured, leaning against him. 'The local women bathed me and dressed me for the ceremony, do you remember?'

Good memories of hot days, warm nights and long, languorous lovemaking.

'How could I forget?' He lowered his head to kiss her neck and she felt the pleasure welling up inside. He released her with a sigh. 'I have tried so hard to resist you.'

She did not move away.

'Why should you?' she whispered, letting the towel fall to the floor. 'I am your wife.'

Green fire blazed in his eyes. As he lifted her into his arms she wanted to say how much she loved him, but he had made it plain he did not want that. She was afraid such a declaration might drive him away again and she could not bear for him to leave now, when her body was crying out for him. Instead she put her hands around his neck and buried her face in his shoulder while he carried her through to the bed and laid her gently on the covers. In one fluid movement he shed his banyan and stretched himself beside her. He propped himself on one elbow and looked at her, devouring her with his eyes, and it was all she could do not to reach out for him. When he lowered his head to plant a gentle kiss on one shoulder she breathed out on a sigh. Her head went back as he trailed kisses across her collar bone, pausing at the little dip at the base of her throat.

Ellen closed her eyes and reached for him. She pushed her hands through his hair, feeling the silky softness of it, breathing in the scent of him, damp skin and warm, woody spices that excited her senses. She burrowed against him, urgently seeking his mouth, and when at last their lips met the whole world exploded. She clung to him, touching, caressing, revelling in the feel of flesh on flesh as they came together in a tangle of limbs and a frenzied consummation that was over all too soon.

In a silence broken only by their gasping, panting breaths, Ellen rolled away from Max, on to her side. Gently but firmly he reached out and pulled her against him, curving himself around her back and cradling one breast in his hand as he kissed her neck. Smiling, Ellen closed her eyes and enjoyed the delicious sensation of his body wrapped about her. It felt as if she had come home.

She had slept then, but at some point Max must have given orders for dinner to be sent up on a tray, for when she awoke he coaxed her to sit up and they fed each other with delicious slivers of meat and fruit washed down with sweet wines. It was a magical, other-worldly experience, curled on the bed within the glow from a single branched candlestick. They barely spoke and Ellen knew it was a truce, of sorts, and she was content to shut out the problems of the past, for a while at least.

Afterwards Max pulled her back down into his bed and they fell into a deep sleep, but before the last of the candles had burned itself out Ellen stirred. Max was still curled about her, but now he was pressed against her, hard and aroused.

The hand on her breast was caressing her, his thumb gently circling the nub. She moved restlessly and his other hand slid over her hip. She gasped as his fingers slipped into the hinge of her thighs and he began to stroke her, slowly at first, but going deeper, faster until she was bucking against him, crying out as he carried her to the very edge of consciousness. Her body was trembling with anticipation as he rolled her on to her stomach and pulled up her hips. Then, kneeling behind her on the bed, he entered her, driving deep into her core. He smoothed his hands over her aching breasts, ran his fingers over her belly and down again between her thighs to caress the tender spot there until she was moaning with pleasure. Every thrust brought a gasp as he took her higher and she knew he was keeping his own desires in check until he had tipped her over the edge into ecstasy. Only then did he let go and with a shout of triumph he buried himself deep inside her. They fell on to the bed, sated, exhausted, and as Max gathered her against him she heard his murmur, soft against her skin.

'My wife. My Duchess.'

But in the morning she was alone.

Jupiter flew across the park, Max crouched low over his neck, urging him on, pushing the horse to its limit. Deer grazing peacefully on the rise scattered in panic as the black hunter and its rider continued their headlong flight. They skirted the Home Wood and galloped towards the ridge, where the pace slowed as they ascended the hill. Max had hoped an early morning gallop would purge the lust from his blood and he would be able to think rationally, but it had not worked. He could not forget the sight of Ellen as she rose, naked from the bath, the feel of her, fragile and defenceless in his arms. Then watching that rosy mouth brush his fingertips as he fed her delicate morsels, fulfilling his need to protect and cherish her. He had vowed he would not fall under her spell again, but desire had overwhelmed him, fierce as ever.

For a few hours last night he had forgotten the pain and anger and guilt that had dogged him for so long. Perhaps he was wrong to blame her for everything. Perhaps it was not too late to start again, if he could trust her. If she loved him. Max brought Jupiter to a stand on the edge of the ridge. Yesterday's storm had cleared the air and his lands lay spread out below him, Rossenhall looking serene in the morning sun.

Was she awake yet, his Duchess? Was she lying in those tangled twisted sheets and thinking how glorious the night had been? Of course not. He was not fool enough to think her first waking thoughts would be of him. She would go directly to the nursery, to assure herself that Jamie was safe. His hands tightened on the reins and Jupiter snorted and sidled nervously. Max leaned forward and stroked the glossy neck.

'I cannot blame her, I suppose, since it was the first place I went this morning.'

He thought again of peeping in at the little scamp as he slept, the way his heart turned over at the sight of that tousled head, of being assured by Matlock that the young lord was none the worse for yesterday's adventure.

He is all I have, Max.

He could not forget Ellen's words. They had echoed in his head when he woke at first light to find her still sleeping in his arms. He had slipped out of bed, knowing if he stayed he would give in again to the desire that was still raging through him. Last night she had wanted comfort, reassurance, but that did not mean she loved him, any more than he loved her.

It was simply desire.

Max turned Jupiter and headed back the way they had come, but there was a nagging suspicion in his brain that there was nothing simple about his desire for his wife.

Chapter Twelve

She was in the Duke's bed.

Ellen stretched luxuriously, aware of the feeling of well-being that still enveloped her, despite the fact that she was alone. Their union last night had been borne out of need, but it had been satisfying for both of them, she was convinced of it. But if that were so, where was Max now? She must be cautious, it would not be wise to read too much into what had happened. They had comforted one another, it was nothing more than that and she must not expect some miraculous reconciliation. Nevertheless, the tiny flame of hope would not be quenched.

Ellen sat up and looked about her. The curtains around the bed were tied back and on top of a chest of drawers by the window she could see the tray of dishes from last night's meal. It reminded her of the intimate dinner they had shared, the gentle way Max had coaxed her to eat. As if he really cared. She pushed away the thought and concentrated on studying the room. It was as ostentatious as her own bedchamber, but in darker, more masculine colours that made it even more oppressive. She spent a few moments lost in a pleasant daydream of how she would redecorate it, but she soon gave up. Max would never allow it.

Birds were singing outside the window and there were sounds that indicated the household was awake. What she would give at this minute to have connecting doors between the Duke and Duchess's apartments! Her eyes fell upon the garishly coloured dressing gown laid across the end of the bed. Max's banyan. Had he left it there deliberately, so she would have something to wear as she made her way back to her own room? How thoughtful of him. She slipped it on, shivering a little as the cold silk touched her bare skin. It was far too long, puddling the floor around her feet, but at least it covered her completely. A quick peep into the dressing room showed her that everything was as they had left it last night, the bath still full of water and their clothes scattered over the floor. She smiled. No doubt Max had given instructions that she was not to be disturbed and his excellent valet was complying in full.

Still smiling, Ellen checked that the banyan was securely fastened and swept out of the Duke's apartments and back to her own, as composed as—well, as a duchess.

When Max returned from his ride he shut himself away in the offices with Tony for the rest of the day, dealing with estate matters. He knew he was avoiding Ellen, but it had to be done. He needed time to rebuild his defences against her allure. Yet he could not ignore the whisper of anticipation as the dinner hour approached. He was eager to see his Duchess again.

The Dowager was alone when he entered the drawing room. She had heard of Jamie's escapade yesterday and was eager to discuss it. Not so much a discussion as a diatribe, he thought grimly as Dorcas launched into a long lecture on managing a family.

'I was never in favour of moving a laundry maid to the nursery,' she declared. 'It was the height of folly. I knew no good would come of it and after this incident I hope you will turn her off, Maximilian.'

'You are talking of Eliza,' said Ellen, coming in at that moment. 'I spoke to her this morning. The poor girl is as sorry as can be that she let Jamie out of her sight. I am confident it will not happen again. Jamie, too, has been told he must not go out of doors unaccompanied.'

Dorcas sniffed. 'I still say the girl is not fit to look after a child.'

'The running of the household is the Duchess's province,' said Max.

Ellen threw him a grateful look. 'I am sure Eliza has learned her lesson and I believe she will be a much better nursemaid in future.'

Since Matlock came in at that moment with the little Marquess, the subject was dropped. Jamie was in buoyant mood, he had enjoyed another riding lesson and was eager to tell them all about it.

After half an hour Dorcas declared she had a headache coming on and as Matlock had not yet returned to collect Jamie, Ellen whisked him away, back to the nursery.

The door had barely closed before Dorcas turned to Max.

'You are too lenient, Your Grace. This is your house; it is up to you to decide if the nursemaid goes or stays.'

'I have told you, Dorcas, this is a matter for the Duchess.'

'Duchess!' Dorcas gave an angry titter. 'The Colnebrookes can trace their lineage back to the

Conqueror. What is *she* but a…a tradesman's chit?'

'She is my wife, madam, and the mother of my child.'

'But is she a suitable consort? If she truly cared for you, would she have kept the boy hidden for three years? Oh, do not attempt to deny it, Maximilian. I know you—if you had known about your son you would have fetched him here immediately.'

'But you will not share your theory, Dorcas, is that understood?'

The Dowager's thin lips almost disappeared as she fought with her temper, then she inclined her head.

'Naturally, if that is your wish.'

'It is. If I discover you have mentioned the matter to anyone else I shall be extremely displeased, do I make myself clear?'

'She has bewitched you with her beauty.'

'Perhaps.'

Unbidden, thoughts of the night returned and he could not prevent a smile breaking out. The Dowager saw it at once and her eyes snapped angrily.

'She is making a fool of you, Maximilian,' she said, her voice rising. 'She left you once, what is to stop her doing so again? Who knows how the twisted minds of the lower orders work?'

Max frowned. 'Now you are being foolish.'

'Am I? Your brother knew what was due to his rank, he would never have married beneath him as you have done! And as his heir you should have applied to him for permission to marry. If only you had written to him, asked for his advice before throwing yourself away on a nobody, this disastrous *mésalliance* could not have occurred!'

The Dowager's strident voice cut off abruptly. She was staring past him and Max turned to see Ellen had come into the room.

Ellen forced herself to move away from the door. Dorcas was glaring at her, a mixture of chagrin and defiance in her face as she realised her words had been overheard. Max was scowling and Ellen wondered if he would contradict the Dowager, but the heartbeat's silence that followed gave her the answer. He, too, thought their marriage a disastrous *mésalliance*. But she was already aware of his opinion. Silly of her to think last night would make a difference. She put up her chin.

'Eliza was in the nursery, eager to make up for her lapse yesterday,' she said. 'I left Jamie with her and Matlock and promised to look in later to kiss him goodnight.'

Max took a few steps towards her. 'Ellen—'

Ellen turned aside, determined not to let him finish. Last night's moment of weakness was over. She was herself again. In control.

'Perkins tells me dinner is ready for us,' she said, moving to the door. 'Shall we go in?'

And so we continue.

Ellen smiled and conversed during dinner as if she had not overheard Dorcas's comments and no one referred to it. The Dowager was stiff but polite and when the meal ended she retired immediately. Ellen went up to the nursery, where Jamie was sleeping peacefully. After a brief word with Matlock she slipped away, wondering if she should return to the drawing room and wait for Max, but in the end she too decided to go to bed.

Memories of the previous night returned, making her body ache with longing, but she had little hope of Max coming to her room. However, she kept her candle burning and her reading book open before her, although she scarce read one word in twenty, but after an hour she gave it up and settled down to sleep. The darkness pressed around her, tense and expectant. Ellen realised she was waiting, listening, and at last she heard it. Max's firm tread in the passage. She heard him pause outside her door and her hands clenched at her sides. Would he knock? Would he come in? After what seemed like hours he walked on, his footsteps quickly dying away into the night and she heard the soft, distant thud as he closed the door of his own bedchamber.

The days fell into a pattern. Max spent most of his time with Tony or out on the estate. He came in only for breakfast and dinner, where he and Ellen made polite conversation on unexceptional matters. Any questions about the estate he answered politely, but advised Ellen to address her enquiries to Tony Grisham.

'I thought you might like to ride out with me, Your Grace,' she said, after one such conversation. They were in the drawing room after dinner and she glanced out at the glorious sunset. 'It promises to be a fine day tomorrow. I have another gown to take to Mrs Phelps for repair and I thought I might call upon Mr Martin to see how the work is progressing on his roof. I should like to show you how well Belle has come on.' When he said nothing she added quietly, 'You have not seen her in action since that first ride we took together and that was almost two weeks ago.'

Dorcas tutted. 'My dear Ellen, you must realise the Duke has more important matters to concern him than riding out with you. Your son and this house should be more than enough to fill your days.'

'Jamie is my first concern, naturally,' Ellen replied, 'but you know yourself, ma'am, that Mrs Greenwood is such a superior housekeeper there is really very little for me to do. I want to learn more about Rossenhall and the estate.'

'Then the steward is quite the best person to acquaint you with everything you need to know.' Dorcas told her, adding with a note of censure in her voice, 'the Duke is far too busy to indulge you with pleasure jaunts.'

'I was not suggesting we ride out purely for pleasure,' said Ellen mildly. 'But the more I learn about the land and the future plans, the more I can help. Then the Duke would be less busy.'

Her eyes were on Max, who felt the frown furrowing his brow as he tried to ignore the attraction between them. He knew he was being unfair. She was trying to atone for the past by helping him to run Rossenhall and perhaps she *could* help him, if only he could be in her presence without wanting to drag her off to bed. Just the thought of it sent hot desire slamming through his body. He wanted to lose himself in her again, to forget the past. But how could he? What right had he to be happy?

He said at last, 'I am busy for the next few days, but Tony will ride with you, if you wish.'

He saw the flicker of disappointment in her eyes before the thick lashes dropped, veiling her thoughts. Nothing more was said of it, Ellen turning the subject and discussing with Dorcas the plight of a local family. Listening to their conversation, Max admitted to himself that even after such a short time at Rossenhall, Ellen already had a better understanding of its people than her sister-in-law.

The long case clock was chiming four when Max went to the library the following day, ostensibly looking for a book to while away the time until dinner, but in fact he positioned himself by the window so he would be able to see Ellen when she returned. He knew she was not riding out with Tony until later in the week, but when, shortly after noon, he had chanced upon Stevens, the groom had told him his Duchess had taken Belle out with only a stable hand for company.

Hell and confound it, why had he not gone with her? They could have ridden to the woods beyond the seven-acre field and he could have told her about his plans to sell the timber, and from there they might have enjoyed a gallop up to the ridge. Instead he had spent a fruitless afternoon poring over the accounts, unable to draw any conclusions since his mind was continually wandering to Ellen, wondering where she was and what she was doing.

A movement at the edge of the park caught his eye and he saw Ellen cantering towards the stables, the groom a respectful distance behind. By heaven, she looked good, the blue skirts of her habit billowing out around the white mare. He wished more than ever that he had gone out with her, to hear her merry laugh as they raced neck and neck across the park. He would give no quarter and she would ask none.

He forced himself to turn away from the engaging sight. He was only torturing himself and for what? He was determined to keep his distance and he must learn to ignore her, to go about his own business and let Ellen get on with hers. But as he browsed the shelves, picking up one novel after another and putting it back, he was alert, listening for her footsteps as she crossed the hall. Perkins would be looking out for her, ready to greet her as she came in, as much under her spell as the rest of his staff. He could not help his spirits lifting, his heart beating a little faster when he heard her voice as she spoke to the butler. He pulled another volume from the shelves and flicked through it, imagining her crossing the hall, lifting her skirts and revealing her dainty ankles as she ran quickly up the stairs to change for dinner. He needed to change, too, but he must wait until she was in her room, he did not want to meet her on the stairs, not while the hot blood was hammering through his body like this.

'Perkins said I would find you in here.'

At the sound of her voice he snapped the book shut. With slow deliberation he replaced it on the shelf. Ellen had come in and closed the door behind her. She was standing now with her back against the door, a shy smile on her lips.

The riding habit is the exact colour of your eyes, do you know that?

He cleared his throat. 'You wanted to see me?'

'Yes, if you can spare me a moment. I know you are very busy.'

'Of course.'

He clasped his hands behind his back to stop himself reaching for her. With a grateful nod she came further into the room.

'I called upon Mrs Arncliffe and Georgiana on the way home. Mr Grisham was there, taking tea with the family.' She chuckled, a rich, warm sound that made something in his chest contract.

'He and Georgie looked most discomposed when I walked in.'

Max watched her, enjoying the graceful way she moved, the slight tilt of her head while she considered her words. She turned to him, clearly requiring him to say something.

'Discomposed?' He tried to concentrate. 'Why should that be?'

'I do not know,' she replied. 'From their conversation I think they have been meeting quite frequently. Perhaps they believe you would object to their friendship.'

'Not at all,' he said, surprised. 'I should be delighted if they were to become good friends.'

'And perhaps something more,' she suggested. 'I know it is very early days, but should you object, if at some point they should wish to marry?'

'No, not at all.'

Her sudden smile lit up the room.

'Good, I am very glad of it, because I think it would be an excellent solution. However, I would not promote it if you were not in favour.'

'Promote it? Are you matchmaking, Ellen?'

'No, not at all. Georgie was so devoted to Frederick I know there is nothing further from her mind than marrying again, but I do think they are a comfort to one another. And Mrs Arncliffe thinks so, too. I wish they might all come to

the summer ball, but with Frederick so recently
buried that will not do at all, will it? Never mind,
I shall invite Georgie and her mama-in-law to
join us for dinner beforehand and Mr Grisham
shall escort them home before the ball itself be-
gins. I do not think he will mind that, do you?
And there will be other opportunities for them
to meet here, especially now I have ascertained
that I shall not be going against your wishes.' She
threw up her head as the clock chimed the hour.
'Heavens, is that the time? I must fly if I am not
to be late for dinner.'

'Is that all?' he asked, unable to resist a smile.
'You have a genius for promoting everyone's happiness.'

She blushed, shook her head and went out.
Max's smile faded as soon as he was alone.

Except mine.

With the August Ball fast approaching Ellen
found herself busier than ever and it helped to
keep her thoughts from the continuing coolness
between herself and the Duke. She still felt that
familiar swooping in her stomach whenever she
saw him, especially if she surprised in him that
glinting smile, but, knowing it could never lead
to anything more, she threw her energies into
looking after her son and managing Rossenhall.

There had been a gratifying response to the invitations, including one acceptance that pleased her immensely, and a week before the ball the new Duchess welcomed her first guest to Rossenhall.

Ellen was at the door just as the dusty post-chaise drew up and she hurried down the steps to hurl herself into the arms of the little figure who alighted.

'Oh, Mrs Ackroyd, I am *so happy* to see you!'

Mrs Ackroyd was a small woman with a mop of unruly black curls and dark, bird-like eyes that saw everything. She had been widowed at an early age and left with a large property, but no money to run it. Instead of selling up she had decided to open her house as an academy for young ladies, taking in the daughters of the very rich and giving them an education that she hoped would prepare them for the world. Her girls were taught all the usual accomplishments necessary for any young lady wishing to make a good match. However, as well as the lessons in music, dancing and drawing, her pupils were provided with the very best teachers of languages, the classics, arithmetic, logic and all the other subjects available to their male counterparts. There was no doubt that some of Mrs Ackroyd's charges had no interest in such an education, but those students who wished to learn were given the means to do so and Ellen was eternally grateful for that.

Ellen knew her greeting was not the dignified welcome her old friend would expect from a duchess, but Mrs Ackroyd said nothing. She returned the embrace warmly and accompanied Ellen into the house, leaving her maid to oversee the unloading of numerous trunks and bags.

'Have you come direct from Portsmouth? How long did it take you? Would you like to rest and change your clothes before we talk?'

As they moved into the hall Ellen fired questions until her guest stopped and raised her hands.

'My dear Ellen, you must give me time to breathe! I am not at all fatigued and would very much like to take a glass of wine with you, if you do not mind my sitting down with you in all my dirt. Then I may answer the rest of your questions in a civilised manner.'

Ellen laughed and begged pardon. 'Come along, then; I know where we may be comfortable and Perkins shall bring us a decanter of claret. That was always your favourite wine, if I recall.'

And with a glance to ensure the butler knew what was required, Ellen swept her guest off to the morning room. Her heart was lighter than it had been for a long time and she knew it was because her friend and mentor had arrived.

'Now,' said Ellen, when they were seated with glasses of wine and a plate of tiny sweet biscuits before them, 'tell me first of all how long you will be in England. You are welcome to stay here for as long as you wish, you know that.'

'Thank you, but it can only be for a few weeks, I am afraid. I am off again on my travels in September.'

'And you have had no recurrence of the fever that laid you low when we came home from Egypt?'

'None at all. The Harrogate waters were most efficacious.'

Ellen smiled. 'I think your iron constitution had more to do with it. Where do you go next?'

A mischievous twinkle lit the black eyes. 'I am going to Turkey.'

'You are going out to join Lady Hester Stanhope,' said Ellen, laughing. 'I knew you would not be able to resist, when you told me she had written to you.'

'It was too tempting.' Mrs Ackroyd savoured her wine, nodding in approval at Ellen before she continued. 'She is trying to arrange a visit to France to see Bonaparte, you know.'

'Truly? And will you go with her?'

'I cannot think she will succeed, but if she does, no, I shall not go with her. I have no interest in pandering to that monster's conceit. Instead I will go on to Alexandria and renew my acquaintance with Monsieur Drovetti. I thought I should tell you that at once, Ellen, then we need not mention it again.'

'Thank you, you are right in thinking Max would not want to hear of that.'

'Did the Duke cut up rough about our leaving Egypt under French protection?' she asked in her forthright way.

'Max has every right to be aggrieved that I did not follow his advice.'

'Monsieur Drovetti got us away safely, though, did he not? The Duke should be grateful to him.'

Ellen's hand fluttered. 'He does not see it quite like that—'

She broke off as the door opened and Max came in.

'I heard our guest had arrived,' he said, bowing over the lady's hand. 'How do you do, ma'am? I trust you had a good journey?'

'Very good, thank you, Your Grace. I travelled post from Portsmouth and spent only one night on the road.'

'Ellen told me you have been in Greece.'

He took a seat, perfectly at his ease as he asked

Mrs Ackroyd about her travels. Ellen watched them, waiting for some comment that would bring up all the ill feeling and acrimony of the past, but it seemed that her old teacher and her husband were determined to maintain the harmony of their first meeting in four years.

It was not until Ellen showed Mrs Ackroyd to the charming guest bedchamber that the subject Ellen had been dreading was broached. As soon as they were alone in the room the older lady fixed her bright, shrewd eyes on Ellen.

'When I left you in Harrogate you were convinced your marriage was a sham. Clearly that cannot be true, or Jamie would not be heir to a dukedom.'

'It turned out that was a misunderstanding.' Ellen had been preparing her explanation for some time and it came out smoothly. 'We met at Harrogate and resolved our differences.'

'That could not have been easy.'

'True, but that is all past now.'

'What you mean is you would rather I did not ask you any more about it.'

Ellen knew she was blushing under Mrs Ackroyd's direct stare.

'I would be grateful if we did not mention it again, yes.'

'Very well, my love, if that is your wish. As long as you are happy.'

'Of course,' said Ellen. 'Now, it wants but an hour until dinner and your maid will be eager to get you out of your travelling clothes, so I shall go away. I will come back later to take you to the drawing room. Then you shall meet Max's sister-in-law, the Dowager Duchess of Rossenhall.'

Ellen knew she was running away and it made her uncomfortable. She had never before hidden anything from Mrs Ackroyd, who was almost like a mother to her, but if she took Ellen's part against Max, it could reawaken old resentments and Ellen wanted to avoid that at all costs.

The meeting between Dorcas and Mrs Ackroyd went as well as one might expect between one widow, indolent and prone to ill health, and another so full of restless energy she found it hard to sit still.

'I am glad you are here to support the Duchess,' declared Dorcas with regal calm. 'The Rossenhall Ball will be the first real test of her marriage.'

'Indeed?' Mrs Ackroyd raised a brow. 'It is to be a grand occasion, then.'

The Dowager gave a thin, deprecating smile. 'Well, not *grand*, precisely. A few of my London friends have been persuaded to grace the occasion. However, you may be sure that everyone will be watching to see how the new Duchess conducts herself.'

'I am sure the Duchess will conduct herself perfectly,' replied Mrs Ackroyd, bridling. 'She has been very well trained.' Max gave a crack of laughter, which brought those shrewd dark eyes around to him. 'And will you be at her side, Your Grace?'

'Of course.'

There was a touch of hauteur in his voice, but Ellen's guest was in no wise daunted and continued, 'I ask because you have not always been there to support your wife.'

The meaning of those words was only too clear. Ellen saw Max stiffen and she rose quickly from her seat.

'Let us go in to dinner. Your Grace, if you will escort the Dowager, I shall follow on with my old friend.'

And with that she ushered Max and Dorcas out of the room.

Ellen was grateful that nothing else occurred to mar the evening. Mrs Ackroyd set herself the task of drawing out the Dowager and succeeded very well. Despite her chosen profession, Mrs

Ackroyd was very well connected and they soon discovered several mutual acquaintances whose reputation they could spend the evening cheerfully ripping to shreds. When the ladies retired to the drawing room Ellen left them to their verbal assassination and wandered out on to the terrace. The evening sky was darkening rapidly and the first faint stars were appearing.

'It promises to be another fine day tomorrow.'

She jumped at the sound of Max's deep voice at her shoulder.

'I hope it will be,' she said, smiling. 'I want to take our guest for a drive and it will be so much better if we can do so with the hood down.'

'I am surprised she is getting on so well with the Dowager.'

'Mrs Ackroyd has the ability to get on with everyone,' said Ellen. 'She will tailor her conversation to suit her company.'

'And the Dowager loves nothing more than gossip and scandal.'

Ellen did not reply. He was standing beside her and if she breathed in deeply she could detect a faint trace of him in the air, the hint of warm spices that set her heart beating faster and brought back memories of the days—and nights—they had spent together under the eastern sky.

She had a sudden memory of the first time she had smelled this particular fragrance. Max had taken her, in disguise, to a local market where the dusty air was thick with the pungent smell of camel and goats and he had given her his handkerchief to hold over her nose. When she had remarked on its scent he had told her a Cairo perfumer blended it for him. The heady mix of sandalwood, musk and agarwood had caressed her senses, just as it was doing now. She wanted to lean closer, to breathe deeper.

'Talking of scandal,' murmured Max, 'what does the lady know of our…er…reunion?'

The warm sensation of well-being that had been wrapping itself around Ellen leaked away. She said cautiously, 'She knows only that you found me in Harrogate.'

'You told her I came looking for you?'

'I implied as much. I thought it better she believes that, rather than the truth.' She gazed out into the darkness, trying not to sigh. 'That you would have divorced me, if it were not for Jamie.'

He caught her arm and turned her to him, saying angrily, 'Is it not also true that you are only here because of the boy?'

His fingers dug into her flesh. She wanted to deny it, to reach up, to kiss away the anger and the hurt, but what if he rejected her? Her confidence, the certainty that she could achieve anything, deserted her when she was with Max. No one else had ever made her feel so vulnerable, so powerless, but she was not about to admit it. Not with two women sitting only yards away, one willing to defend her to the death, the other only too ready to see her humiliated. She stepped away from him, gently pulling her arm free.

'We should go in.'

'Ellen.'

The single word stopped her as she turned towards the drawing room and she waited for him to continue.

'About the ball. I will be there, at your side. I know my duty to my Duchess.'

I do not want you to do it out of duty!

The words screamed in her head, but she would not utter them, since she knew duty was all that was keeping them together.

Silently she inclined her head and stepped back inside.

Chapter Thirteen

The final days before the ball flew by. Rooms had to be prepared for the ball itself as well as chambers for the guests who were staying overnight. Rossenhall had relatively few guest rooms and these were to be occupied by the Dowager's brother, Giles, and her acquaintances. Max had invited only a few friends and they were putting up at the Red Lion. Ellen's invitation to her own step-mama had been regretfully declined, as they were making a tour of the north and would not be back in time. Ellen smiled at the irony of it; if she had still been in Harrogate she might have welcomed them, now she could only write back with an invitation for them to visit Rossenhall during the winter.

The Dowager eyed all the activity with disfavour and kept to her room during the day, complaining of headaches and feverishness.

'The Duchess is turning the house upside down,' she complained to Max, as they waited for Ellen and Mrs Ackroyd to join them for dinner three days before the ball. 'The household is running around doing her bidding and it will all come to nought. She has left herself far too much to do at the last minute. It will be a disaster and we shall look ridiculous.'

'She will not fail.' Max allowed himself a little smile. 'I think I know enough of my wife to know the ball will be a success, as is everything she does.'

'Yes, she has you all under her spell,' said the Dowager spitefully.

He silenced her with a look and she relapsed into self-pity.

'I would help her if I could,' she said, a quaver in her voice, 'but I feel so ill, I fear it is the ague.'

'Then I suggest you stay out of the way, as I do, and let Ellen get on with it,' he replied, showing no sympathy. 'She has Mrs Ackroyd to help her and they seem to have everything in hand.'

Max felt a little guilty that he had absented himself so much over the past week, but Ellen assured him she could manage everything with the help of Tony and the housekeeper, and he was glad to keep his distance. That way it was easier to fight the desire that would not be conquered and could only be assuaged by hard, physical work. Consequently, he spent his days on the estate, helping to fell trees, dig ditches and repair walls. But even then he could not forget her. His people had nothing but praise for the Duchess and naturally they wanted to tell him. He should be pleased they thought so well of her, but it only increased his guilt, because he would not allow himself the pleasure of loving her. Not that she ever asked it of him. She had accepted the situation and went about her daily tasks with an equanimity which, he convinced himself, showed how little she cared. It was only Jamie she loved. Had she not told him as much, that day she feared the boy had drowned?

The Duchess and her guest came in at that moment, and Dorcas immediately went on to the attack about the progress of the ball. But to everything Ellen had an answer, and in the end she silenced her sister-in-law by going across and hugging her.

'I know how anxious you are that we put on a grand show, Dorcas, but trust me, it will all work out well.'

Max felt the iron band tighten around his chest. She always responded with such patience and good humour to the Dowager's grumblings, and she never complained of his lack of attention. He had never known a woman so self-sufficient.

That was why it came as such a surprise when he found her crying, the morning before the ball.

Guests were arriving at Rossenhall that afternoon and he knew Ellen would be busy with her last-minute preparations, so he went up to the nursery to take Jamie out for a while. He was secretly relieved the boy wanted to sail his yacht rather than take out the drum and play soldiers, for with all the windows thrown wide to air the house, they would have to go some distance to avoid upsetting Dorcas's delicate nerves. It was around noon when he delivered Jamie back to the nursery and Max knew he was late for his meeting with Tony in the estate room. The quickest route was down the backstairs and past the storage rooms that were part of the housekeeper's domain. As he approached the linen closet he noticed the door was ajar and he heard a definite sob.

Max hesitated. If one of the maids was distressed, then she would be embarrassed to be discovered by the master of the house. He decided he would not disturb her, but would mention the matter to Mrs Greenwood. He proceeded quietly, but as he passed the door he caught a glimpse of yellow-silk skirts. Definitely *not* a servant's dress. He stopped and pushed open the door.

'Ellen?'

She was standing with her back to him, her face in her hands.

'Oh!' She whipped a napkin from one of the shelves to wipe her eyes, keeping her back to him. 'I, um, Mrs Greenwood is so busy I said I would come and check we had sufficient clean table linen.'

'And what is there in that to make you weep?' He reached out and turned her to face him, cupping her chin in her hand and forcing her to look up at him. She gave a shaky laugh and eased herself out of his grasp.

'I beg your pardon. I am being very foolish. I am a little tired, that is all.'

'I can well believe you are tired, but that is not enough to overset you.'

He saw the shadow flit across her face, a hunted look. He thought that if he had not been blocking the exit she would have run away from him.

'No,' she said at last. She looked down at her hands, pleating the napkin between her fingers. 'I am crying for us, Max. We are neither of us truly happy, are we, trapped in this marriage?'

It took every ounce of willpower not to reach

out and pull her into his arms. He might claim
it was to comfort her, but it was as much for his
own comfort, that he might lose himself in her.
Quickly he reminded himself that Ellen did not
really want him. She was only with him because
of Jamie.

He is all I have, Max.

By heaven, he was jealous of his own son!

He made a decision.

'I am going away,' he said. 'I have been discussing it with Tony for a while now. I need to
visit the other properties, talk to the stewards
there, see the land for myself. Then I shall be in
a better position to decide what must be done. I
shall be gone some months. It will give us time
to…adjust to the situation.'

'I see.' She did not look up. 'Will you not take
me with—?'

'No!' He dragged in a breath and tried to
soften the refusal. 'You will want to remain here,
with Jamie, will you not? And you need to organise your court dress for the spring. The dress-
maker is coming today, is she not? You must tell
her to get working on it. Spend whatever you
need, you will hear no objections from me.'

'Yes, of course. Thank you.' Still she would
not look at him. 'When will you go?'

'As soon as I can. The morning after the ball.'

'Jamie will miss you.'

And you, Ellen, will you miss me?

'I shall write him notes and enclose them in my letters to you.'

'Thank you.' She folded the napkin and went to place it back on the shelf, then changed her mind and put it on the windowsill instead. Even Max could see the sad, crumpled square would need laundering again before it could be used at table.

She drew herself up. 'If you will excuse me, I must get on.'

He flattened himself against a cupboard as she squeezed by him and disappeared. Max leaned back and closed his eyes. It would tear his heart out to leave, but would it really be any worse than seeing her every day? Perhaps a few months apart would clear the confusion in his mind. He remembered his meeting with Tony. He would have to tell him of his decision to begin his tour of the estates as soon as the ball was over. He would have to think of a reason why he was in such a hurry to be gone. Max breathed deeply, preparing himself, and became aware that the air in the room was redolent of herbs, placed between the sheets to keep them fresh. His mouth twisted. He would never be able to smell lavender again without remembering the pain and sadness of this moment.

* * *

Ellen flew up the stairs to her room, praying the expected guests would not arrive early. She needed time to compose herself. She had thought she could cope with Max's coldness, with the distance he put between them, but this morning it had all become too much and she had given in to a moment's weakness, only to have him discover her weeping. And now it was all so much worse. He was going away and she would not see him for months.

Somehow she got through the rest of the day. She left Dorcas to greet the houseguests while she met with the fashionable French *modiste* employed to make her ball gown. When she put it on, the voluble seamstress declared she looked *ravissante,* but the compliments only brought a lump to Ellen's throat as she recalled the moonless night on the Nile that had inspired it.

Max had said to her then, 'When we get back to England I shall buy you a gown just like the sky, blue-black satin, seeded with diamonds. We will dance until midnight, then I shall take you to bed and undress you.'

She had hoped to charm Max and remind him of that magical night. That was why she had ordered the midnight-blue silk spangled with crystals, but that was before Max had told her about the lives he had risked and lost because he had been desperate with grief for her. She had killed his affection for her and she must come to terms with the fact that it would only ever be lust that fuelled his desire for her, not love.

And that was not good enough.

'So that is everything, Tony.' Max put down his pen and sat back. 'You have all you need to run Rossenhall in my absence. I will leave you my itinerary, so you will know where I am if you need me.'

'And you are determined to leave, the morning after the ball?'

'I am.' Max frowned. 'What is it? Why do you look at me like that? Do you think I am wrong to go so soon?'

'It is not my place to censure Your Grace.'

'My Grace be damned,' said Max brutally. 'Out with it, Tony. We have been friends too long for such fustian.'

For a tense moment Tony held his eyes, then he looked down at the desk, idly pushing the papers into a pile.

'As a friend, then,' he said slowly. 'It occurs to me that you are running away.'

Max pressed his lips together to prevent an angry denial.

'I had hoped,' Tony continued, still not looking up, 'that you would settle at Rossenhall. With your Duchess.'

The air was so charged a spark might have ignited it, but Max knew it was time to be honest with his friend.

'It is *because* of the Duchess that I must go.' Max pushed back his chair and walked to the window. 'That letter I wrote you from Harrogate, about Ellen and I agreeing that she should live incognito until I was ready to bring her to Rossenhall, it was all lies. She left me, because she thought our marriage was a sham, that the soldier she met in Egypt was an imposter.'

'Well…' Max heard the hesitation in Tony's voice, knew he was picking his words carefully '…since you were never officially in Egypt surely that is understandable.'

'I know it and I could forgive her that, if it wasn't for what followed.' Max felt the guilt welling up in him again, black and painful as ever. It was like uncovering an old wound and finding it had not healed at all. 'When I thought I had lost her for ever I became reckless, taking on every thankless, dangerous task the army threw at me. It cost lives, Tony, but unfortunately not mine. Don't you see? It was all very well for me to risk my own life, but I had no right to condemn my men.'

'You did not condemn them. Every one of those missions was composed of volunteers.'

'Hah!'

'You were a good leader,' said Tony simply. 'They would have followed you anywhere.'

Max dismissed his words with a wave of a hand and he shook himself, as if trying to shoulder away the guilt that haunted him.

'I led them to their deaths. You cannot deny it, Tony. You were there. You and Fred Arncliffe were but two casualties of my actions. Actions that I would not have carried out, if Ellen had not left me.'

'And you blame her for that?'

'I blame myself for allowing her to drive me to such depths of despair!'

'So you are punishing her for your own guilt.'

'I suppose I am. I know that is not right, but I cannot look at her without thinking of all the good men who lost their lives.'

Behind him, Max heard Tony exhale and say slowly, 'It is my belief that you would have volunteered for those missions, even if your wife had been safe in England.'

'Never!'

'Very well, let me put another argument. Have you ever thought, Major, that if you had *not* been there to lead them, your men might have ended up with one of those incompetents that the army likes to put in charge? Someone like that fool, Bennington Ffog.'

'That is enough!' snarled Max, finding relief from his guilt and grief in anger. He swung round. 'We have already said too much on the subject.'

'Not quite.' Tony pushed himself to his feet and met Max's eyes steadily. 'You may give me notice to quit, if you wish, but I will say my piece, Major. If it was because of your Duchess that you took on those well-nigh impossible missions then I can only thank her, from the bottom of my heart. Those attacks would have gone ahead, even if you had not been there, and without your excellent leadership even more good men would have died. I am also pretty sure that I would have lost a lot more than an arm and Freddie Arncliffe would never have got home to see his wife and daughter. Now, if you will excuse me, I have work to do. The Duchess has invited me to join the dinner party tomorrow, but if you wish me to leave, I will do so as soon as I have prepared those reports for you.'

'Dammit, Tony, of course I do not want you to

go and I will not accept your resignation!' Max rubbed his hands across his eyes. 'I suppose you think I am a damned fool.'

There was the hint of a smile in Tony's voice as he replied, 'As a matter of fact, I do, Your Grace.'

'Then answer me one question,' said Max. 'Why, since she professed to love me more than life itself, did she not tell me I had a son?'

Tony did not flinch under Max's searching stare, but there was no mistaking the sympathy in his face as he shook his head and said sadly, 'That I do not know, Your Grace.'

Another dinner to be endured and house guests to be entertained. Ellen changed into a fashionable white-satin robe trimmed with gold chenille, draped with a green crape sash which was pulled in around the high waist and fastened on one shoulder with a large emerald brooch. Emeralds also glinted at her neck and ears. They winked back at her when she looked in her glass, reminding her of the laughing glint she had surprised in Max's eyes occasionally when he looked at her. But not any more. Stifling a sigh, Ellen put on her long gloves, fixed her smile in place and went downstairs.

Ellen was introduced to Lord This and Lady

That, to simpering misses and knowing matrons, all friends of the Dowager. The last to be introduced was the Honourable Giles Wendlebury, the Dowager's younger brother. He was as thickset as Dorcas was thin and, in contrast to his sister's pale complexion, his face had the ruddy glow of a heavy drinker. He squeezed Ellen's hand as he lifted it and pressed a wet kiss upon her gloved fingers.

'So this is the new Duchess. Delighted to meet you, Your Grace. And now Max has brought you home perhaps we will have more parties at Rossenhall. You might even be able to find me a rich wife. Old Max would appreciate that, ain't that so, Duke?'

He laughed heartily and Ellen glanced at her husband. Max was talking with Mrs Ackroyd and affected not to hear, but she knew from the stony look on his face that he was not amused by his brother-in-law. Well, at least they were in accord upon that. She smiled, murmured something innocuous and moved on.

To Ellen's mind the party was too loud and cheerful. The men behaved with a false bonhomie that she could see Max disliked and when Jamie was brought into the drawing room the ladies cooed and petted him in a way that made the little boy squirm. It was all so disingenuous.

Max studiously avoided Ellen's eye, but she knew in her bones that he hated it as much as she. Their guests admired the house, applauded the dinner, praised their host and complimented their hostess. Mrs Ackroyd had little time for such insincerity and confined most of her remarks to her hostess, but even this did not help Ellen, for the weight of unhappiness pressing upon her heart cried out to be shared and there was no time for such a luxury now.

At last the interminable evening was over. All the guests except Mrs Ackroyd retired, the Dowager graciously offering to accompany her guests, since she had to pass their chambers on the way to her own apartments in the west wing. The Duke was also eager to quit the room.

'I shall leave you, too,' he said with a brief smile that covered both his wife and Mrs Ackroyd, sitting together on a sofa. 'I am sure you will be pleased to have a little time to yourselves.'

With a bow he was gone and silence fell over the room.

'How very considerate,' remarked Mrs Ackroyd. When Ellen made no reply she continued, 'Perhaps he thinks if he leaves us alone you will tell me why you are so unhappy.' Ellen's eyes flew to her face and she nodded. 'You may be able to hide your sorrow from everyone else, but I know you too well, Ellen. Have you quarrelled? I was surprised when the Duke announced he would be leaving Rossenhall so soon after the ball.' She reached out and took Ellen's hands. 'Come, love, you were always wont to confide in me and you can do so now.'

It was too much. With a shuddering sob Ellen threw herself into her arms and Mrs Ackroyd held her, crooning softly. It did not last long and soon Ellen was drying her tears and apologising for her weakness.

Mrs Ackroyd patted her hands. 'Do you know, that is the only time I have seen you cry, apart from the first day you arrived at my school, a homesick little girl who had never known a mother's love. You have always kept your true feelings hidden behind a smile. So I know something must be very wrong.'

'It is.' Ellen wiped her damp cheeks. 'Max did not come to find me,' she confessed, 'we met by chance in Harrogate and when he found out about Jamie, he thought I was deliberately hiding the boy away from him.'

'But you had written to him, telling him about James.'

'He never received my letter.'

'But you explained that you had tried to contact him?'

'He would not believe me, without proof.' Ellen sighed. 'I had thought, *hoped*, that things would improve once we were under the same roof, working together. I thought we could learn to be happy, but it has not been so. He cannot forgive me.' Her head bowed as fresh tears welled up. 'He is going away because he thinks I shall be more comfortable without him. In fact, it will be the opposite.'

'My love, you cannot take all the blame for this estrangement.'

Ellen raised her head at that. 'I can and I will. If I had not been foolish enough to doubt him, if I had done as he asked, returned to Portsmouth in an English frigate and waited for him, this could never have happened.'

'You must tell him again that you wrote to him,' said Mrs Ackroyd. 'And that you also contacted the late Duke. I will vouch for it.'

Ellen shook her head. 'He would merely think I was trying to put the blame on to his brother, who is no longer here to defend himself.' She saw the sparkle in her friend's eyes and clutched her hands. 'Promise me you will say nothing, ma'am. Max thinks badly enough of me as it is. I will not make it any worse.'

Mrs Ackroyd looked closely at her for a long moment. At last she said, 'Tell me, Ellen, do you still love him?'

'With all my heart.'

'Then tell him so, my dear. You were always one to keep your feelings hidden, to smile when you felt like crying, but now you must tell him the truth.'

'But what if he spurns me again?'

The older woman squeezed her fingers. 'What if he does not?'

Max deliberately extended his morning ride to keep him away from the house until well past noon. He had no wish to spend more time than was necessary with the Dowager's friends. Ellen's step-mama was on a protracted tour of the north and she had declined his suggestion to invite other members of her family to Rossenhall for the ball, so Max could then hardly refuse to let Dorcas fill the guest rooms with her cronies. Thankfully they were confined to the west wing, so with any luck he could avoid seeing them until tonight's grand dinner. Truth to tell, he wanted to avoid everyone for a while.

Yesterday's conversation with Tony refused to leave him and he went over it in his head as he cantered away from Rossenhall, Jupiter covering the ground with his long, easy stride. The sun had passed its zenith before the confusion in his mind settled. He had been too hard on Ellen. Perhaps he was even being too hard on himself. He knew there was some truth in what Tony had said about all those desperate military campaigns: a lesser commander might well have lost even more men. As Max acknowledged that fact, the weight on his spirits eased a fraction. It was wrong of him to blame Ellen for his actions and he must ask her to forgive him. But the devil on his shoulder demanded if he could forgive *her* for concealing the fact that he had a son.

But she said she had written to him.

Max frowned. He had blamed her for not trusting him, for believing he would deceive her. Surely he must now give her that same trust. Yet Hugo would have told him if any such letter had arrived. One letter might have gone astray, but two? Perhaps... For the first time he allowed himself to consider other possibilities. Ellen would not lie, he would stake his life on it, but could he trust his own judgement, where his Duchess was concerned? Every fibre of his being told him he could. He touched his heels against Jupiter's flanks, anxious to see Ellen, to make his peace with her.

* * *

Max reached the stable yard just as Tony was dismounting.

His steward nodded towards his sweating horse.

'You have been riding hard, Your Grace.'

'Yes, I have urgent matters to attend.'

'Then let us walk to the house together.' Tony fell into step beside him. 'Is it anything I can help with?'

'No. That is…' Max wavered as a thought struck him. 'Your predecessor kept meticulous records of all the correspondence here, is that not so?'

Tony laughed. 'Aye, Your Grace, Atherwell kept everything. Letters received, copies of letters sent, laundry lists. There's boxes full of it in the small anteroom beside the library. I have been going back through it, trying to weed out the dross and clear some space, but I have by no means finished.'

'Have you gone through the papers for four years ago? From January 1807, to be exact.'

'Why, yes, I have.'

'And was there…?' Max paused, took a breath. 'Did you find anything pertaining to my wife, my marriage?'

Tony threw him a glance, clearly guessing the reason for Max's question. 'No, Your Grace.'

The letters must have gone astray. Max no longer doubted that she had written. He had spent long enough now in Ellen's company to know she would have wanted him to know about Jamie. He would trust her with his life. The revelation was like a weight lifted from his shoulders and it took him a moment to realise his steward was still speaking.

'I beg your pardon, Tony, what was that?'

'I said there might be something amongst your brother's private papers.'

Max stopped. 'Private papers?'

'Why, yes. They are in a separate trunk, but I do not have access.' Tony looked genuinely confused. 'I thought you had the key, Your Grace. If not, then it must still be with the Dowager.'

Max did not need proof that Ellen had tried to contact him, but there was another, darker suspicion that he needed to allay. With a nod to Tony he set out to find his sister-in-law.

Dorcas was in the hall, preparing to walk in the gardens with her guests. Max indicated by a look that he wanted to speak to her and she excused herself from the chattering throng.

'I understand my brother's private correspondence is locked in a trunk in the library.' She immediately looked wary and he said impatiently, 'I would like the key to it.'

'I am about to take everyone out of doors, can it not wait?'

'No, it cannot.'

'But why do you want the key? It contains only Hugo's private papers. Mostly our correspondence when we were first married. There can be nothing in there to interest you.'

'No?'

Her eyes slid away from his.

'I... I am not sure just where to lay my hands on the key, can you give me a little time to find it? Until after dinner, perhaps.'

'No, Dorcas.' Max's instincts were screaming at him. 'You will find me the key now, if you please, or I shall break open the lock.'

The library anteroom was lined with shelves, half of them piled high with a haphazard collection of boxes and papers while the rest, where Tony had been at work, were filled with orderly boxes, each one clearly labelled. Max easily found the large metal box containing his brother's private papers and carried it across to the small desk. Then he took the key Dorcas had so grudgingly given him and fitted it into the lock.

In the top of the box were Hugo's journals.

Max pulled one out and flicked through the pages. His brother had always been more of a sportsman than a scholar and he was not surprised to see it held only a sentence or two on each page, and sometimes a whole week between entries. For the first time he allowed himself to admit that Hugo had been more interested in the esteem that came with being Duke than in looking after the estates. He searched for the journal containing entries for 1807, but there was nothing of interest. He stacked the books on the desk and lifted out the papers beneath. There were a few bundles neatly tied together, early letters between Hugo and Dorcas. Max quickly put these to one side and began to make his way through the remaining pile of correspondence.

Everything was in a rough order, beginning with a few letters of condolence upon the death of their mother, while they were both at school. Then Max's occasional letters from Oxford. Max had gone there just as his brother was leaving. Hugo had learned to run the estate while Max finished his studies and joined the army, where he received rapid promotion. He sifted through the papers: invitations, family letters and his own infrequent notes. A few words had been scratched on each one by Hugo, instructions to the steward on how to respond. Max realised now that he had not received one personal note from Hugo once he became Duke, not even when Max had been injured in battle. Fred had described his family as cold and Max could see it now. Cold and unfeeling. How different from the warmth that Ellen had brought to Rossenhall. To his own life.

He worked quickly through the pile, his frown deepening. Six years ago—condolences upon their father's death. He went slower until he found his letter explaining that he would be going to Sicily with his regiment. He had been unable to tell his family anything more, it was a highly secret operation, not even the English Consul would be told.

He put the paper down carefully, scanning the next and the next. Ellen had returned to England the following January, when the records still showed him to be in Sicily. Was it any wonder she had thought ill of him? As he turned over another sheet his breath caught in his throat.

The letter from Ellen was dated June 1807. It described her marriage and her current condition and she asked for the Duke's help in finding Major Max Colnebrooke. It was brief, barely filling one side. On the other was the direction, and across one corner a few lines in Hugo's untidy scrawl, instructions to Atherwell on how to respond.

Tradesman's chit. Make it plain neither she nor her bastard are welcome here.

Max stared at the date against the response. It was only weeks after he had been home on leave. He had told Hugo he had been in Egypt, although he had not mentioned his marriage. Max had preferred to conduct his search for Ellen privately and, if he couldn't find her, well, at least his humiliation would be a secret. But even so why had Hugo not written to him? He must have known there might be some truth in the letter.

Tradesman's chit.

Ellen had used that same expression to describe herself. Had Atherwell been crass enough to use his master's derogatory term in the reply he had sent her? Max knew he was more than capable of it. To Hugo and his wife breeding was everything, they believed their blood was superior. His mouth twisted. He had seen enough blood during his years in the army to know that wasn't true. Would it have made any difference if Hugo had known that Ellen was one of the wealthiest heiresses in England? He doubted it.

Max went back to the pile of letters. Ellen said she had written twice. He turned over leaf after leaf, finally coming full circle. He was reading condolence letters again, this time for Hugo's untimely death. Most of the letters were addressed to the widowed Duchess, only a few directed to the new Duke. All carried a brief instruction from the Dowager for Atherwell to reply.

Max felt again the blow of Hugo's demise. Not so much grief as guilt. Guilt that he should be inheriting, that he had not perished on the battlefield. He had not been able to face returning to Rossenhall and had used his military duties as an excuse. After all, Atherwell had been steward for thirty years, he and Dorcas would manage very well without him. It wasn't until the death of the old steward last winter that Max forced himself to return and he had brought in Tony Grisham as his steward. It must have been at that point, when Dorcas handed over responsibility for running the estates to Tony, that these private letters had been locked away.

Max scraped up the sheets into a pile and was about to put them back into the box when a folded letter dropped on to the desk. He recognised at once the neat, sloping hand that had written the direction. He picked up the letter. It was addressed to the Duke of Rossenhall. The seal was broken and he slowly unfolded the paper.

He read the date on the letter three times: fifteenth of March, 1810. Three weeks after Hugo's death. He swallowed hard and read the formal words of sympathy on the loss of his brother and then stopped at the final sentences.

> *I beg you will forgive the presumption, but despite assurances to the contrary I believe that you are the same Major Colnebrooke with whom I was acquainted in Egypt. I thought it only right that you should know, Your Grace, that you have a son. James is a very happy, healthy little boy. I ask nothing from you, but I am writing in the hope this knowledge may be a comfort to you, as it is to me.*

The page shook in his hand. Here it was, proof that she had not abandoned him. She had even given her address in Harrogate. But Dorcas had scrawled thick, angular letters across the top of the sheet.

Received: 20th March.
Answer: None required.

Chapter Fourteen

The house was very quiet when Max left the library. He suspected that he was the only one who was not in his room, changing for dinner. He made his way quickly to the Dowager's apartments. She was resting on her *chaise* and sat up with a jolt as he entered without knocking.

'Heavens, you startled me! What do you mean by bursting in like that?'

He glanced at the hovering maid. 'Leave us.'

Dorcas eyed him nervously. 'I hope you are not going to shout, Max, for I have the headache. If it is about the money I have given Giles then you have no cause for complaint, it came from my widow's jointure, not the estate.'

'I have not the slightest interest in your brother.' He ignored the vinaigrette bottle that she was waving ominously and held out the letter. 'Why did you not tell me about this?'

She stared at the paper, but made no attempt to take it from him.

'You were away, you instructed me to deal with everything.'

'And you did not think to send this on to me?' He stared at her, incredulous.

She shrugged. 'I did not want to trouble you.'

'This letter says I have a son and you did not want to *trouble me*?'

He spoke quietly, but anger was bubbling up like hot oil as he thought of how Ellen must have felt, first of all to receive that rejection from Hugo and then to think he himself was ignoring her.

'It was not my decision,' cried Dorcas, shrinking from the fury she saw in his face. 'It was Hugo who said we must ignore her, after that first letter!'

'So you knew of that, too?'

'Of course. Hugo discussed the whole matter with me.'

'But why did Hugo not discuss it with *me*? I was in England then, he had my direction.'

'We agreed it was an imposter, trying to wheedle her way into the family.' She added defiantly, 'What else were we to think? After all, you had not informed us of your marriage. When this second letter came, naturally I thought she had seen the notices of your elevation and had decided to try again.'

Max forced down his anger, acknowledging the truth of her argument. Hugo would never have believed he would marry anyone outside his own sphere, and he— Max rubbed a hand across his eyes. If only he had told them, but pride, blind, stubborn pride had made him keep his marriage a secret. Dorcas sat up, her lip curling derisively.

'Do not blame me for this, Maximilian. You were clearly ashamed of your marriage, or you would have spoken of it.'

'I was ashamed to admit she had left me,' he said slowly. 'But she had good cause to doubt me.' He fixed her with a steely look. 'And you did not think to tell me any of this, even when I brought my bride to Rossenhall?' Max paced the room, unable to keep still. 'I thought Ellen had made no attempt to contact me.' He stopped before her, frowning. 'You encouraged me to believe that.'

'I should have burned those letters,' she muttered.

His shook his head, his spirits lifting as he realised with blinding clarity that he had not needed the letters to prove Ellen had told him the truth.

He said, 'It would not make the slightest difference, not now. I trust my wife. I know she would not have hidden herself away if she had not been convinced that I did not wish to find her.'

He turned and made for the door.

'Maximilian! What are you going to do?'

'I am going to find Ellen and tell her what a damned fool I have been.' As he grasped the handle he looked back. 'You will make arrangements to remove to the dower house as soon as the ball is over, madam. I will no longer have you in my house.'

Max went back to the east wing, but he was too late to catch Ellen alone. He was informed that the Duchess had already joined their guests downstairs. Curbing his impatience, Max went off to change.

The drawing room was bustling, full of noise and chatter. All the guests invited to join the family for dinner were gathered there, including Tony Grisham who was talking to Georgiana and her mother-in-law.

Ellen watched them for a moment, noted the slight blush on Georgie's cheeks and the way Tony was looking at her. It would be a match, she felt sure. The Lodge was certainly large enough for a family and would do very well for them if it was redecorated. She must talk to Max about it.

Max. The knot of anxiety in her stomach tightened a little more. She had been trying to find him all day, but he had been avoiding her, she was sure of it, and now time was running out to tell him how she felt. She looked around the room again and a momentary anxiety flickered. She could not see him or Dorcas amongst the throng. With the ball to follow it would be difficult to put dinner back, but she was considering the possibility when she saw the Dowager come in. She looked pale, but after a venomous glance towards Ellen she sought out her brother and began to talk to him. Ellen shrugged. She was growing accustomed to her sister-in-law's coldness and if there was nothing she could do about it then it must be ignored. A movement caught her eye and she turned just as Max entered the room.

Her heartbeat quickened when she saw his tall upright figure filling the doorway, the shoulders of his dark coat almost touching the frame on either side. His hair gleamed golden in the bright light of a summer's evening and she thought he had never looked better. Or perhaps that was because he was leaving her tomorrow. He stopped to exchange a word and a smile with Mrs Ackroyd, who was standing near the door, then he turned to scan the room. When his eyes fell upon Ellen her heart stopped altogether. She had become used to him avoiding her, not meeting her gaze unless it was necessary, but tonight there was no hesitation. He came directly towards her, his eyes fixed on her face.

Even as the Duke reached out to her, Perkins came in to announce dinner. Ellen was finding it difficult to breathe with Max holding her hands, but she managed a shaky laugh.

'I was on the point of delaying our dinner, Your Grace.'

He carried her fingers to his lips in an unexpectedly tender gesture.

'Could anything be more badly timed?' he murmured. 'We must talk, as soon as possible.'

'Indeed we must.' She kept her smile in place for the benefit of their guests. 'As soon as we can both slip away.'

There was no time for more. Max went off to give his arm to an aged duchess and Ellen organised everyone into an orderly procession to the dining room. There were twenty couples to be seated and Ellen could not even see Max at the other end of the table, such was the quantity of candles and silverware between them. Not by the flicker of an eyelid did she show her impatience to discover just what it was he wanted to say to her, but her mind rampaged upon endless speculation.

* * *

The dinner dragged on interminably. Max listened to the elderly Duchess, a distant relation whom he had felt duty-bound to invite, but his mind was on Ellen. She had told him nothing of the gown she had ordered for the ball, but as soon as he had entered the drawing room he was transported back to the Nile and the nights they had shared beneath the stars. Seeing her standing across the crowded drawing room, the dark silk enhancing the blue of her eyes, it had been as much as he could do not to drag her away there and then and lay his heart and his hopes at her feet once more.

But it must wait. There were several more courses to be sampled and he could not sit there smiling like an idiot through it, he must drag his mind away from his wife, sitting at the other end of the table, and make conversation, however much it irked him.

'At last I have you to myself.'

In the general hubbub of guests leaving the dining room, the Duke caught Ellen's hand and whisked her into the small sitting room. Much as she wanted to talk to him, she was acutely aware of her duties as a hostess.

'Yes, but we must not be long, Max,' she told him. 'People will soon be arriving for the ball, to say nothing of our dinner guests, who will be expecting us to join them in the drawing room.'

'Let them amuse themselves for a while. This is important.'

'Please.' She put a finger to his lips, knowing if she delayed she might lose her nerve. 'Before you say anything more, let me speak. I—I wanted to tell you that I love you, Max. I have always loved you, from the very first moment I saw you. I know you c-cannot love me, I am reconciled to that, and I will do my best not to embarrass you again with an excess of emotion, but please, I do not want you to go away. I would rather live in the shadows than without you...'

She trailed off, unnerved by his frowning look, but the next moment he was dragging her into his arms and kissing her. It was the miracle Ellen had dreamed of throughout the protracted dinner and now she almost swooned with relief as his mouth found hers in a ruthless, demanding kiss. When at last he raised his head she gave a small sigh of disappointment, but she put her hands against his chest to prevent him kissing her again.

'You said you wished to speak to me,' she reminded him.

He caught her hands and stared down at them, silent and brooding.

'Max?' she prompted him, trying to ignore

the distracting way he was rubbing his thumb over her fingers.

'I found your letters today.'

'I see.'

His grip tightened. He looked into her face. 'Why did you not tell me? When I accused you of not trying to find me, why did you not say that Hugo had replied and in such degrading terms?'

'The letter I received was from your steward,' she said cautiously.

'Atherwell wrote it at my brother's behest. I saw for myself Hugo's instructions and I am ashamed that he should be so ill mannered. Why did you not tell me what he said to you?'

'Because I did not want to tarnish your memory of your brother.' She hesitated before adding, 'Besides, would you have believed me?'

'No, not then.' He sighed. 'But you had every right to expect that your second letter would reach me. Ellen, I cannot tell you how sorry I am.'

'It is not your fault, Max. When you told me you had not returned immediately to Rossenhall, I guessed you had not seen my letter. I never believed you would ignore it.'

'But you suspected Dorcas had kept it from me?'

'Once I had met her I was sure of it, but I had no proof.'

'And you have borne all her unkindness with patience and goodwill.' He shook his head. 'I could not have been so generous.'

'What good would it have done to stir up the coals? You would have had to choose between her and me—' her smile went a little awry '—and I had already given you cause to hate me.'

He dragged her close again. 'Not hate,' he murmured, kissing her. 'I hated myself, but I never stopped loving you. I know that now.' After another long kiss he raised his head, but only to enfold her against his chest and rest his cheek against her hair. 'Having lived with you these past months I know you would never lie to me. That is not why I needed to find the letters. I did not want to believe that Hugo would serve me such a trick. Damn his abominable pride!'

'He must have thought it for the best.' She sighed. 'And the Dowager made it very clear she thought me too far beneath you to be worthy of notice.'

She spoke lightly, but could not keep the quiver of hurt from her voice.

His arms tightened. 'She is so very wrong. You are far, far above all of us. I knew it when I married you. But we can do better than this, love. I want us to start again, if you will agree to it. I have already told Dorcas she must remove to the dower house as soon as possible. Then we can make Rossenhall our own. Oh, Ellen, I have been such a fool. I have been blaming you for my own failings and do not deserve that you should love me. Can you ever forgive me?'

'Oh, Max.' She reached up and put her fingers against his mouth to silence him. 'You deserve much, much more than I can ever give you,' she whispered. 'But first you must forgive yourself. Fred said you were an excellent soldier. He told me you saved his life and countless others.'

He sighed. 'Yes, Tony said as much to me the other day.'

'Then you should believe it.' She buried her face in his shoulder. 'I only hope you can forgive *me* for doubting you in the first place.'

'There is nothing to forgive.'

He cupped her face, turning it up towards him, and as he did so she could not prevent a few hot tears escaping and rolling over his fingers.

'Ah, my love, do not weep.' He took out his handkerchief and began to wipe her cheeks.

'I thought I had lost you,' she whispered.

'I was *sure* I had lost you.' He bent his head to place another kiss upon her lips. 'My love,' he whispered, covering her face with kisses. 'My Duchess.'

The faint sounds of voices and laughter dragged them back to the present. He raised his head.

'We had best get back to our guests.' His eyes searched her face. 'Would you like me to go on ahead? Do you need a few moments to compose yourself?'

She shook her head, taking the handkerchief from him to dry her eyes before she smiled mistily up at him.

'No. Let us face them all together.'

'Dorcas knows the truth about our separation,' he warned her. 'She could damage your reputation.'

'She could try.' Ellen smiled, supremely confident now that she knew he loved her. 'Let us go in, Max. If we show the world we are united, no one can harm us.'

Epilogue

Max and Ellen were back at Rossenhall the following summer in time for the August Ball. Ellen's redecorations were complete, the reception rooms looked very much as they always had, only more magnificent with fresh paint and gilding on the ornate plasterwork, but the family's apartments had been transformed. The oppressive ornamentation and tapestries had been removed and the ceilings and walls repainted in pale colours that made the most of the elegant stucco. The heavy damask curtains had been replaced with light floral silks around the bed and windows. The Duchess's light touch was also evident in the nursery, where the young Marquess and his baby sister were sleeping peacefully while their parents welcomed everyone to the ball.

Ellen was again wearing a gown of midnight-blue silk, but this time it was seeded with diamonds, not crystals. Max wanted to signal to the world that the Rossenhall fortunes were once more in the ascendant. As he led his Duchess into the marble hall, ready to meet their guests, he lifted her hand to his lips.

'You look magnificent,' he murmured, his eyes gleaming with love.

'I think I have done very well, for a tradesman's daughter,' Ellen teased him.

'A tradesman's daughter with a very shrewd brain,' he replied. 'The investments your father's advisors recommended are already paying dividends, you and Tony run my properties with such efficiency that you leave me nothing to do except marvel at my good fortune.'

'That is not true and you know it,' said Ellen, slipping her hand through his arm. 'I think we make a very good team, you and I.'

There was no time for more, the guests were arriving. It was less crowded than the previous year, the Duke and Duchess having declared the occasion was for Rossenhall people, their close friends, neighbours and tenants. The ball had been preceded two days earlier by a party for the servants, for Ellen was anxious that their labours should not be forgotten.

The Duke could only marvel at his Duchess's

stamina. He watched her circling the room, talking, laughing and dancing with their guests. She was a beautiful, elegant hostess, endearing herself even more to the people of Rossenhall. At last he caught up with her, insisting that they go in to supper together.

'It is a success,' he told her, sitting down beside her. *'You* are a success.'

'Are you sorry we have kept it to local families?' she asked him, 'I know Dorcas was disappointed that it was not to be a grand society event.'

'If the Dowager had had her way the house would be filled with lords, ladies and even royalty,' he said. 'No, we see enough of those people in town. This celebration is for us. For you.' He lowered his voice. 'The fact that Dorcas declined to attend, because we have not invited *"her sort of people"* shows why she was never loved at Rossenhall, as you are.'

'I was sorry Mrs Ackroyd could not be here,' said Ellen as Max refilled her wineglass. 'Her last letter from Greece was full of condemnation of Lord Elgin for removing so many artefacts from the Parthenon. I think she would like you to raise the matter in the House.'

Max shook his head. 'I have enough to do supporting the war in the Peninsula. When we have finally defeated Bonaparte, perhaps I may have more time for your friend's crusades.' He put up his head. 'Listen, the next dance is about to begin. Will you join me, Duchess?'

'With pleasure, Duke. But only one dance: I am determined that you must stand up with little Clare Arncliffe tonight. It will be good practice for her come-out later this year.'

'And may I also dance with Georgiana?' he asked.

'Of course, if you can tear her away from Tony. You know how it is with new brides.'

'Not only new ones,' he growled.

He slipped an arm around her waist and Ellen felt the familiar rush of desire. Max was right, she thought, as he led her on to the dance floor. It was not only new brides who were besotted with their husbands.

Later, when the guests had gone, they made their way up to the ducal apartments. Max's only stipulation in the refurbishment had been that the Duchess's apartments should adjoin his own and a connecting door had been added, although they never made any pretence of retiring separately. Max led her directly to his bedchamber, where he proceeded to undress her between long, languid kisses that made Ellen shiver voluptuously.

The slow thrust and parry of tongues was like a ritual dance that aroused them both with its sensuous demands.

Leaving their clothes pooled on the floor, Max lifted her effortlessly on to the bed and in the pale moonlight they continued to caress one another, his hands skimming her soft flesh while her fingers explored the muscular hardness of his back. Almost too soon the languid kisses gave way to fierce desire, a giddy rush of blood that carried them to the final consummation and left them to fall into a sated, exhausted slumber, entwined in each other's arms.

In the morning Ellen stirred, stretching luxuriously, revelling in the closeness of Max's body, measuring his length against her. She rolled over and kissed him.

'Max, wake up. It must be late. I can hear Flynn moving about in your dressing room.'

'He will be leaving our morning coffee.'

She nibbled his ear. 'What an excellent valet. I have always thought so.'

'Yes, he is,' he agreed, sitting up. 'I suppose you want me to fetch the tray?'

Ellen's eyes rested on his naked chest with the fine smattering of hair like a shield across his breast.

'Perhaps not quite yet,' she murmured.

He laughed and pulled her to him. 'You, madam, are incorrigible.'

He kissed her, but when he released her she remained with her head against his shoulder, looking up at him.

She said wickedly, 'If I am, it is only what you taught me, all those years ago under the desert stars.'

She saw the flame of desire in his eyes then, as memories stirred, but he fought it with teasing words.

'Nonsense. You were always headstrong and wilful. A termagant.'

'I was not!'

'No? Then let me go and fetch in our coffee. I need to make an early start today. There is a great deal of work to do.'

She snuggled closer. 'In a while.'

'You see,' he muttered. 'Wilful, headstrong, totally spoiled.'

'No, merely determined!' Her hand slid under the covers and she grabbed him.

'Ah!' he yelled. 'Don't do that. I won't be able to—'

But he could. And he did.

* * * * *

*If you enjoyed this story,
you won't want to miss*
THE INFAMOUS ARRANDALES *quartet,
four more great reads from Sarah Mallory:*

*THE CHAPERON'S SEDUCTION
TEMPTATION OF A GOVERNESS
RETURN OF THE RUNAWAY
THE OUTCAST'S REDEMPTION*

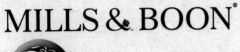

MILLS & BOON®

AWAKEN THE ROMANCE OF THE PAST

7/04

MILLS & BOON®

EXCLUSIVE EXTRACT

When Lady Sara Herriard's husband dies,
she decides it's time for her to live as she pleases.
She won't change for anyone—and certainly
not the infuriating Marquess of Cannock!

Read on for a sneak preview of
SURRENDER TO THE MARQUESS

The hoofbeats behind her were getting closer, much
closer. She risked a backwards glance and realised that
the only danger to her just at that moment was the
Marquess himself. He looked as though he wanted to
throttle her.

Sara twisted back round, wishing she was riding
astride and not wearing this so-fashionable habit with
its trailing skirts and broadcloth that slid on the saddle.
As she thought about sliding a buzzard flapped up out
of the long grass, a rabbit in its talons. The mare jinked,
stiff-legged, swerved back and Sara lost her stirrup, lost
her balance and went over Twilight's shoulder down to
meet the turf with a thud.

Instinctively she rolled, tucking herself up into a ball
as her great-uncle the Rajah's *syce* had taught her. The
clifftop was almost as hard as the sun-baked Indian plain,
she thought as she tumbled, arms around her head, braced
for the hooves of Lucian's horse.

There was the sound of furious, inventive, swearing,

then she came to a stop, untrampled, and lifted her head warily in time to see Lucian dismount from a rearing horse in a muscular, controlled slide.

'Sara!'

He was by her side and she closed her eyes strategically to postpone his anger and in sheer self-preservation. He had looked like a god just then and she could put no reliance on her own self-control. 'Mmm?' she managed.

'Are you hurt?'

Yes, was the honest answer. Her left shoulder hurt, her right wrist stung and her pride as a horsewoman was severely dented. 'No,' she said and opened her eyes.

'Excellent,' Lucian growled. 'Because I fully intend wringing your neck.'

'Why?' Indignant, Sara moved too quickly, found several other things that hurt and was hauled into an upright sitting position. 'Ow! What are you doing?'

'Checking.' His hands worked along her collarbone, wriggled her fingers and prodded her ribs. 'Move your feet. Let me see your eyes, your ears. What day of the week is it?'

'Thursday.'

'Correct.' Then he kissed her.

Don't miss
SURRENDER TO THE MARQUESS
by Louise Allen

Available March 2017
www.millsandboon.co.uk

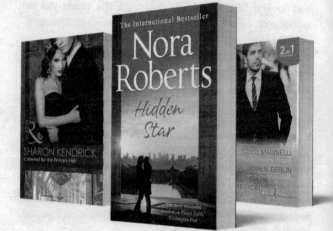

Join Britain's BIGGEST Romance Book Club

50% OFF your first parcel

- **EXCLUSIVE offers** every month

- **FREE delivery direct** to your door

- **NEVER MISS a title**

- **EARN Bonus Book** points

Call Customer Services
0844 844 1358*

or visit
illsandboon.co.uk/subscriptions